# HOOD RATS

by
E.R. McNair

Compilation and Introduction copyright © 2008 by
Triple Crown Publications
PO Box 6888
Columbus, OH 43205
www.TripleCrownPublications.com

Library of Congress Control Number: 2008936566
ISBN 13: 978-0-9799517-8-7
Cover Design: Triple Crown Publications
Typesetting: Holscher Type and Design
Editors: Maxine Thompson, Nikki Jenkins
Editorial Assistant: Sarah Kennedy
Editor-in-Chief: Dany Ferneau
Consulting: Vickie Stringer

First Trade Paperback Edition Printing
10 9 8 7 6 5 4 3 2 1

Printed in the United States of America

# Acknowledgements

In the Name of Allah Most Merciful the Most Gracious. You alone we worship and to you alone we turn for help.

Thank you to Triple Crown for believing in this project and taking a chance on little ole me I hope we can continue to make beautiful reading together. Thanks to Dr. Maxine Thompson whose editing took my book to a whole different level. Terreece Clarke for working with me and helping me through this process. Thanks to Mia for taking all of my crazy questions and being patient with me. Thanks to Danielle for picking up where Mia left off. Thank you to Vickie Stringer for having a dream and believing in it and not only for making your own dream come true but for reaching back and making others dreams come true too!

Thank you to my close friends and family that stood by me while I was writing this book for your input and endless proof reads.

Thanks, Aunt Bonnie for telling me to take a chance at having this published I cannot believe that it is really happening.

Thank you to my favorite writers Toni Morrison, Maya Angelou, Nikki Giovanni and Zora Neale Hurston. The beautiful thing about reading is that it allows you if only for a minute to escape your world around you and to live in someone else's.

Please check out my webpage http://aaids.blogspot.com/ it provides information on the HIV/AIDS epidemic that is currently destroying the black community. To my people caught up in the system know that in everything, there is a lesson but with Allah in your lives, even the impossible is possible.

# Dedications

This is dedicated to my daughter, Kamira, and my son, Kamren, the loves of my life. Everything that I do is for you.

To my Mom, thanks for giving me a love for reading and writing.

To my Nana thanks for being the one I can talk to about anything, my best friend.

To my Pop's, Rest in Peace. I miss you!

To the man that forever changed my life—you stole my heart forever and you know exactly who you are!

# one

### *Bre*

Gary, Indiana isn't known for much; steel mills and high unemployment rates. And one of the most famous, or infamous, people from here is Michael Jackson. While his song claims that, 'I'm going back to Indiana, Gary, Indiana here I come,' he's not been back in years and he probably has no intentions of coming back any time soon.

My girls and I live in Gary. We watch as crime rises and the will to find gainful employment decreases. We're creative in our methods of getting money to fund our habits. But that's the life of a Hood Rat.

The hood has been popping all week about Big Tone's coming home party. He's been locked up for three years on cocaine possession charges, and now he's coming home. My girls, Nesha, Nicky and I are at CeeCee's crib, hanging out before we hit the party up. CeeCee has just gotten her food stamps and we're doing

*E.R. McNair*

it up, ghetto-fabulous style. The first of the month is the bomb at CeeCee's. But by the end of the month, the cupboards are bare.

I feel sorry for her kids. Because I don't want her kids to be hungry, I'm careful about how much food I take. There is so much food, I think I'll bust—burgers, hot dogs, chips, soda and more.

I'm in my favorite spot, CeeCee's chaise lounge, eating the hell out of some pizza and, of course, Nicky, Cee and Nesha are doing their usual, smoking up some shit. I don't mess with that shit. I got high one time and climbed up a damn tree. I broke three nails, scratched up my knees and ruined my favorite pair of boots. I can laugh about it now, but back then it was a sensitive subject. So I leave that shit alone. I don't drink either so I'm pretty much the square out of the crew.

Nicky says between puffs, "Y'all know the club is going to be hot tonight. Big Tone just got out of jail and Jay and Slick are going all out for that nigga. The Upscale is going to be on and popping for real." She stands up and moves her body from side to side, as if she were already at the club and on the dance floor.

CeeCee pulls out her bags from her trip to the mall earlier. She snatches out an outfit, waving it around with flair. "Bitches, don't hate!"

She leaves the room, laughing loudly, and comes back a few minutes later wrapped in a tight-ass Juicy dress. It hugs her curves and shows a bit more than I would be comfortable with. But that's CeeCee; she's

*E.R. McNair*

comfortable with the curves God gave her and doesn't care who sees them. The more who stare the better.

Even though it's September, it's still warm outside so she bought a halter dress and the bitch even got the matching shoes.

"Damn, bitch, where you get that shit from?" Nesha asks, shouting over the music from the CD player in the corner.

"DayDay picked it out for me." CeeCee twirls around, modeling her outfit, raising her feet up so that we got a good view of the matching shoes. Her laugh moves through the room and is contagious. We all join her on the imaginary dance floor, laughing and spinning around, preparing our moves for the night.

DayDay has been CeeCee's man for almost twelve years now. They met in middle school when she was fourteen and he was fifteen.

They have three kids together—DJ, Ashley and Alexis.

But everybody in the hood knows that CeeCee was kicking it with Tone before he went to jail. I'm wondering how she's going to pull off being with Tone tonight. Everybody who is anybody in the hood will be at this party, and that includes DayDay. That CeeCee sure loves to live dangerously.

"CeeCee, how're you going to wear a dress that your man bought you to a party for the nigga you've been cheating on him with?" Nesha asks laughing.

"Whatever, girl. Please, DayDay knows what's up. And he better not question me, either." CeeCee flips her hand. "Please, like he ain't doing one, two, three other girls in the hood." She counts on her fingers. "As long as that nigga pay me my money, don't bring no diseases back to me and asks me no questions, I don't give a shit what he does and he don't question me about what I do." She raises her hand in the air and Nesha gives a high five. "Hollar!"

CeeCee has it like that. Day knows what was up. Shit, she was driving Tone's car around the hood like it was hers. It was obvious CeeCee has no shame to her game. She figures because she's pretty, she can get away with the shit she does. But we all wonder how long it will last.

"Girl, you know you're an asshole," Nicky says. "One day that nigga is gonna whoop your ass and you gonna deserve that shit, for real."

CeeCee rolls her eyes at Nicky. "Do you all hear what I hear?" She cranes her neck, as if she's heard something that we all can't hear. "You can't hear that?" She asks again, a huge smile on her face.

We all listen, trying to figure out what CeeCee is talking about. Nesha even turns down the CD player and she pushes back the window shades trying to get a good look out the front window to see if someone is out there.

"What, what do you hear?" we all ask in unison, paranoid by her question.

"I hear a hater up in this piece!" CeeCee screams, laughing loudly and dancing around the room, her outfit still on and hugging her large, round hips. "Hater!" She points at Nicky. "Hater! Bitches, don't hate the player,

*E.R. McNair*

hate the game."

Nicky rolls her eyes and sticks her middle finger up at CeeCee. She twists her lips and folds her arms across her chest.

We all know that Nicky had a thing for Tone and she was mad as hell when she found out that CeeCee was doing him. They didn't speak for months behind that shit. But Nick got her revenge though. She did DayDay in CeeCee's house. But I think that was a one time thing.

It's fucked up what Nick did, but CeeCee is wrong, too. She knows that Nicky was gone off that nigga Tone. Nicky was so jacked up when she found out about CeeCee and Tone, she was sick, literally, throwing up and everything. No one knows if Tone was interested in Nicky or not. He never gave her any holler. But what does that mean? Niggas are always trying to play it cool as if nothing fazes them. So, just because he was hawking CeeCee, doesn't mean he didn't feel Nicky too.

CeeCee goes to change her clothes and she returns with a large red plastic cup filled to the rim with alcohol. She's getting her drink on, talking about what she's going to do to Tone. "I can't wait to see that nigga tonight."

"What are you going do to that nigga, girl?" Nesha asks, easing herself into the large arm chair across the room. She kicks her shoes off and drops her feet onto the coffee table disturbing the loose herb that lays in a shoe box lid.

"I can't reveal too many of my tricks, but I'm going to

*E.R. McNair*

bring tears to that nigga's eyes." CeeCee laughs.

Nicky just sits there listening and you can see that she's still mad as hell about CeeCee fucking with Tone. You can almost see steam rising from the top of her head. You would think Nicky would have learned to deal with CeeCee's brash demeanor, but it's still affecting her. It seems like Nicky is jealous of CeeCee. But she'll never admit it.

"Y'all just don't know. That nigga's dick is so damn big, I can't wait to get that shit tonight." CeeCee stares into space, daydreaming about what's going to happen tonight after the club. "You gotta think. It's been three long ass years since he's had *any* pussy. I'm gonna give him all he needs and then some."

I didn't want to burst her bubble, but I had to ask CeeCee how she knows she's going to be the one giving it to Tone tonight.

"CeeCee, you know how many hoes there will be up in there tonight? What makes you think you will be leaving with Tone at the end of the night?" I smile, teasing her. "And you know his baby's momma is going to be posted up right next to him."

"Y'all no-getting-dick broads kill me," CeeCee says. "I'm a professional at my game. I get what I want when I want it. And tonight, I want Tone. You bitches mark my words. I will be leaving the Upscale with Big Tone tonight." CeeCee drains her cup and rises from her chair for a refill.

"Besides, do you really think I give a damn about that

*E.R. McNair*

that bitch, Sharmel?" she asks. "She's in his life as the result of one drunken night of pleasure and from what I hear, it wasn't all that pleasurable. Please, that ugly-ass broad is the last thing on that nigga's mind. Girl, have you seen her lately? Can you say 'hot mess?' Trust me, the only thing those two have in common *is* a baby."

"Shit," CeeCee continues, almost half way through her second drink, "that nigga was at my door as soon as he got out." She pulls something out her purse that lays it on the dining room table. "And I got the key to the hotel room they got downtown right here." She picks it back up and waves the hotel key around, proving her point.

The way CeeCee's drinking, she'll be too drunk to execute any of the tricks she described. Sometimes I hated being the no-dick-getting chick in the crew. I was really living vicariously through my girls' lives. And even though sometimes their lives were full of unnecessary drama, I stuck through it with them.

Nesha smiles. She's pleased that her girl is still at the top her game. "Damn, bitch, I taught you well, didn't I? Your ass is on it. Did you give Tone a taste of what's to come?"

CeeCee smiles and describes how she gave him a sample of her goodness. She brags that he came after one lick and we all bust out laughing, even Nicky has to laugh on that one. A one minute brother. Now I have had my share of getting my groove on, but I was nowhere close to CeeCee and Nesha's league. But don't get me

*E.R. McNair*

wrong, now, I'm not a beginner.

From what CeeCee and Nesha say, there is an art to giving head. I just need a little more practice until I develop their artistic ability. They joke about teaching classes at the community recreation center because the talk around the hood is that their head game was top-notch. I tell them that I might not be able to blow back brains like they can, but I can ride a pony with the skill of jockey and so after their class, I'll teach Pony Riding 101.

After we laugh about CeeCee's morning escapade with Tone, I tell Cee, Nicky and Nesha that I need to run to the mall if I'm going out with their asses tonight. I know that Mello is going to be at the club tonight, and I've been hot for him for a minute, so I want to look my best.

Mello is DayDay's best friend. CeeCee thinks he's just what I need. She warns me, "Girl, you'd better come correct because Mello has been over here with Day and he asked about you."

I don't know if that's a good or bad thing, though. CeeCee says Day told him I was a good girl, nothing like my friends.

"I'll ride to the mall with you." Nicky says. "I need to pick up something and I want to get a manicure and pedicure." She takes one more hit on her blunt, knocks back the last of her drink and grabs her purse.

I can tell she's getting tired of sitting here with CeeCee listening to her describe, in detail, what will hap-

*E.R. McNair*

pen while she'll be at home, lying alone in her bed. I can tell that CeeCee picked up on that too. But of course, CeeCee doesn't care. I think she fucks with Nicky on purpose.

"We'll see you later, around eight," I tell Nesha and Cee as I search through my purse for my car keys and my sunglasses.

"Don't be late, bitch," Nesha says, another blunt burning between her lips.

"We need to be up in the club, sitting in VIP with drinks in our hands before all the chicken heads get there"

I raise my middle finger at Nesha as we're leaving CeeCee's house. "You just be ready when we get back."

## two

**Bre**

I don't know who came up with the term "hood rat." I mean, back in the day, me and my girls wouldn't have considered ourselves rats. But, if you ask anyone around Gary, Indiana, they may think otherwise. But they're just haters. We know we're ghetto fabulous. I mean, don't no broads do it the way we do it.

Take my girl CeeCee, or Cecelia Jones, Hood Rat number one. She gets her shit when she wants it. I mean, her crib has nice furniture, she's always in the mall and she drives a bad ass car. But truth be known, she isn't the cleanest person I've ever met, yet the niggas love her. They will drop that cash on her ass without even thinking about it twice. And they could care less about her man Dayonte Jackson or DayDay.

CeeCee didn't always have her shit together, though. She comes from dysfunction at its finest. Her mother, Ms. Joyce, started smoking Crack when CeeCee was real

*E.R. McNair*

young and who knows where or who CeeCee's daddy is. All we know is that he was some white man that her mom had been kicking it with back in the day.

I used to feel real bad for CeeCee when she was thirteen. She was always stuck taking care of her brother Shane and her sister Shaneka, while her mother was out kicking it.

CeeCee was the only mom the kids ever really knew. She didn't finish high school because she was always taking care of them, making sure that they ate and were clean and clothed. And that was too bad because she's a smart girl.

Then CeeCee met DayDay. At first, he chased her so bad. It was so funny. I have never seen a nigga get rejected that many times, but he would keep coming back for more. He was a glutton for punishment.

I remember when Day first started making money hustling. He was doing anything and everything to try to win CeeCee over. One time at school during lunch, Day handed CeeCee a shopping bag full of new clothes. Day was determined that he was going to make CeeCee his girlfriend. He really won her over when he helped her take care of her brother and sister. He made sure they had food on their table, that the electricity stayed on and that they had clothes on their backs. Every day he would come to her with something new. It was crazy.

You know how it is when you come from not having anything and a nigga starts dropping cash on you and showering you with gifts? It's kind of hard to resist. Or so

CeeCee's told me.

They had been together for a couple of years when CeeCee got pregnant. She figured the baby would be her ticket away from her crazy mother.

CeeCee delivered a healthy son that looked like he could be Day's twin. They named him Dayonte Jackson Jr., but called him DJ. He was so cute and he had curly, jet black hair and he was dark chocolate; nothing like his mom, who was very light skinned.

As much as she hated playing Mommy to her brother and sister, I never thought CeeCee would have a baby. But, I guess love will make you do crazy things. When the baby was a month old, Day moved CeeCee out of her mom's house and into his mother's house. That only lasted about one week because CeeCee and Ms. Jackson didn't get along. Ms. Jackson hated CeeCee; and she had no problem telling CeeCee just how much she hated her.

On a daily basis they would argue and fight about how to take care of DJ or how to cook dinner or how to clean the house. Eventually, it got to the point where one of them had to go. It was Ms. Jackson's house, so it was CeeCee who got the boot. Day got some fiend to rent an apartment for CeeCee.

CeeCee had been out of her mother's house for about two months when she found out that Children's Services had taken her brother and sister away. She cried for days believing that it was her fault.

The girls and I tried to tell her that it wasn't her fault and that if she had been there, she would have been

*E.R. McNair*

taken away, too. But, she felt it was her responsibility to protect them and to take care of them in their mother's absence. And so in CeeCee's eyes, she let them down. I don't think CeeCee has ever forgiven herself for Shane and Shaneka being put in foster care. I'm not even sure she knows where they are now. Maybe that has something to do with the way she's raising her kids.

You would think that it would make her a better mother. But, unfortunately, CeeCee is just like her mother. No, she's not doing drugs. But, her mothering skills are non-existent. If it wasn't for Day's mom, her three kids might have ended up in the same predicament as her brother and sister.

Then you have Nicky, or Nicole Hampton, Hood Rat number two. She keeps her hair tight and her gear fly. Nicky and I have been best friends since kindergarten. She was the first person I met when my mother and I moved to Gary.

Nicky lived with her mother down the street from me. She also lived with her dad and her big brother, Anthony. Nicky and I always had fun. We would have sleep-overs and play Barbie dolls when we were little, and later on, we would double date and hang out at the mall. But that was until her brother was arrested on a murder charge and he was sentenced to life in prison. Her family fell apart after that. Her father felt that he failed his family and he was so upset that he split. Nicky hasn't seen him since.

Nicky felt that it was her mother's fault that her

brother was in jail. Because of this, for a long time she didn't speak to her mother. Mrs. Hampton allowed Anthony's ass to run wild and she wouldn't allow Mr. Hampton to discipline him. What did she expect?

Anthony was crazy, but in the years Nicky and I ran together he had become my big brother, too. I remember when this guy who I was dating in high school tried to smack me around. Anthony went off; dude was so scared he pissed his pants. Anthony had gotten a reputation as a person that you didn't want to mess with. He was probably six feet tall and at least three hundred pounds. He was a big dude, but to those that knew him, he was a sweetheart. But, if you crossed him or those he loved, it was a done deal.

Just like a mother, Mrs. Hampton, to this day, claims Anthony is innocent. She's sold her car and mortgaged her house to appeal his case. But we believe her case is moot. Everyone in the hood knows Anthony did that nigga in. The story is that the guy owed Anthony money and that when Anthony approached dude, dude basically told him to suck his dick and chalk it up as a loss. Well, Anthony wasn't trying to hear that shit and apparently he punched dude so hard that when he went out, he never woke up. Nicky became very depressed when her brother went to jail. Not only did she lose her brother, but her father, too; she was a daddy's girl.

One summer not too long ago, Nicky was about twenty, she met this dude named Tay Marshall at Club Crazy. Tay was from Little Rock, Arkansas and he was in

*E.R. McNair*

town to escape some trouble he had fallen into in Little Rock. He was staying with his aunt, who lived not to far from Nicky.

Tay was fine as hell and he and Nick really hit it off, right from the beginning. They were hanging out with each other every day; going to the movies and dinner and to the mall. If I needed to find Nicky and she wasn't at home, all I had to do was go to Tay's aunt's house to find her. We all thought she had found "the one."

When it was time for Tay to return to Little Rock, Nicky cried like a baby. She was almost as devastated as she was when her brother and daddy left; but she managed to get through it because Tay promised her that he would be back to see her and that they would call each other all the time. There was even talk of her moving to Little Rock to be with him.

Tay called Nicky the second his plane landed in Little Rock and she told me they talked for three hours straight. She said her mother was going to kill her when she got the long distance phone bill. Nicky told me she loved Tay and she wanted to be his wife. A week went by and she hadn't heard from him. She tried to call, but his phone went straight to voicemail. Nicky was crushed by what she thought was the brush off, but she chalked the experience up as a lesson learned and that niggas will be niggas.

Two months after Tay had returned home, Nicky found out she was pregnant. She tried again to get in touch with him but now the number she had for him was disconnected. She went by his aunt's house, wanting to give her the good news, only to find out that Tay had been killed in a drive-by shooting not too long after he had gotten back home.

Nicky took the news hard; I was worried about her. She felt like everyone that she loved was leaving her. And who wouldn't think that?

A couple of months later, Nicky gave birth to a bouncing baby boy. She named him Ty and she tried to get back to her old self. I suggested that she go to Tay's aunts house and tell her the good news about Tay's son, but Nicky refused. She said it would be better for everyone if she stayed away and that she didn't want any problems with his family when it came to her baby.

Once Ty was a couple of months old, Nicky started hanging out with some real unsavory dudes. That was around the time I started to hear stories about her smoking and hanging out in clubs on the opposite side of town. I never saw any of this for myself. So, I just hoped what I heard wasn't true.

Then there is Nesha, or Danesha Perry, Hood Rat number three. She's on something totally different. Nesha will do whatever and whoever to get what she wants or needs. Others would call her a hoe more than a rat. Nesha gives the term "one-night-stand" a whole new meaning. She's like a nigga when it comes to sex. She'll have one nigga coming in the front door while another one is going out the back.

To each his own, I guess. Niggas do that shit all the

*E.R. McNair*

time and nobody has a damn thing to say. She gets her paper, so talk all the shit you want. I know plenty of chicks who wish they could be like Nesha. She doesn't give a damn what anybody says about her, and that's what I like about Nesha. But you better believe a bitch won't say anything foul behind her back. Nesha's rumble game is tight. They'll never bring that shit to her face.

Nesha has four brothers—Tito, Michael, James and Marlon. Her mother was a fan of the Jackson 5. She's the only girl. Her mother is white and we guess her dad is black. But no one has ever seen him. She always says her dad is some famous singer that her mom met when she was a groupie back in the day. But Nesha's mother will never tell her who he is. We all bet she doesn't even know. But Nesha swears that one day she's going to find him so he can take her ass away from the hood and her irritating family. But he won't want her ghetto ass. He probably knows about her and that's why he stays as far away from her as he can.

Nesha's probably the way she is because she lives with four males who proclaim to be players. None of us girls tried to get with Nesha's brothers, even though they were all fine as hell. We've seen too much. We watched as the girls would come to their front door, crying when their phone calls weren't returned or begging for one more try when the relationship was ended. Talk about hoes! Nesha's brothers were "Grade A" hoes. They went through more ass than underwear.

Nesha has three kids. They all have different daddies

because Nesha gets down like that and she doesn't care at all what anyone thinks. Her mom wasn't much of an example; she was just as much of a hoe as Nesha's brothers. Ms. Perry had a different dude living at her house every other month. The apple doesn't fall far from the tree.

Nesha is a hustler. If it's going to make her some money, she's going to do it. She's sold weed, crack and cocaine, anything she thinks will bring her the cash. She hustles harder than some dudes we know.

Nesha is CeeCee's other half. They've been best friends since kindergarten. They are, as the niggas say, the dime pieces of the crew. They're both biracial. They both have straight hair and light complexions. All the shit a nigga from the hood looks for. But they're grimy as hell and the two of them together are scary.

Nesha will cut a bitch quick. Hell, she'll cut a nigga if she has to and her mouth is worse than a knife. To have four brothers, she did not need them at all to come to her rescue. If anything, they came to stop her crazy ass from tearing shit up. She's who she is and she makes no excuses about it.

Nesha and I aren't as close as Nicky and I or even as close as CeeCee and I. But she is still my girl. Nesha and Nicky are cool, but they have their moments when they are like oil and water.

I'm the quiet, shy one; nothing like CeeCee, Nicky or Nesha. It's true, opposites attract. People always wonder why I hang out with my girls. But we have fun together

*E.R. McNair*

and I can't think of hanging with anyone else.

My mom and I are close. My father left us when I was little. So we moved to Gary from Toledo when my mom and dad divorced. Mom decided that she was going to punish my dad and move us 300 miles away from him. I can't say I blame her after all of the cheating he did.

I was little, but I remember what was going on. I could hear them fighting all the time about phone calls and visits from other women.

My mom and my dad met in high school. She was a little square, but she was so pretty and smart and she had a good head on her shoulders. She was a cheerleader and an honor student. My dad was a player and he was the handsome basketball star. I think I got my academic skills from my mom.

They stayed together throughout high school and then my mom got pregnant with me her sophomore year of college. My grandparents kept me so she could graduate. Once she did, she and my dad got married. I think he only married her because my mom got a good job working with the city. My dad never worked. He was a hustler from the beginning and my mom took care of everything, including him. My grandparents hated him. But my mom was in love, or at least she was until the women started calling our house. Some even had the nerve to come to our house. The gossip in the streets was that my dad had six other kids. But I'm not sure. As far as I was concerned, I was an only child.

My mom was born in Gary, Indiana. She still had

family here so she moved us back to get away from my dad. When we moved back to Gary, Mom got a job as an assistant director at the city's Human Resources Department and she found a house in Miller, not too far from Duneland Village. That's where CeeCee and Nesha lived.

I met Nicky when I was six years old. She was outside her house playing jump rope. I stood and watched her for a while then she asked if I wanted to play with her, and we've been cool ever since.

Nicky and I walked to school together and on the first day I met Nesha and CeeCee. Nicky already knew them, and we all became close. When my mom met CeeCee, she couldn't stand her. CeeCee tried to steal five dollars from my mother's wallet and ever since that day she's been banned from our house. Mom didn't have a problem with Nesha or Nicky but she would always warn me that my girls were trouble waiting to happen.

My girls and I, we've been through a lot together. We love each other and we have each other's back. And nothing anyone can say will stop us from kicking it together. The life of the Hood Rats isn't always what it seems to be, especially when you're on the outside looking in.

Oh, who am I? I'm Hood Rat number four. I'm LaBrea Watkins, or as my girls call me, Bre for short.

*E.R. McNair*

# three

**Nicky**

I decide to hit the mall with Bre to find something fly to rock to the club tonight. I'm the flyest of the Hood Rats, you better believe it. So, I have to maintain that image with these niggas in Gary.

I had to get out of there before I said something to CeeCee *she* would later regret. I'm sick and tired of Nesha, and even more tired of CeeCee. She thinks she got it going on, but I can show her better than I can tell her. That's why I fucked her man. Yes, I fucked him and I fucked him well, and it was right in her shit, too. Right up in her bed. So, while she's thinking DayDay knows where home is, he likes to vacation away from home sometimes and when he does, I'm right there to make him comfy and cozy.

CeeCee's popping all that mess about what she's going to do to Tone tonight. Well, while she's fucking Tone, I'll be boning the hell out of DayDay. Mark my words.

"What are you thinking about?" Bre asks me.

"Nothing," I say, not feeling like elaborating on my plans.

Bre's not to be trusted either. Look at her sitting over there. We used to be such good friends, but that was before she got all brand new and started trying to act like she was better than me.

"Let's go to the Cat's Meow," I suggest. "I want to get my nails done." I check out the chipping polish on my hands and realize I'd waited too long to make this trip. Besides, DayDay just brought the money over to me today. He's bankrolling this trip to the mall. I smile to myself. If Bre only knew.

"Is your mom watching Ty tonight?" Bre asks as she pulls her car into a parking spot.

"Yeah," I say, remembering that I need to call her, "I need to make sure mom and Ty are all right. My mom wasn't feeling good today." I grabbed my cell phone from my purse and dialed my mom's number.

After making sure my mom is cool, I think about what I'm going to wear tonight. I grab the money out of my pocket and count it. I smile again. It's only a matter of time before DayDay sees just what he's got and what he could have with me.

"I'm not wearing anything hoochie, for real. I need some classy, stylish shit," Bre says, peering through the store windows to see if she sees anything that catches her eye.

*E.R. McNair*

I nod. "Yeah, I feel you," I say. "That was a mess, what CeeCee had on. When will she realize that just because they make it in your size, doesn't mean you should wear it?"

"You didn't like what CeeCee's wearing tonight?" Bre asks, staring at me.

"I mean, we're grown-ass women. We need to leave that hoochie shit for the chickens," I tell Bre. "Why, did you like it?"

"Nicky, you sound like you're hatin' again. You know I have to call you on your shit," Bre chastises.

I look at Bre. What does she know? If she was my dog like she used to be, she'd get me and understand what I'm going through.

"Come on, Nicky, are you sure you're not just pissed because CeeCee is fucking Tone tonight? Sounds like a little hateration and holleration up in this dancery." She laughs, nudging me in the arm.

Again I look at Bre and I'm beginning to get an attitude.

"Fuck that nigga," I say. "He can't handle this shit right here. That's why he had to settle for CeeCee's ass. When he's ready for an upgrade, I may give him a chance, if the price is right."

"Nicky." I hear someone call my name. Finally an opportunity to get away from Bre before I cuss her out.

I look to see Slick walking toward us and he has some troll on his arm.

"Nicky," he calls me again and I see that the girl has

*E.R. McNair*

an attitude.

"What's up?" I ask Slick.

"You, girl." Slick waves at Bre who has walked toward Neiman Marcus.

"What's up with your girl?" Slick asks.

I shrug. I do know what's up with Bre. She's got a big stick stuck up her ass.

"I know you and your girls are coming out tonight. It's going to be all that," Slick says. "We're going to do it up pimp style tonight, boy," Slick brags. He pops the girl on her ass and she turns up her lips like she wants to say something but she knows better.

She then puts her hands on her hips and I look at her and roll my eyes.

"I'll see you tonight, Slick." I say. "I better get out of here before I have to smack a bitch up in this piece."

Slick laughs and grabs the girl by her arm. "See you tonight, Nick. I got something for you. Just let me know when you're ready for it."

I nod. And I think. What if Slick is offering me an opportunity to make some money? My own money and I wouldn't have to depend on a nigga for cash to pay my rent, or to buy stuff for my baby.

"How's Tone?" I ask Slick before he can get too far down the mall. I'm anxious to hear the answer.

"Good," Slick answers, smiling and walking away. He pulls the girl down the mall walk way and I can hear her cussing at him for talking to me.

Here comes Bre. I look at her and wonder what she's

*E.R. McNair*

about to say. I'm not in the mood for her shit tonight.

"Nicky, I know how you really feel," Bre starts back up.

Can't she just drop this shit? I'm only half way listening to her. I remember an outfit I saw in BeBe.

Bre continues. "Yeah, you say you don't want Tone, but if that nigga said that he wanted you, you would be right with him and you know it."

I just roll my eyes and let what Bre's saying to go in one ear and out the other. And then I have to laugh. "Okay, Bre, you got me on that, but come on, he was mine. I had my eye on him first. CeeCee's ass does this shit all the time. And she's got a damn man! The shit's fucked up, and you know it. Then she has the nerve to flaunt it in my face like it's some kind of joke."

"Look, Nicky, I know you were hurt, but come on, you did the ultimate sin." Bre pushes the issue. She stops walking and allows people to pass us. "You fucked DayDay, her baby's daddy. You know they are still together no matter what she does. You and Tone were never a couple." We walk some more and Bre stops to get something to drink. "You liked him and he liked her, that's the game, baby. The chips don't always fall your way."

I notice the girl handing Bre her drink is listening to close to our conversation. I give her the eye and say, "What the fuck, get back to work." Then I look at Bre.

"Whatever, Bre! You say that now. Wait until CeeCee fucks someone you like. Then let's see if you're talking the same bullshit." I twist my lips and roll my eyes.

"But we're girls, Nicky. We're not supposed to get pissed with each other over a nigga. Niggas come and go, but we're supposed to be girls for life."

"Sounds good, Bre. But life ain't like that," I say.

I find the perfect outfit in BeBe and then Bre and I head to her car.

"Can we run by my mother's house?" I ask. "I need to take her some money."

Bre pulls into my mother's driveway and she honks the horn. Ty runs out the front door.

"Hey, baby," I say as I plant kisses all over Ty's face.

"Mommy, stop!" he whines as he squirms to free himself from my grip. He wipes at the wet spots left from my lips.

"Here Ty. Take this money to Nana." I hand him the rest of the money DayDay brought me this morning and I pat him on the bottom. "I'll see you in the morning. Mommy loves you."

"Love you too, Mommy," Ty answers and he runs back to the front door.

I look at my son and wonder if I'm really doing the best I can with him. It's hard not having his father around. But there are a million bitches doing it alone. I can do it, too.

Bre drops me off at home.

Before she leaves she shouts, "Be ready when I get back."

I nod my head, flash the peace sign and walk into my

*E.R. McNair*

house. I can't shake this attitude. For some reason I'm pissed at the world and I have to find a way to make all this shit better.

## four

**CeeCee**

"Nesha, turn that shit up!" I holler at Nesha from my bed-room. "That's my motherfucking jam!" I am so high. I look at myself in the mirror, turning to check the angle from all sides and I'm happy with what I see. And I know that nigga Tone is going to be happy, too. I am the shit!

I'm tired of DayDay. We've been together way too long and I'm just ready for something else, something new. Plus, I'm sick of his mother. She gives me shit all the time and I know one time she's going to say the wrong shit and I'm going to blast her one.

Thank the Lord she didn't come to the door when I dropped the kids off this afternoon. I know she would have said something about me going out tonight. I'm young, I'm supposed to go out and kick it with my girls. She doesn't say anything when her son is missing in action for weeks at a time. Oh, hell no, that nigga can do no wrong.

"Nesha, roll another blunt. There should be some more in the drawer in the kitchen. The one by the sink."

The door bell rings and Bre walks in. I hope Nicky decided to leave her stupid ass at home. I know I'm tired of her. She's always saying shit about DayDay. I know that bitch better stay as far away from him as she can. She's just pissed because Tone wants me and he doesn't want her trifling ass. Don't hate me!

"Hey, bitches!" Bre calls out over the loud music. She turns down the CD player and pushes the off button. "Let's go, CeeCee."

"Here I come," I say. "I know I look good," I tell the girls. "Don't hate!"

Nesha comes out of the bathroom with a blunt between her lips. "Your ass thinks you look good."

Nicky edges her way into the living room. "I have to pee."

"Damn," I say to myself. Nicky better watch herself.

Nicky zips past Nesha and bumps into me on her way to the bathroom. I give her an evil look but I hold my tongue.

"Who's driving?" Bre asks.

"Bre, you know the drill. Why do we always have to go through this shit? What is your problem?" Nesha asks, painting her lips with a scarlet red color.

"You're the only one who doesn't drink or smoke," I tell her. "It only makes sense that you drive. Why are you tripping?"

"What if I want to have a drink tonight?" Bre asks, her

hands on her hips.

Nesha and I look at each other and bust out laughing.

"Yeah, right, bitch." Nesha says, her voice bellowing throughout the room.

"I even have to laugh on that one," Nicky says, exiting the bathroom zipping up her pants.

"Okay, bitches, you can stick me with the driving, but I'm putting you all on notice that if I hook up with Mello, all three," Bre points to us, "of you hoes are on your own for a ride home."

"I'm straight. Do I need to show you the hotel room key again?" I remind them, grabbing for my purse.

Nicky sucks her teeth and sashays to the front door.

I laugh my head off. I love fucking with her. Shit, I don't know why she doesn't just get over it.

"Whatever, CeeCee, while you're doing Tone who's gonna be doing your man?" Nicky asks.

I cut my eyes at her. "Oh, Nicky, I really don't give a fuck who's doing DayDay tonight. I just know who I'll be fucking the hell out of. Hell, you want him so bad you can have him for all I care. DayDay knows where home is. Don't get it twisted, Nicky." That bitch is on thin ice.

"CeeCee, there's a thin line between love and hate," Nicky says. "Don't make that nigga hate you."

"Why are you so worried about my man and who I'm doing? Do you want my man or is it that you're still mad because I'm doing Tone when you want him?" I ask with a smirk on my face.

"Fuck you, CeeCee. I'm tired of this bullshit. If we're

*E.R. McNair*

going, let's fucking go," Nicky demands. She switches to the car and jumps into the passenger seat.

I can see Bre giving me some fucked up look, like she's admonishing me for pissing off her friend. Shit, fuck her too.

"What?" I look at Bre.

"Nothing," Bre says and she walks outside to her car.

Nesha and I laugh our asses off and we follow them to the car. I can't wait to see Tone. He's in for the ride of his life tonight.

"You look cute," I tell Bre. "Is that outfit new?" I ask her, noticing it's not something I've seen in her closet.

"Yeah, I picked it up at the mall," Bre answers. She's still a little pissed.

I tell Nicky she looks cute, too. "Who're you trying to be all cute for?" I ask her.

I guess I'm the better bitch. I don't let that shit affect me. I've been around player- hating bitches all my life. I know how to deal with their asses. I can tell Nicky's getting pissed off and it makes me want to fuck with her more. I nudge Nesha in the ribs, but she's so into the argument she's having with one of her babies' daddies on her cell phone she's not following what's going on.

Finally, Bre pulls her car into the parking lot of the Upscale and the music spills out into the lot from the club. It's obvious the club is off the hook. I think everybody in Gary is in there. The club sits on the corner of Grant and Harrison Streets. It's a two-story brick building with lots of windows. The inside looks like a big warehouse and the VIP section is a loft that overlooks the club.

There are dozens of people waiting in line in front of the club and we go right to the door. Nesha says, "We're on the list."

Donell Patrick is at the door and Nesha whispers in his ear. He smiles and pushes the front door open, allowing us to walk right through, leaving a pissed-off group behind us.

It's wall-to-wall people. The DJ is spinning old school hip hop. Eric B and Rakim's *"Eric B is President"* is playing. "That's my jam!" I tell Bre. She nods her head and we look around to see who's here. The hoochies are out in full force. It's some shit to see.

"Damn, do you see these bitches?" I ask. "Where the fuck did they think they were going, to work at the strip club?"

I know it will at least be a few hours before the shit gets started, but I'm sadly mistaken. As soon as we hit the VIP, the shit hits the fan. Nesha gets into an argument with some girl who claims Nesha fucked her man. I tell that girl all the time that she needs to stop that shit. This is just one more broad who's made that claim. Damn, we've only been in the spot for ten minutes. But when drama's your middle name, it's only a matter of time before it finds you no matter where you go.

I stand next to Nesha as she cusses this girl out. I always have my girl's back, but I'm waiting for my man and I'd rather not hook up with him after tussling with some females. Nesha needs to squash this shit quick, fast and in a hurry.

# five

### Nesha

We hit the VIP and I can see that these bitches are staring already. I peel my jean jacket off and let my double D's do the talking for me. These niggas love my big-ass chest and the bitches love to hate them. That's why I got me a tattoo that says "born to be hated."

The VIP area is upstairs and it's surrounded by glass. The people on the dance floor can see the party in VIP, they just aren't privileged enough to take part in it.

I'm standing by the bar, minding my own business, waiting for my drink when this bitch comes up behind me asking me what my name is.

"Who the fuck wants to know?" I ask as I'm paying for my drink.

She tells me her name is Tasha and she thinks I've been kicking it with her husband, Steve. Now, I'm not opposed to sampling what another woman has at home, but when this broad tells me her man's name, I can't place him and I'm not one to forget a name nor a dick.

*E.R. McNair*

"I don't know who the fuck you're talking about," I tell her and I walk away. I'm trying to do better, especially now that I'm dealing with this custody battle.

"What the hell is going on?" CeeCee asks me, shouting over the ear-piercing music.

"This bitch thinks I fucked her man," I tell CeeCee. I know my girl always has my back. I never take my eye off of the tramp standing across the room.

Tasha follows me to where I'm standing and she continues talking. Says that she doesn't believe me, that she's heard about me and she better not hear about me fucking with her man again. I count to ten, still trying to maintain my cool, but then this bitch steps up on me and pokes me in the arm.

"Oh, hell no!" I say and I throw the drink in my hand in her face. "Bitch, don't you ever touch me again!" I say, pissed, because I had to wait twenty minutes on that drink.

CeeCee and Bre grab me and pull me away from the girl who is now dripping wet with my seven and seven.

"I tried," I tell CeeCee. "I tried to keep my cool."

"I know you did, girl," CeeCee tells me.

We find four seats overlooking the whole club. The bartender places drinks in front of us, courtesy of Slick, who shoots us all a nod from the other side of the room. We nod back and we're finally in our groove.

CeeCee, always the clown, starts in first. "Damn, look at these chicken heads up in here. Why would she wear that?" She points to the girl in the jeans that are cut in the front like shorts and long in the back like a skirt. Bad fashion move! It looks like something she made at home.

I'm checking out the dance floor and I see Charles Young. Charles is the father of my youngest son, Chuckie. I just talked to him on the phone and he said he wasn't coming out tonight. I'm pissed. I point to Charles and the skank he's dancing with.

"Look," I say to Bre, pointing at Charles.

"What? I can't see who you're pointing to," she says. This bitch is so blind.

"You need to have her eyes examined. It's Charles!"

"Is that Felicia?" Bre asks, her mouth twisted into a frown.

I nod and mirror her same expression.

"I heard that bitch has herpes," Nicky says.

"I heard that too," I say. "But that nigga is fucking her."

They all look at me as if I've told them that the building would explode in two minutes.

"Yep," I say, "and that nigga is trying to get custody of Chuckie."

They repeat the same look.

I drain my glass and push it across the bar to the bartender. I stare at Charles and hope he can feel my deathrays penetrating his skull. These niggas are a trip!

"What's up, ladies?" DayDay asks.

I throw him a head nod and then continue to stare at Charles. I know some shit is about to get started. Nicky

*E.R. McNair*

and CeeCee up here, both fighting over these sorry-ass niggas. I say we treat them like they treat us, like toys. That's why I fuck freely. I'm playing the game they started.

I have to watch what I do up in here tonight. One slip, and I'll hear about this shit at my court date next week and Charles will try and take Chuckie from me. And I'm not going to let that shit happen. Hell, no!

## six

**Bre**

So far, so good. I can't figure out why these bitches don't get along. We used to be so tight, but as we got older our relationships have changed. But this is when we need each other the most. I wish I could bring back the old times, but I guess we're all so far past jump ropes and pony tails, there is no going back now.

We've been in the club for about a half an hour now. So far, we've almost been in a fight and now I'm just ready to have some damn fun. I can't keep still, the music is hot and I want to get my groove on, for real. Jason Rogers, a guy I went to high school with asks me to dance. "Don't let nobody take my seat," I tell Nicky.

Jason and I hit the dance floor. We're stepping to *"Step in the Name of Love"* and dude is stepping his ass off. I can tell he's looking at my ass but I don't care just as long as he doesn't touch me. We're kicking it and I can feel sweat

*E.R. McNair*

pouring down my back. When the song goes off Jason tries to hug me, but I push him away. I shake my head at him and tell him, "I don't think so." I turn to go back to my seat and when I look up I see Mello walking in the door.

He's staring at me. He waves for me to come to him. I point up to my girls in VIP and I say, "I have to get back to my girls," and I run back upstairs. "Shit! Shit! Shit!" I say to myself, pissed that I may have blown my only chance to be with Mello. I could just kick myself. I can't understand why I'm so scared of this dude.

When I get up to VIP, my girls are cracking up. Nesha starts in on me first.

"Damn, girl, are you scared of that nigga or what? Mello won't bite, not unless you want him to." She starts laughing. "What the fuck is wrong with you? If you don't want him, pass his ass on over here. I'll give him the goody-goody."

"Shut up." I snarl at Nesha. "Mello don't want some shit every nigga in Gary has had."

Nesha shoots me a look I've seen reserved for bitches she was ready to cut.

So I try to clean it up, not prepared for Nesha's mess tonight. "Girl, you know Mello has my head all messed up," I say. "I just couldn't think straight." I kind of laugh, a little nervous by the situation.

"Yeah, bitch," Nicky says, "get it together. You know he'll be up here in a minute."

"He gives me butterflies," I admit, hoping they don't

laugh at me too much.

"Butterflies? What the fuck? How old are you, twelve?" Nesha shouts and she almost falls over onto CeeCee. I can tell that she's drunk.

"Girl, your ass don't have butterflies, more like the wet drawls. Shit, I would have wet drawls, too, as good as that nigga looks tonight, damn!" CeeCee says, pushing me.

"You better not leave that man alone too long tonight. One of these chickens that don't have butterflies—she might have something else, but you best believe she won't have butterflies—will volunteer to keep him company tonight." Nesha laughs.

She's right. He looks so good I thought I would lose it right there. Mello lives up to the term balling out of control. He has a crispy hair cut. As usual. He's blinging in both ears, and this nigga has on a fly-ass button-down shirt with canary yellow diamond cuff links.

I know I saw the same shirt in some men's fashion magazine. It's something like three hundred dollars. Once he comes closer I get a better look and he has on these fly jeans that look fresh from the cleaners with a pair of square-toe Kenneth Cole shoes. He's topped it off with a platinum and diamond chain and his platinum Presidential Rolex watch. Hot to death!

I can't tell for sure, but I would bet money that Mello has bow legs, and that just makes him look extra yummy. He came in with DayDay, who's looking just as fly. But I'm not the only one who's noticed how fly Day is look-

*E.R. McNair*

ing.

"Damn, CeeCee, DayDay's ass is looking good as hell," Nicky says, sitting with her pinky finger in her mouth looking like she wants to eat his ass up or something.

It was her turn to fuck with CeeCee. Nicky continues, "You'd better put a leash on that shit before somebody snatches it up."

"Yeah, I must say, Nicky," CeeCee says, giving it right back to her, "my man does look good, but he's not the reason I'm up in this club tonight, baby." Her eyes are focused on somebody across the room. "There's my reason right there."

We all look up to see Tone walking into the club. It seems as if the party stops when he enters. It's been three long years and he's finally back on the scene and the Gary, Indiana hustlers, chicken heads and hood rats are happy to have Tone back. He can't walk a few feet without having to stop to speak. He's like a celebrity. Throwing dap here, hugs there, it takes Tone about twenty minutes to make it up to the VIP.

Slick and Jay are the first to greet him.

"What's up, Dude?" Jay asks, slapping Tone on the back, his arms wrapped tightly around his shoulders.

Tone's fly, black ass smiles, happy to see the love that everyone has for him. "It's good to be back."

I can't hear him. His voice is so deep it blends in with the rumble from the speakers above my head.

CeeCee can't take her eyes off of Tone. She shoots

him a wink and a smile from where we all sit and he throws her a head nod right back. They're communicating telepathically. I can just imagine what they're saying. Tone's probably saying, "Girl, you ready for tonight?"

And then CeeCee responds, "No, the question is are *you* ready for tonight?" I think about the key in CeeCee's purse. I guess I don't have to worry about her getting home tonight.

Nicky's staring at Slick with a look in her eyes that says, "Yeah, nigga, it's on tonight." She has been kicking it undercover with Slick for a few years. And since she can't have Tone, she's going for the next best thing, his boy.

I guess Slick's all right, if you like thugs. But Nicky has had better and can do better. Slick's a disrespectful ass. He's one of those niggas who thinks he can say anything he wants to a female, but with Nicky he has met his match. She doesn't take any shit from him or any other nigga.

Nicky's brother taught her well. He taught her to demand respect from these niggas out here. So Slick knows what's up with Nicky and he tries his best to abide by the rules.

I see Mello and DayDay coming toward us. Again, my stomach starts to talk to me.

"What's up, DayDay?" CeeCee says, her face twisted up as if she smells something bad. "You're looking pretty fly tonight. Who are you trying impress?"

"CeeCee, like you care. Bitch, please, I know why your

*E.R. McNair*

ass is here tonight. Don't fucking play me."

I look over at Nicky. She has a sinister smirk on her face even though she's sitting comfortably between Slick's knees. She called it though. It was like she knew this shit was going to happen tonight.

Nesha decides to throw her shit in the mix. "Come on, DayDay, you know how shit is. Why are you disrespecting my girl in the club?" She hits a cigarette Jay hands to her and blows the smoke in the air. "I know your ass ain't get all fly to just sit up in this motherfucker tonight. You're trying to find you some new ass to get into tonight, right? We're just following your lead, nigga."

"Hoes, man!" DayDay says, looking behind him at Mello. "You bitches are some damn hoes! Where are my kids at, CeeCee?" DayDay steps up on CeeCee. "Your ass left them at my mom's again?" He puts his finger in her face.

CeeCee stands up to show DayDay she isn't afraid of him. "Why are you worried about where they are tonight? You haven't been around for a week now. Now all of sudden you want to act like you care? You want to act like you're father of the year? Nigga, please." CeeCee turns her back on DayDay. He pushes her and she falls forward. Nesha catches her before she can drop to the ground.

CeeCee laughs, taunting him for losing his cool.

"DayDay!" Mello grabs him, stopping him from doing any more damage.

CeeCee catches her footing and continues to laugh. "Is that all you got, big man?" She's not fazed by his aggression. "What the fuck! Why are you in my face, DayDay. You didn't care about my ass when you disappeared for a week. Now that another nigga is showing me some attention, you want to act all possessive. Shut the fuck up and move around, dude, you're messing up my play."

CeeCee and DayDay have a crazy relationship. They love each other, but have a crazy way of showing it. I think CeeCee is getting DayDay back for all the cheating he's done over the years.

CeeCee sashays away and goes over to where Tone is sitting with his boys. She sits right next to him and she plants a big kiss on his cheek and says, "Welcome home, baby." She then looks over to DayDay and kisses Tone one more time.

DayDay sits down with us and I can tell that he's fuming.

Mello sits down next to me. And Nicky shoots me a look that says, "What are you going to do?" I smile still not sure how to handle this situation.

Nesha gets up. "I'll be back."

Nicky is still talking to Slick. He's kissing her on the neck and plying her with alcohol. She's already on the edge of drunk, and Slick is making sure she's all the way there so she won't turn him down tonight. From what I've heard a girl needs to be drunk to have sex with Slick. Most times, girls leave his bed more than a little disappointed. He's not holding as much as he brags to be.

"You want to dance?" Mello asks me.

*E.R. McNair*

I shake my head no. *Idiot*!

He looks at me seemingly surprised by being turned down. "So," Mello asks taking a sip from his glass, "you always this quiet or you just get that way when I'm around?" He looks around the club.

I hope he's not checking for another female. I laugh nervously. I can just kick myself.

"Is it that obvious?" I ask.

Mello moves his chair a little closer to me and leans in. He talks directly into my ear. His cologne smells delicious. I feel myself begin to float as if what I've been sipping on is more potent than soda. "A little. Can I get you something to drink?"

"No, thanks. I don't drink," I answer, loosening up.

"Get the fuck out of here. For real?" Mello asks, as if I'm lying to him.

"No. Not everyone drinks, Mello."

"Everyone I know does."

"I'm not like everyone you know," I answer, flashing him a little smile.

"I hope not," he shoots back. "How else aren't you like everyone I know?" Mello asks, taking another sip of his drink and moving even closer to me.

I feel his breath on my neck and I'm excited.

"Wouldn't you like to know?" I tease.

"I would." Mello flirts with me, touching my hand. He stares at me, trying to hypnotize me with his eyes.

I jump a little when I feel the warmth of his hand on mine. But then I feel a whole lot better.

*E.R. McNair*

"You know you're looking real fly tonight, I like what you have on, " Mello says.

"You're not looking too bad yourself," I say, checking him out.

"You like my swagger? I just threw this on. You know how it is. A brother got it going on." He shows me his best vogue.

I smile. "Yeah, I know how it is when you've got an image to uphold."

"Now who said I have an image?" Mello asks. He leans in close and whispers to me, "I love your smile. You have pretty teeth."

I smile again. "I'm just like you, aiming to please, that's all."

"Besides, there is only one person's eye I was trying to catch tonight," Mello says, draining his drink.

"Oh, really?" I begin to sweat and it isn't because the club is heating up. "Well, I hope you get what you're look-ing for," I tease.

"I do, too." Again he touches my hand. "So, I'm just going to ask you straight out," he pauses, trying to read me, "am I what you're looking for?"

I almost choke on my soda! Here is the guy who has been on my mind for months, years, and now he's asking me if I'm interested in him. I'm not sure how to answer the question. I want to make sure I don't fuck this up. Is he still with that crazy girl? Or is he with another one and he just wants a little something on the side? Sorry, Charlie, that's not going to fly with me. I know some girls

*E.R. McNair*

don't have a problem being the "girl on the side," but I'm not rolling that way.

"I guess it depends on how you answer my next question," I get out.

"Shoot," Mello says, calmly.

"What about your girlfriend?"

"Who? Who are you talking about? What girlfriend?" He feigns ignorance.

I twist my lips at him. *Don't try to play me like boo boo the fool.*

"Lacy?"

"Who?" Mello asks as if he doesn't know who she is.

"Lacy? She was your girlfriend when I met you a while ago over at CeeCee's," I say, annoyed by his lack of cooperation.

Mello shifts his eyes toward the ceiling as if he's seriously trying to place the name with a face. He's shaking his head from side to side. And then as if a light bulb turns on. "Oh! Her?" Mello starts to laugh. "Forget about her. Old news."

I stare at him, trying to decipher his words as fact or fiction.

"Scout's honor," Mello responds, his two fingers in the air. But it's the wrong hand.

How would he know about scout's honor? I'm sure he was never in a scout troop and the only reason I know which two fingers to use is because I attended a Brownie meeting with this white girl named Shelly when I was ten years old. I realized quickly that that shit wasn't for me.

*E.R. McNair*

I laugh.

"You don't believe me?" he asks, trying to look all innocent. "Call her." He hands me his cell phone. "She might curse you out, but you'll get your answer. We didn't end on good terms."

"That's quite all right." I push his cell phone back at him.

"Do you think I'm lying to you?"

"I'm not sure."

"Why would I lie to you?"

"Why wouldn't you?" I ask.

"I thought you were different?"

"I am. That's the reason you wouldn't lie to me, because I'm different?"

"Yeah. These other girls make you lie to them. So, if you're not like them, there would be no reason to lie. Right?"

"I guess," I answer, not sure how I feel about his rationalization.

He flips the script real quick, moving back to our original conversation.

"I'm glad you like what you see. I love what I see right now," he says. "So tell me, where are you going when you leave the club tonight?"

Wow, forward aren't we? I wasn't really sure how to answer his question. I mean, there was no doubt that I wanted to be with him, but the last thing I wanted was to be a booty call.

"I'm not sure, it depends on what my girls want to do

*E.R. McNair*

since I'm always the damn designated driver," I say with an attitude.

"Those hoes can find a way home."

I'm more than a little offended by Mello calling my girls hoes.

"Now why are you calling my girls hoes?" I say, my hands on my hips and my head moving from side to side.

"My fault," Mello apologizes. "I mean, I thought they could find their own way home if we want to hang out after this and get to know each other a little better."

I give Mello a dirty look. "I'm just saying we rode here together so I don't know about leaving them stranded."

He looks like a wounded puppy. What happened to the thug nigga in him? I smile to myself.

"Okay," Mello concedes. "I was just thinking we could hit up IHOP or something but I can deal with that. I tell you what, I'll give you my number, and you can call me when you're ready to see me again. Maybe we can go to dinner and a movie or something like that."

I'm sitting there in a daze. I can not believe this is really happening. Finally. He writes his number down and hands it to me. Then he kisses me on my forehead and tells me that he'll talk to me later. I'm tripping.

I look over at Nicky to see if she's been paying attention, but what I see makes me forget everything else. Now Nicky's ass is sitting with DayDay. What happened to Slick?

## seven

**Nicky**

This is the shit. I really do like being with DayDay. I'm so much better for him than CeeCee. One day he'll finally see that and kick her ass to the curb.

I'm feeling better tonight than I have in a long time. I hooked up with Slick in the back room and he took care of me. I take a sip of the drink DayDay bought for me and I put my hand on his thigh. He smiles at me and I ease my hand closer to what I've been missing.

"You have beautiful eyes," I say to DayDay.

"You do, too, baby."

I can do nothing but watch his lips move. When they stop, I move closer and cover his mouth with mine. I slip my tongue in between his lips and I can taste the vodka he's been sipping on.

"Nicky."

I hear someone calling my name but I'm too busy right now and I don't want to be disturbed.

*E.R. McNair*

"Nicky!"

I recognize the voice as Bre's but I continue to ignore her. The bitch is bringing down my high.

Then I feel her grab me by my arm and pull me up.

"Nicky, we need to talk," she says and I just want to blast her one good time in the face. I might just do it if she doesn't leave me alone.

I snatch my arm back. "Wait a minute, bitch! I'm busy," I say and I kiss DayDay again.

"Nicky, I'm not playing with your ass. Let's go." Bre stands over me and folds her arms across her chest.

I look at her and twist my lips.

"I'll be right back," I say to DayDay. I lean down and plant one more kiss on his lips to hold him over until I get back. "I've got something for you," I tell him, throwing him my sexiest look.

DayDay grabs for me. But Bre pulls me away, causing me to trip over the heel of my shoe.

"What the fuck's wrong with you?" I ask, trying to right myself. I straighten out my clothes and wipe at my mouth. I'm more than a little fucked up but I'm having a good time and this bitch is ruining everything.

"What are you trying to do?" Bre asks me, pulling me through a small walkway to the bathroom.

I can barely see where I'm going the club is so dark and by now it's so crowded I'm sure everyone that's anyone is here. I wonder where Tone is. I bet somewhere up under that fat-ass CeeCee.

Once in the bathroom Bre pulls me around the crowd

of girls that stand in front of the mirror and into a stall. She jabs her finger into my face. "Nicky, what the fuck are you doing?"

This bitch ought to be glad I'm so high. I should fuck her up. I laugh in Bre's face. "Man, I'm kicking it. Shit, if the bitch don't care, why should I? Come on, Bre, CeeCee did the shit to me," I say, having a difficult time focusing. I can feel my head bobbing back and forth and I try to steady myself on the closed stall door.

"Nicky, this isn't a fight you want to start! It will end badly. DayDay is the father of her kids or did you forget that shit? Whatever they have going on is between them, but what you're doing is wrong, dead wrong," Bre says. "She's supposed to be your girl. What's up?"

"Bre, fuck her, for real. CeeCee ain't shit, never has been, and never will be shit. All she cares about is herself. That's why she never has her kids because she's all about herself. So look, Bre," I can't keep my footing and I slide down the door until I hit the floor. Me and Day are going to keep on kicking it like we have been for a while now. When he ain't with her, he's with me." I finally tell my secret. Or at least I tell one of them. "He's a good guy, and if she can't see that and treat him with some respect, then I will." I put my head down. It's starting to ache. If I sit here long enough I know I could fall asleep. "If you don't like it, then fuck you, too. Bre, Miss Goody fucking Goody, I'm sick of your ass, too!"

"Fuck you, Nicky!" Bre says. "I'm trying to help you and all you're doing is causing yourself more problems."

*E.R. McNair*

I look up at Bre and adjust my focus. "Who the fuck are you, Oprah fucking Winfrey? Don't lecture me and I don't need your God damn help."

"Nicky, I'm going to ignore what you're saying because I know it's the alcohol that's talking. But don't come to me crying when all this shit hits the fan."

Fuck Bre. Why should I listen to her? I deserve to be happy. I'm a good person. I can feel tears begin to sting my eyes.

We've been in the bathroom for at least twenty minutes when some chick busts through the door and says that DayDay is about to get fucked up!

Bre helps me up from the floor. She gets me to the sink and helps me clean myself up. I splash cold water on my face and we leave the bathroom to try to find out what's going on. When we get up to VIP, we see DayDay and Tone standing nose to nose. CeeCee is off to the side of them.

"Motherfucker, I told you I do what the hell I want!" CeeCee says, waving her hands in DayDay's face. "Why you have to come over here and mess my groove up?" She has her other hand on her hip and her head is wobbling back and forth like a bobble head doll.

"Look, bitch, I'm tired of you disrespecting me all over town like I'm some punk-ass nigga. Do I ever bring my shit in your face?" Mello is standing behind DayDay keeping him from jumping on CeeCee. "You think you're going to sit here with this nigga right in front of me? Hell no, it's not going to happen, not today." DayDay turns to

Tone. "So look here, nigga, I know you've been fucking my woman, but that shit ain't going down now, for real. No disrespect to you, dog, but CeeCee is leaving with me tonight."

Tone is a cool-ass dude. He stands in front of DayDay and doesn't move. His demeanor is calm and he doesn't blink an eye.

"I think that's up to CeeCee. You know how the game works. If your bitch chooses me, then you have to respect that shit."

Both of them turn to CeeCee.

That hoe, she's got these niggas fighting over her. I look at her and I feel sick to my stomach. What is it about her? I see Slick off to the side, that trick he was with at the mall standing beside him. I think I saw her in the bathroom when I was with Bre. I can't believe this shit is happening.

I want to scream at DayDay, "You don't need her, you've got me." But I can't. The words are stuck in my throat. I want to tell him that his mother likes me better than she does CeeCee, but I can't get the words to form in my mouth.

"CeeCee, what the fuck are you going to do because if you leave with this nigga, that's it," DayDay says. "I'm done with your ass, and my kids, they're coming with me 'cause your raggedy ass don't give a shit about them anyway."

Why can't DayDay see that she's already made up her mind? She's been sitting up with that nigga all night.

*E.R. McNair*

They were damn near fucking over in the corner. She's not going to stop fucking with that nigga. I even heard that she was going to visit Tone while he was locked up. She was putting his money on Tone's books. Come on DayDay, forget that bitch! We can raise the kids, me and you, together.

"Nigga, you think you're going to sit here and threaten me about my kids? Are you crazy?" CeeCee jams her finger into DayDay's forehead.

And then DayDay snaps. All hell breaks loose. DayDay turns around and punches CeeCee dead in her face. I can't believe it. I run up behind him and try to grab his arm to stop him from hitting her again, but he spins around again and I'm thrown to the ground. CeeCee drops to the floor like a ton of bricks and she and I are laying side by side; the only difference is that she's out cold.

Then DayDay, even though he's got nothing on Tone when it comes to size because Tone is a big-ass nigga, hits him square in the jaw. The next thing we know these two are going at it.

Out of nowhere someone yells, "Gun!" and everybody starts running everywhere. I'm knocked down, and I can't see Bre; she was just holding me up. I hear pop, pop, pop and then I see people running and screaming.

I can't move. I'm in so much pain from being stepped on. And all of a sudden someone grabs me and snatches me up. It's still a little dark in the club but when I catch a little light I can see that it's Slick.

"Let's get the fuck out of here," Slick says and he pulls me through the crowd.

Once in the parking lot he's on his cell phone and then within a couple of minutes a car speeds around the corner and abruptly stops in front of us. Slick jumps in and the car races away.

I'm alone in the lot except for the people running around to find their cars. But where are my girls? I slowly walk back toward the Upscale and the pain in my head stops me in my tracks. I hold the front of my head. It feels as if it's going to crack open any minute.

Sirens cut through the dark Gary, Indiana night air filling it with even more confusion. Police cars zoom to a stop all around me.

Bre and Mello rush out the club as I'm heading toward the door. Mello plants a kiss on her cheek and she blushes. How can that she play bashful during this mess? Then he takes off as soon as the cop cars begin to swarm around them.

The door to the club swings open again and Nesha and CeeCee stumble out. CeeCee's leaning on Nesha barely able to hold herself up. She still seems as if she's half asleep. They look as if they've just awakened from a horrible nightmare.

"Where the fuck have you been?" Nesha asks me. Her hair is a mess on top of her head and her wife beater is splattered with blood. Is it hers or someone else's?

I ignore her, still holding my throbbing head. Bre comes and stands beside me. "Let's go, the car's over here." She tries to guide me, but I stagger, almost falling to the ground. I grab onto her arm and again I try to walk.

Paramedics are wheeling club patrons out of the club's emergency exit toward ambulances and police officers are escorting others out to squad cars. Then we see another stretcher being wheeled out and we all recognize the victim. It's DayDay!

CeeCee screams and lunges toward the gurney, missing it and falling to the ground.

"Oh, my God! DayDay, wake up! Please wake up!" CeeCee rushes toward the ambulance where they have placed DayDay, but she's stopped by two big, burley police officers.

I want to smack the shit out of her and tell her to cut the shit. She's so drama.

DayDay's eyes are closed and I want to touch his face. He doesn't need all that screaming. I just want to whisper in his ear that I'm here for him if he needs me.

I feel everything that I put in my stomach all day rise to the top of my throat and I want to release it all, all over the ground. I try to suppress the urge but before I can stop myself, I'm leaning over and it's all coming up.

Bre's beside me and I can feel her hand rub my back and pull my hair up so that I don't ruin the weave I just had put in a week ago. I can still hear CeeCee screaming and making a scene.

I stand up and scream, "Shut the fuck up! Shut the fuck up you stupid bitch! This is all your fault. All this

*E.R. McNair*

shit is your fault!" I wave my hands around.

People are staring at me. I know I probably look a mess. But I don't care. I start to cry.

I walk over to CeeCee, who is still screaming. Nesha is at her side and I don't care. The way I feel, I'll fight them both right now. I stand right in CeeCee's face. "This is all your fault."

And before I know it, she slaps me. "Bitch!" CeeCee screams at me.

I raise my hand to slap her back and someone grabs me. The big rough hands of a man, I can't see who, carries me over to Bre's car and throws me in the front seat.

I'm pissed. I'm worried. I'm sad. I'm friendless.

I see Bre talking to a police officer. CeeCee's still acting like a damn fool. Now everyone is around her, showing her the attention she thrives on. I can't stand that bitch.

Finally, we all get in the car.

CeeCee's whimpering in the back seat. "I can't believe this shit," she says over and over again.

"We're going to the hospital," Bre tells me.

"Take me home," I say. I can't be around this shit all night.

"What the fuck?" Nesha shouts at me. "What the fuck do you mean take you home?"

"I said, take me home." I can't even scream back at her.

"Look Nicky, you live on the opposite side of town. We don't have time to take you home," Bre says.

*E.R. McNair*

I can feel my blood begin to boil. I get so hot and I think I might vomit again.

"I fucking want to go home!" I scream. "I want to go home!"

"Stop acting like a fucking baby!" Nesha screams. "Sit your ass still and ride to the hospital. You can take a cab home from there."

We drive in silence to the hospital. I'm not ready for what I'm about to see. My heart is aching for DayDay and I'm pissed because I can't let anyone know my true feelings. I feel tears in my eyes but I can't let them fall.

# eight

**Bre**

CeeCee runs into the emergency room lobby and searches the room for someone to guide her to DayDay. She grabs on the white coat of an older, gray-haired man with a mop in his hand. "Excuse me!" CeeCee shouts in his face.

"CeeCee, let me." I pull her away from the man, it's obvious he's disturbed by her loud voice and her abrasive behavior. I hand her over to Nesha. "Who can give me information about a patient brought in by the ambulance?" I ask, trying to equal out CeeCee's roughness with my calm.

The man points to the desk across the hallway.

Before I can ask the question I hear CeeCee scream, "Here he is! DayDay, DayDay, baby! It's me, Cecilia! DayDay talk to me! Please!"

"Can someone get her away from here?" a nurse covered in blood calls out.

*E.R. McNair*

CeeCee moans, her cries louder than the commotion that was the emergency room.

I know we're in for a long night and once DayDay's mom finds out about all of this it's going to be an even longer night. We sit in the emergency room waiting area and CeeCee continues to cry, ignoring all the other patients and guests that are waiting there who have their own concerns. She has a black eye and a nurse asks if she needs to be seen by a doctor.

CeeCee growls at her, "Go fuck yourself."

I apologize to the nurse with a smile and she turns to go back to her station a little wounded by CeeCee's words.

I try to console my friend. "CeeCee, sweetie, it's going to be okay. Day's strong. Girl, we just have to pray for him, you have to be strong for him. Can I get you some coffee or a soda?"

I think she's going to tell me to go fuck myself too. But instead she says,

"Bre," her acrylic nails ripping into my skin, "I don't know how to be strong for him. I can barely be strong for myself. How could I do this to him? It's my fault that he is in this situation." She moans and rocks back and forth.

Her buzz is completely gone.

Nicky barks, "Well, at least you can admit that this shit is all your fault. You can be such a selfish-ass bitch sometimes. It's always about CeeCee."

"Nicky..." I try to shut her up. Her buzz has disappeared as well.

But she continues, "You knew what the fuck you were doing like always, anything to get some attention. It's always about you ain't it, CeeCee?"

"Nicky, shut the fuck up please!" I scream irritated by her insensitivity. "This is not the time for this shit, okay?" I feel eyes on me from other patients and I shoot them a look that says leave me alone.

Nicky is adamant. "Whatever, Bre..."

"Nicky, I'm going to take your ass out in the parking lot and beat you down!" Nesha jumps up.

"When you feel froggy, jump bitch!" Nicky shouts back at Nesha.

I move between them. "Do you want security to ask us to leave? Can't you two be civil for a few minutes? Nicky sit your ass down and Nesha..."

"What?"

"Chill out, damn! Look what this shit is doing to CeeCee!" I say, looking down at CeeCee who's crying into her hands.

"I'm just saying," Nicky continues, her voice not as loud as before. "What's she going to tell his mom or better yet, his kids? 'I was trying be a hoe and I got your son and dad shot?' She needs to take responsibility for her actions, and you fucking know it."

"Nicky!" Nesha snaps again, "I'm not going to tell your ass again. Shut the fuck up, bitch!"

"I got your bitch right here, slut!"

"Look, Nesha and Nicky, please. Both of you can shut the hell up," I say again. They both act like sisters fight-

*E.R. McNair*

ing in the back of the family car. I wish I could backhand them both and shut them the fuck up.

They both sit down and decide to be quiet. CeeCee continues to cry.

"CeeCee, sweetie, do you want me to call Ms. Jackson?" I know the call needs to be made and I know that CeeCee is in no condition to make it.

CeeCee nods her head and it seems as if her moans are less frequent.

I punch the number into my cell phone and I try to be as calm as I can.

Ms. Jackson answers the phone and I can tell that I've disrupted her sleep. I know that this conversation will be even more difficult.

"Ms. Jackson, hi, this is LaBrea Watkins. I'm a friend of Dayonte and CeeCee's."

She pauses, waiting for the reason for my call. Everyone knows that no one calls in the middle of the night just to say hi.

I tell her that DayDay has been in an accident and that he's at Methodist Hospital on Grant Street and that we haven't heard from the doctor about his condition yet but we have no reason to expect the worst. I try to get everything out in one breath hoping she won't ask me too many questions I don't have the answer to.

After she screams, one loud ear piercing shriek, she tells me that once she can find someone to watch the kids she'll be right here.

"What did she say?" CeeCee asks. She's a bit more

coherent now. "I know she hates me and all hell is going to break loose once she gets here." Again she grabs my arm.

"Maybe it won't be as bad as you think." I look over at her and we both start laughing knowing that it'll be worse. "Can I get you something to drink or eat?"

CeeCee shakes her head and she closes her eyes.

DayDay's mom can't stand CeeCee. She says that CeeCee fucked up her son's life. She believes that Day was this good all-American guy before he started messing with CeeCee. Yeah, he used to play basketball for our high school and he was really good. But he was hustling weed long before he started messing with CeeCee. She didn't do it to him, he was already done. Ms. Jackson swore that DayDay to going to college and she blames CeeCee for him not going. And Ms. Jackson believes that CeeCee got pregnant on purpose to trap her son into staying at home, but that nigga wasn't going anyway.

A doctor comes out. "Is anyone here with Dayonte Jackson?" CeeCee jumps up and runs toward the doctor.

"I'm his wife, doctor," CeeCee lies, wiping at the tears in her eyes with a tissue I hand her.

The doctor hesitates but continues, "Good morning, I'm Dr. Lewis," he holds out his hand and shakes CeeCee's. "Right now your husband is stable. We found two bullets and one is very close to his spine. We think it's best to not remove that one right now. We're going to monitor him and then make a decision."

"Can I see him, doctor?" CeeCee asks.

*E.R. McNair*

"Not right now, we're still trying to make him comfortable. I'll send someone out to tell you when you can see him. But I would suggest that you wait until morning."

CeeCee looks at the doctor, irritated by his explanation. She looks like shit. "No, I'll stay right here." She begins to walk away.

The doctor nods and turns to walk away and just as he's leaving, DayDay's mom comes in. She's crying hysterically. "Where's my baby!"

"Is this your mother-in-law?" Dr. Lewis asks CeeCee.

Sheepishly, CeeCee shakes her head no as she's backing away from the doctor.

"Hell, no!" Ms. Jackson shouts, her good friend Ms. Gomer at her heels. "That tramp will never marry my baby."

Ms. Jackson grabs the doctor by his lab coat and screams over and over, "Please don't let my baby die!"

"Ma'am, you'll have to calm down." The doctor looks helplessly for security. "Ma'am, please, I can't explain to you what's happening if you don't calm down."

It takes a minute for Ms. Jackson to regain her composure.

The doctor explains to her what he's already told us and then he leaves to get back to DayDay.

As soon as the doctor leaves, Ms. Jackson starts in on CeeCee. "I guess you're happy now! Like you didn't fuck up his life enough when your ass tricked him and you got pregnant to trap him."

*E.R. McNair*

We probably could have recited word for word Ms. Jackson's rant. It was the same thing every time as if she rehearses it.

She continues, "I know you did this to my son, didn't you?" Ms. Jackson jumps in CeeCee's face. And she continues, "I know you had something to do with this, and so help me God, if my son dies, I will have your little ass killed! Do you hear me, you little slut? Dead!"

Security comes over, "Ma'am, I'm going to have to ask you to leave if you can't keep it down."

"Me? Me leave? What about her? She's the reason I'm here and you want to ask the mother of the man who's fighting for his life to leave? What kind of place is this?" Ms. Jackson falls down on the floor, moaning as if her heart has been broken.

Ms. Gomer helps her up and onto a chair and holds her in her arms as she shoots daggers from her eyes at CeeCee and anyone who is around her, guilty by association.

"Who called me? Which one of you called me?" Ms. Jackson asks, her voice hoarse from screaming, but also due to the three packs of cigarettes she smokes daily.

Hesitantly, I step forward. "It was me, Ms. Jackson."

She flashes a crooked, yellow, missing teeth smile. "Tell me what happened." Her whimpers are almost nonexistent now.

I explain to her that DayDay had gotten into an argument with Tone and that one thing led to another, shots were fired and it was DayDay who was shot. She asked

*E.R. McNair*

if CeeCee had anything to do with it and while I tried not to lie, in order to save the people in the emergency room an earful, I told her I didn't know why they were fighting.

"He's my only baby," Ms. Jackson tells me while she touches my face with her rough, dry hands. "I don't know what I'll do if something happens to him." Her tears return.

I search the room for Nicky and Nesha. Nicky is on the other side of the room on her cell phone and Nesha is MIA.

I dial Mello's number prepared to give him all the information I have. The phone rings four times and then goes to voicemail. I get ready to leave a message and then my other line clicks and it's him.

"Hey, Mello, I just wanted to call and let you know what's going on with DayDay."

"Is my boy okay? I'm on my way there right now. Methodist, right?"

"Yeah. He's stable. The doctors want him to rest so we haven't been able to see him. Ms Jackson is here, though, and she's been tripping." I try to whisper.

"How is she right now?" Mello asks.

"Calm now, but how long that will last, no one knows."

"I'm pulling up now. I shouldn't ask because it's that bitch's fault we're in this shit, but is CeeCee okay?"

"She was flipping there for a minute, but she's much better now. We're all real tired and we need to go home, but she won't leave. So, I'm staying with her. I'll see you in a few."

We sit in the waiting room for what seems like hours before the doctor comes back out. Nesha returned and she and Nicky are asleep on a couch. I fell asleep on Mello's lap and when I open my eyes, CeeCee is looking out the window, a cup of coffee in her hand. I don't see Ms. Jackson's friend, but Ms. Jackson is sitting in a wheel chair by the nurse's station and I wonder what drama went down while I slept.

"Hi, Ms Jackson, we met earlier," the doctor speaks to DayDay's mom. "I wanted to give you all an update."

CeeCee moves closer to the doctor so she can hear what he's saying.

"What do you want? Haven't you done enough?" Ms. Jackson shouts at CeeCee.

"Look, I care about him, too. I want him to get better." CeeCee throws her cup down and the remaining coffee splashes onto the floor. "Why are you doing this to me?" She starts crying.

Mello walks over and tries to defuse the situation. "Momma Jackson." He holds her hand.

She smiles up at Mello. "Go ahead, doctor."

"Right now is going to be touch and go. It's all really up to your son and how much fight he has in him. He's on a ventilator and unfortunately, he's unconscious. So we don't know exactly how much damage is done. We won't know until he wakes up." The doctor looks at us all. By now Nicky and Nesha are awake. "The next twenty-four hours will be the most critical. That's all I can tell

*E.R. McNair*

you right now. Now I need to get back, but if you have any questions you can talk to someone at the nurse's station."

That's all that CeeCee and Ms. Jackson need to hear. CeeCee loses it, and so does Ms. Jackson. We all try to calm them both down but to no avail. The nurse tells us that it would be best for us to take both of them home so that they can get some rest. There isn't really anything that we could do at this point.

"I'm not leaving my son," Ms. Jackson cries.

The nurse says, "Ms Jackson, you and this young lady, if you promise to go home and get some rest, you can go into Dayonte's room, but only for a minute, and only if you do not cause any disturbances."

"Thank you, nurse. We'll make sure not to disturb my son. I promise."

Once the nurse leaves, Ms. Jackson lights into CeeCee, but she keeps it to a whisper. "I shouldn't let you see shit, you little bitch. I don't know what happened to my son yet, but I know your little whorish ass had something to do with it. When I find out what went down, and if you had anything to do with it, you won't ever see my son again, ever."

"Look, Ms. Jackson, it's been a long night. I'm tired, you're tired. Do we have to do this right now?" CeeCee says. "Let's just go see DayDay."

While Ms. Jackson is in the room, Mello comes back inside from using his cell phone. "Where's Momma Jackson?"

E.R. McNair

"She's in with DayDay. Can you take her home when she comes back out?"

"Of course." He puts his arm around me. That was the boost of energy I needed.

Ms. Jackson comes out and CeeCee rushes in the door bumping DayDay's mom out of the way. Mello grabs the older lady stopping her from going back into the room and disturbing her resting son.

"I'll call you later," Mello says to me as he escorts Ms. Jackson and Ms. Gomer to the elevator doors.

Once CeeCee comes out, we all leave the hospital.

I drop everyone off and head home. I'm tired as hell, for real, and the sun has come up. When I get home, the first thing I do is take a bath.

Afterwards, I doze off. My phone rings and I answer it, pissed that the caller is cutting into my sleep.

"Bre?" It's Mello.

"Hey, Mello, what's going on?"

"You made it back home from the hospital?" he asks.

"Yeah, I'm just getting into the bed."

He's quiet for a few minutes. "I was just sitting here thinking about everything from last night. That shit was crazy for real. I think I'm still in a daze."

"Yeah," was all I could think of to say. "Did you get Ms. Jackson home?"

"Yeah, I got her home. I was calling to see if you felt like some company. I'm pretty fucked up about my boy and I just wanted to chill with you," Mello confides.

"I feel you but I don't know how much company I'll

*E.R. McNair*

be. But sure, I'd love to see you."

"Open the door. I'm right outside and I brought breakfast. I hope you like bacon and eggs."

## nine

**CeeCee**

I can't sleep. When I close my eyes I relive the whole night and it's hell all over again. I need to get back to the hospital. I need to see DayDay. If I don't, I don't know what's going to happen or what I'm going to do.

The room is silent except for the hum and the occasional beep of the equipment helping to keep DayDay alive. I force myself to look at him and I can feel the tears well up in my eyes. The scars on his face are fresh and his right hand is swollen, probably as a result of connecting a solid punch to Tone's jaw.

I'm cold and begin to shiver. I'm not sure if it's because of the temperature of the room or if it's a result of my fear. I can't bring myself to move closer. I'm scared if I walk I'll disturb something vital to DayDay's ability to breathe, to live. I want to turn and run out the room, but I can't do that either.

*E.R. McNair*

The door swings open and I expect to see Ms. Jackson but instead it's a nurse. She smiles at me, but I can tell she's startled by my presence. "I'm sorry?" She notices that I jump and grab at my chest.

I fake a smile and I open my mouth to explain why I'm there but she nods her head, letting me know that no explanation is needed.

I try to catch my breath and quickly, I wipe at the tears in my eyes and adjust my clothes in an attempt to regain my composure.

"I'm just here to check his vitals," the nurse tells me. She moves quickly around the room reading monitors, scribbling notes on his chart obviously less concerned than I am about disturbing my man.

"Can I get you anything?" the nurse asks.

I shake my head no, still not able to find words.

The nurse leaves and I move closer to the bed. I watch the rise and fall of DayDay's chest and I begin to cry again. I quickly reach out and grab his hand. Even though the room is freezing, his hand is warm.

"DayDay, I'm so sorry." I put my head down on the bed. "Please, baby, don't leave me! Please, the kids and me, we need you. I love you so much. God, please don't take him away. I need him, please."

The words fall freely from my lips and I'm able to say right now what I've never been able to say before. "I love you, DayDay. I know that you can hear me. I just want you to know that I love you so much and I don't know what I'd do without you." I lean in and kiss his full, swollen lips.

Before I leave, not wanting to ruin my chances of being able to visit him again, I touch DayDay's face. When I make it to the door, I turn around and take another look at him, just in case this is the last time I see him breathing.

*E.R. McNair*

## ten

**Bre**

Before opening the door, I look around my small one-bedroom apartment to make sure that everything is in its place. My living room and dining room are one big room and so I use a large bookshelf to divide them into two rooms.

I have a pretty blue sofa with a large comfy blue chair. I love bright colors so I accented the space with red, yellow and orange pillows thrown on my sofa and chair. My tables are silver with glass tops. My dining room has a glass and silver table with high back silver chairs and I have all stainless steel appliances in my kitchen. I like the contemporary look.

Satisfied that the place is neat enough, I open the front door and my heart flutters. Mello looks so good. He's changed his clothes. I can see in his eyes that he's really hurt about everything. I grab the bag of food from him and lead him into the dining room so we can eat and talk.

"Bre, I'm sorry that I left you at the club like that." He puts his head down. "I just can't go back to jail," Mello continues, sadness in his voice. "Man, that place ain't for me, and all I needed was to be caught up in that shit." He looks in my eyes and grabs my hand. "Day is my boy, and I will always have his back. But I got this shit handled, for real."

I nod. "You don't have to explain anything to me. I'm sure Day understands why you left. I just can't believe that Tone shot him like that! That's some crazy shit. You know we hear about niggas getting shot all the time, but I never would have thought it would have been DayDay."

"Me, either. But that nigga, Tone, he's going to get his, believe that. This shit ain't going down without him knowing that he fucked with the wrong niggas. He fucked up when he shot Day." Mello stands up and paces the room. "CeeCee's ass is fucked up, too. She knew that was some foul shit she was pulling. I told my boy to leave her ass alone a long time ago." He looks back at me. "I know she's your girl, but she's a sheisty-ass broad and that's real."

"I know CeeCee does some messed up stuff sometimes, but you have to know her past. She had it real fucked up, and I really don't think she's capable of giving herself to someone, not totally. You know, you've heard of those people that fuck up good stuff because they can't believe that someone could actually be good to them?" I explain.

*E.R. McNair*

"I think she stayed with DayDay because he allowed her to get away with murder and she knew that he wasn't going anywhere. She was able to control him when so many other things in her life were out of control. Last night was the last thing she expected would ever happen." I push the food on my plate around, deciding that I'm really not all that hungry which is surprising since I haven't eaten since yesterday afternoon at CeeCee's.

"You know, DayDay had never been that up front with CeeCee in all the years they've been together. He had never told her ass off like he did last night. I think this whole thing is going to open up her eyes so she sees that she has a damn good thing with him. I hope it brings them closer together and maybe even changes who she is. But come on, Mello, you have to admit that DayDay has fucked up, too. How long has he and Nicky been kicking it?"

Mello looks at me as if he can't believe I know about this information. "Come on, Bre, I can't tell you that. Yeah, it was fucked up that he was doing Nicky, but she was the one who came to him. He's a man, what do you expect him to do when some bitch is throwing her pussy at him? And then, she was treating him way better than CeeCee ever did. Shit, he'd be a fool not to go after that. Really, I think he was starting to think about their relationship and he finally realized that CeeCee ain't the only chick out there. He knew he could find someone who would treat him much better and respect him, which she don't do at all. If she cared about him, she wouldn't have pulled that shit last night. Now you have to agree with that?"

I thought about it. "I guess you're right." I'm unable to argue for CeeCee. She dug her own hole this time. "I don't know though, I think they both were lacking in the respect department."

"Yeah, well, Bre, I can see you're different, and I hope that we can become more than friends. For real." He smiled at me. I start to warm up from the inside out.

"Well, we will have to see about that, now won't we?"

Mello smiles at me. "Thanks for talking to me, Bre. I think I'm going to go." He begins to get up from the couch.

"Don't leave, please," I say and I move closer to him. I grab his hand and lean in, making him put his arm around me again. "I need to be held. I want to be held. That is if you don't mind."

"No, I don't mind."

I stand up and pull Mello by his hand to my bedroom. We lay down on my bed, fully clothed and we talk for what seems like forever. I tell him all about my mom and how I met CeeCee, Nicky and Nesha. He tells me that he met DayDay in the first grade. He says he was this cool little dude. His mom came to class with him and the teachers had to ask her to leave. Mello says that Ms. Jackson was so funny. She said she didn't want to leave her son with strangers. So Mello, being the hero that he is, said that he would be Day's friend and then it would be okay for her to leave him.

*E.R. McNair*

Mello says that he grew up with his dad because his mom died of ovarian cancer when he was two years old. When he met Ms. Jackson, she became like a mother to him and DayDay like a brother. Mello says his dad re-married when he was six and his stepmother was a real bitch. "She and my dad had three other kids and once that happened, I wasn't important to them anymore."

I tell him I could relate a little. I tell him that I have brothers and sisters by my dad, but I never met them.

"I learned to hustle in Chicago. DayDay and I would go to visit his aunt there. Her son was in the Vice Lords. We learned everything we know from watching them." Mello looks up at the ceiling. "I wanted to be just like them niggas. I wanted to join their gang, but they would-n't let me."

I turn on my side, lean on my elbow and stare at him.

"When I was sixteen I got a girl pregnant."

"You're a father?" I ask, surprised and not sure if I'm ready for the drama of a baby's mama.

"Not by her. The girl in high school lost her baby, but I have a baby by another girl, though. He's six. We're close. I have him every other weekend."

I'm not sure I want to know, but I ask anyway, "Mello, what have you heard about Tone shooting Day?"

"I don't have all the information right now, but, I'm being told that he didn't do it. One of his boys did, but it don't matter who it was. Tone is the one that's going to get handled behind it. If it was done, it was because he called for it to be done." He continues. "I made some calls but, it's better if I don't say anything to you. You don't need to be associated with this shit any more than you already are." He rolls over and looks at me. Then he touches my face and runs his fingers through my hair. "This game can be treacherous. I had to learn that from the beginning. But Bre, I like you. I like you a lot. And, I don't know what's going to happen with me and you, but I'm ready for whatever it is. I just need you to know that I have a lot that I deal with and if you don't hear from me or see me it's just business and has nothing to do with you."

I nod my head. But I have to think about what he's saying. I've been strung along by men in the past. But was I ready for this? Mello was letting me know from the beginning that he will be ignoring me and my calls. I'm sure I'm okay with that.

"Yeah," Mello says again, "I think I really like you, Bre. You are different from the others." He smiles, crosses his arms and closes his eyes.

I stare at the ceiling for a little while thinking about everything that has happened. Am I ready for all of this? Eventually, I fall asleep. Mello is right next to me, and I'm glad he's there. I feel safe with him beside me and I look forward to waking up in his arms.

*E.R. McNair*

# eleven

**Bre**

Mello and I are still asleep when the phone rings, waking me up. I strain my eyes to look at the clock and it reads two o'clock in the afternoon. A hint of sun peeks through the curtains. My head aches and I see I have a bruise on my arm from where someone ran into me the night before.

"Hello?" I answer, keeping my voice low as not to wake Mello. I leave the bed and move into the bathroom and close the door behind me.

"Bre."

I can tell it's CeeCee, but her cell phone is breaking up.

"CeeCee, what's wrong? I can barely hear you. You're breaking up."

"Bre, DayDay's mother is over here at my house..." CeeCee is screaming into the phone and it continues to fade in and out.

"Calm down, CeeCee."

"Bre?" Mello is at the bathroom door. "What's wrong?" he asks, knocking on the door.

I pull the door open. "It's CeeCee. She's screaming something about DayDay's mom being at her house?"

"Okay, okay, CeeCee. I'm on my way." I search for a pair of sweats to throw on.

Mello and I stare at each other with a look of "here we go again," on our faces.

When we get to CeeCee's house, the police are there, and every neighbor she has is out for the show. CeeCee's third-story apartment sits at the north end of the square. Those neighbors that aren't outside are in their windows looking down. Ms. Jackson is talking to one of the officers when we pull up.

"Officer, uh, Richards, I don't give a fuck what this bitch says." She takes the last hit of her cigarette and she throws it onto the ground. "I ain't giving her ass shit. This bitch don't want her kids. Do you know how long these kids have been at my house?" Ms. Jackson yells.

"All I want is my fucking kids. They're my kids. I want my kids!" CeeCee yells back. When she sees me and Mello she runs over to us. "Bre, she won't give me my kids back." CeeCee has on a pair of jeans, a T-shirt and her hair is tucked under a navy blue bandana.

"Look, Ma'am, if you don't have legal documents indicating that you have custody or legal guardianship of her kids, then you have to turn the kids over to her,"

*E.R. McNair*

Officer Richards responds.

Ms. Jackson glares at CeeCee. "No, I ain't got custody of those kids. But I should. Ask her how long they've been at my house. They've been there for weeks."

Ms. Jackson's lying, but she's trying to prove a point. I look at her and shake my head.

She continues, "she abandoned those kids, and now all of a sudden she wants them back. I'm their grandmother. I take care of them kids, not her," Ms. Jackson says. "Mello, tell them. That's her friend over there." Ms. Jackson points at me. "That's her friend, ask her, she knows how long them kids have been with me because they've been together."

The officer looks annoyed. "Look, ma'am, I understand your concern, but right now you will have to give this young lady her children. If you wish to obtain custody or become their legal guardian, you will need to do it through the court system. Do you understand?"

"I don't believe this shit! This raggedy bitch gets my son shot, and now I have to give her the only thing my son has to fight for, his children?" Ms. Jackson yells. "I won't do it, you'll have to take my ass to jail!"

"Then take that bitch to jail then. She's breaking the law, Officer. She's kidnapped my kids. I want them back right now," CeeCee demands.

"Look, ladies," the officer intervenes. "We can do this the easy way or the hard way, it's really up to you two. Now, Ma'am, you said your son is in the hospital, and if that is the case I think the last place that you would want to be is in jail. I suggest you give this young lady her kids and worry about your son getting well."

"I can't focus on my son when I worry about my babies, don't you get it?" Ms. Jackson asks, with tears in her eyes.

"I can't believe this bitch! Don't believe those damn tears!" CeeCee yells. "Those are my babies, don't *you* get it? I know how to take care of my damn kids."

"I can't tell. You don't ever have them. I'm surprised they know who the fuck you are, tramp!"

"Okay, that's it," the second officer, Officer Greene, interrupts. She's had enough of the drama. "Ladies, we're going to take you both downtown and straighten this out there. We will need to call youth services to take the children until this is taken care of." Officer Green moves toward the cruiser and proceeds to call downtown for backup.

"See what you did, bitch! Now they're going to take my kids to foster care! Please, officer, I'm sorry, I won't say anything else. Just please take me to get my kids."

"Ms. Jackson you have one more opportunity, what's it going to be?"

DayDay's mom stands still, she lights another cigarette and blows the smoke in the air. I'm exhausted. I can lay down on the ground and fall asleep. I know I'll be going to bed early this evening or it will be a long day at work tomorrow.

"Ms. Jackson?" Officer Richards asks. "What's it going to be?"

*E.R. McNair*

"Fine, I'll take you to get the kids. CeeCee, you are on warning. If anything happens to my grandbabies it's your ass."

"That's enough, ma'am, let's go. Ms. Davis, we'll be back with your kids," Officer Richards says.

"Okay, and thank you, Officer Richards, I really appreciate all of your help," CeeCee says.

"Yeah, well, you can show me by taking care of your kids once you get them. You understand?"

"Yes, and I promise, they'll be well taken care of," CeeCee replies.

We watch the police cruiser leave.

Mello asks CeeCee while fishing money out of his pocket, "Do you need anything; money for food?" He hands her a wad of cash.

CeeCee pushes the money back to him but Mello insists.

"All right, Bre, I'll holler at you later on. I have some things I need to handle," Mello says. We drove separate cars and so I can get home later.

"Okay, Mello, I'll talk to you later." He kisses me on my lips and I think I might melt. "I'm going to hang out with CeeCee for a little."

"CeeCee," Mello turns to her, "take care of my boy's kids. He's fighting for his life and they are all he has right now."

CeeCee nods. It's obvious she's a little choked up. "I really do love my kids. I know sometimes you wouldn't think that I do. But I do. It's just hard for me to show it.

*E.R. McNair*

I know how Day feels about them. I'll take care of them."

After Mello leaves, CeeCee and I talk while I help her straighten up her apartment before her kids come back home.

"I think I'm ready for a change, Bre."

"Oh, yeah? What are you thinking?" I ask her as I folded a basket of clothes.

"I'm not sure. I just can't keep going through this crap. I'm tired of arguing with DayDay. I'm tired of arguing with his mother. Bre, I'm just tired."

"Is there anything I can do to help?" I ask.

"I'm not sure. I don't know what to do myself."

"Well, if I can help, let me know."

"I will. Thanks, Bre."

About an hour later the doorbell rings. CeeCee opens the door and the kids run in. They're so excited to see their mother. Questions are flying at CeeCee from three directions. I wave at CeeCee telling her I'm going to go. She waves back and winks at me.

I can tell that the change she talked about is already taking place. I'm so proud of her and I hope CeeCee's optimism is contagious.

It's been a few days since I last talked to Mello. It made going to work so hard. I really miss him. I remembered our conversation about him not being around because he had things to take care of, but that didn't ease the ache in my heart. I knew I wouldn't like this. I

*E.R. McNair*

try not to be mad but that shit still pisses me off. I mean, niggas act like they can't pick up a damn phone and say 'I'm alive' or 'I'm busy, but I've been thinking about you. I'll get back with you in few days.'

Sunday night before I went to bed Mello called and asked me on a date Friday night. It's now Tuesday and I haven't heard from him since then. I'm hoping that everything is okay and that he's all right.

This relationship is starting to remind me of my first love. His name was Donald and he would pull this same shit all of the time. I called myself saving my woman-hood for him. He had me gone. It seemed like every time I would be ready to say, "fuck him," he would do something to make me stay around. After we had sex for the first time and I thought I was definitely in love with him, Donald had some girl call me and tell me that she was kicking it with Donald and he wanted me to quit calling him. I was so hurt I didn't tell anybody. It was times like those that I wished I had a big brother or my father around so I could get advice.

I'm starting to feel like, "Here we go again." This was the reason I stayed single for so long. Niggas ain't shit.

My thoughts are interrupted by the phone ringing.

"Hello."

"Hey, Bre, what's going on?" Nicky asks.

"What's up?" I ask, not sure if I feel like talking to Nicky. She's part of the problem.

"I haven't talked to you in a couple of days. I just wanted to make sure you're okay. How's it going with

Mello?"

I had just gotten home from work. I was pulling my shirt off over my head trying to balance the phone on my ear. "I haven't talked to Mello in a couple of days either."

"What? Well, what does that mean?" Nicky asks.

I wasn't sure what she was up to. If she'd fuck around with CeeCee's man, the same man she has children with, would Nicky try to push up on Mello, a man I've just been talking to for a very short amount of time?

"I'm not sure what it means. Have you talked to him?" I ask, wondering if she would bust herself.

Nicky pauses. I wonder if she's on to me. "Why would I talk to Mello?" Nicky asks. She sounds a little pissed off.

"I don't know. I just thought I would ask."

Changing the subject, Nicky says, "You know they found Tone in his car last night? He was shot full of bullets and burnt to a crisp. It was on the news and everything."

"For real?" I ask, surprised by the news. "Girl, I've been going to bed early for the past couple of nights. My body hasn't caught up from the sleep I didn't get Saturday night." I look at the bruise on my arm and see that it's fading.

"I knew you wouldn't have seen it. Isn't that some crazy shit?" she asks. "The word is that some of your boy's people did that shit. That's why I was asking if you've seen him."

*E.R. McNair*

"Tone's dead and you think Mello did it and you think he told me about it?" I ask, surprised by her question and worried that if she thinks that, how many other people would think it as well.

"I just asked," Nicky says. "I'm just trying to find out what's what."

"I don't know anything. Like I told you, I haven't talked to Mello in a couple of days."

"Hmmm," Nicky murmurs. I can tell she's skeptical of my answer.

I didn't care. I'm skeptical of hers as well. I don't believe that she hadn't talked to Mello. I hate being paranoid. I need to call CeeCee and see if she heard about this shit.

"Yeah, well, I hope your boy ain't have shit to do with it. I talked to Slick and Tone's boys are ready to murder everybody who's close to DayDay!" Nicky reports.

"Well, thanks, Nicky," I say, dryly, still doubtful of her intention. "I've got to go, I'm on my way to my mother's house," I lie.

"You'd better let your girl know what's going on. She'd better watch out, too."

It sounds to me that Nicky's making a threat, but it's not blatant.

"I will. I'll let her know. Thanks, Nicky."

She hangs up before I can say anything else.

I turn on the television to see if I can catch the story on the seven o'clock news. I try to call CeeCee, but I get her voicemail so I figure that she's at the hospital visiting Day. I try to call Mello again a few more times. I leave a message and tell him what Nicky said and I tell him to call me as soon as he gets my message.

I'm not sure that I feel as safe with Mello as I did before. I just hope Mello is alive and that he's safe and that he has nothing to do with Tone's death, for all our sakes.

*E.R. McNair*

## twelve

**CeeCee**

It's hard to find things to occupy my time. It's not like I don't have stuff to do around my house, there are dishes in the sink, dirty clothes in the hamper and the floors need to be swept and mopped. But I'm just so overwhelmed by my guilt that I'm too tired to do anything else. I'm trying to be patient with the kids when they ask about their dad and whether or not he's going to be all right, but I'm finding that hard as well. I cry all the time and I wonder if the tears are for me or DayDay.

DJ is trying to help with me Ashley and Alexis. I have to smile. I then feel guilty that I took my children for granted, too. Maybe it's true that the apple doesn't fall too far from the tree and I'm more like my mother than I thought.

The phone rings. More often than not, the caller is someone shouting obscenities or someone telling me that that "I'm dead." They call me bitch, hoe, or slut. I've been told that I better watch my back or that someone is watching me. I don't let the kids answer the phone anymore and try to explain to a six-year-old that she can't answer the phone because there are people that are saying bad stuff calling.

This time I pick up the phone and it's Bre.

"Hey, CeeCee what's going on?" she asks. "Are you and the kids okay?"

"Hey, Bre. We're okay. I just haven't been sleeping and so I'm a little exhausted is all," I say.

The kids come into the room and turn on the television. Alexis hands me her broken Barbie doll and I pop the leg back on it.

"Do you need anything?" Bre asks.

"No. What I need you can't give me. I need peace, Bre. Peace. How can I get it?" I ask and I can feel the emotion welling up again. I try not to let the kids see me cry. I don't want them to think anything is wrong. I keep my voice down. "I'm so worried. All the time. I worry when the kids leave, I'm scared they're not coming back. And it's not just from this Tone shit. It's DayDay's psycho mother. I'm worried she'll go to the school and take them. My life is a mess. Not that it was all that perfect before."

"Whose is?" Bre asks.

"I guess you're right." I chuckle. "But then I go and fuck it up and it goes from bad to worse."

"Well, CeeCee, you just have to learn from your mistakes and keep going."

*E.R. McNair*

"I guess you're right."

"What's today's word about DayDay?" she asks.

"We just got back from the hospital not too long ago," I say, trying to find a comfortable spot in the arm chair. "I've been talking to DayDay. The doctors said they think he can hear us. So, I told him about Tone. The police came to hospital today to see if Day was awake yet. Then they questioned me about Tone, like I had anything to do with his murder." I laugh. "I never really thought I could kill somebody, Bre. But right now, I'm glad he's gone."

I think about the idea and still can't see myself shooting him then setting him on fire. "I told them we had been on a couple of dates. But I didn't know much about him. I hadn't even been to his house. But when I told them someone was calling my house and threatening me and my kids, they didn't even seem to care. It was like they thought I deserved it."

"No, you don't deserve it, CeeCee. I'm concerned about them calling your house. Do you know who it was?" Bre asks.

"I have some ideas, but I can't prove anything. That's why I just got my number changed and I didn't even give it to my mother." I stop. "You know, I wouldn't put anything past Ms. Jackson."

"You think DayDay's mom is calling your house?" Bre asks.

"Not many people hate me as much as she does," I say and the possibility makes more and more sense. "I don't know what I saw in Tone," I tell Bre, thinking about the nigga and the last time I saw him. I shudder at the thought.

"He was a trip. Maybe he got what he deserved. Remember that time he took that chick Tasha's son's wheelchair because he said she owed him money and if she could buy a wheelchair then she could give him his money?" Bre says.

"I don't even know what made me fuck with Tone. I mean at the time maybe it was the thrill of just being with a nigga with his reputation. I don't know," I tell Bre, tears returning. I grab a tissue from the table beside the chair and dab at my eyes. Alexis turns around and I smile at her to mask my sadness.

"CeeCee, we can't live in the past. We've all made some fucked up decisions. We just have to go forward. What's done is done."

"I talked to Nesha," I tell Bre. "Her brothers said they heard it was some Chicago niggas that killed Tone. Possibly gang-related. But we all knew Tone wasn't associated with any gangs."

"Gangs, no way," Bre agrees.

"Talk is also that he may have pissed off the wrong motherfucker in jail," I say.

"Possibly," Bre responds.

"I'm just glad the mother fucker is gone," I say. "Now if DayDay is okay, I can get on with my life."

"I'm sure it'll happen soon."

"I hope so," I say, but I'm not sure if it's true.

*E.R. McNair*

# thirteen

***Nesha***

The phone ringing wakes me from my sleep. I look at the caller ID and it's Charles. I don't know if I'm in the mood to deal with him right now. I have a major hang over.

But I don't answer the phone, he'll call me until I do, so I suck it up.

"Hello?"

"I'm coming to pick up Chuckie," Charles says and right off he sounds as if he has an attitude.

"Fine," I say, not wanting to instigate an argument. "What time, I'll have him ready."

"I'll be there in about an hour."

And before I can respond, he hangs up in my ear.

Charles and I never got along. But, the sex was the bomb! He did things to me that no one had ever done before, and I'm a professional. I should have known fucking with him wasn't going to work. We were too different. He has a job, I hustle. He went to college. I barely made it out of high school. He liked the excitement of my life. He liked living dangerously. But he was pissed when I told him I was pregnant. He demanded a DNA test and threatened often to take me to court to get sole custody when he found out that Chuckie was, in fact, his.

I could have Charles taken care of. But that wouldn't be fair to Chuckie. While Charles is an ass to me, he's the best dad ever to Chuckie. I know how it feels to grow up wanting my dad around.

I only wish my other children's fathers were half the man Charles is. Marshawn's dad is a career criminal. I got along the best with him. Shit, we'd be the dynamic duo if he wouldn't have gotten caught up in the last big bust here in Gary, and who knows where Angel's dad is. He split when he found out I was pregnant.

I sure can pick them, can't I? Let me get my ass up and make sure this house is straight before Charles gets here.

The phone rings again and I hesitate answering it. The number is a blocked number.

"Hello?"

It's CeeCee.

"What's up, girl?" I say, trying to straighten up the living room. I peek into Chuckie's room and I see him still asleep. He doesn't have on the pajamas I left out for my brother to put on him. I let him sleep.

CeeCee is quiet and I can tell she's still upset.

"Snap out of it, CeeCee," I holler at her after I close

*E.R. McNair*

Chuckie's door. "The shit is over. Fuck Tone's ass, he's gone."

I can hear her crying.

"CeeCee, I'm not going to listen to your ass feel sorry for yourself. You fucked up. So the fuck what. Get over it!"

My brother, I think it's Tito, hollers at me to be quiet.

"Fuck you!" I shout back at him.

"I'm tired of living like this, Nesha."

"Living like what? What's wrong with the way you're living?" I ask her. Sounds like her ass has been talking to Bre. "Shit happens, CeeCee."

"But it's my fault. I don't know what I'll do if DayDay doesn't make it."

"Yes you do. Your ass will keep living, just like the rest of us. We've been dealt this shitty-ass hand. We'll play it till we die. We've been doing this shit this long, CeeCee, don't wimp out on me now." I turn and kick my brother Marlon and tell him to move because Charles will be here soon. They understand the turmoil between us and try to help me. They don't want Charles to take Chuckie away.

CeeCee doesn't say anything.

Chuckie comes out of his room and he wraps his arms around my legs. I can't help but smile. He has red stains at the corners of his mouth and I know I'm going to hear shit if I don't get him cleaned up before Charles gets here.

"Nesha, I want more. I'm tired of fighting, cussing,

*E.R. McNair*

struggling. I'm tired."

"Then what are you going to do?" I ask CeeCee.

"I don't know."

"When you figure it out, let me know," I say and I hang up annoyed. Our life has been fine so far and now all of sudden things are suddenly wrong and need to be changed? What the fuck?

I throw Chuckie in the bathtub. We laugh, giggle and play. I dress him in one of the many outfits he has courtesy of Charles and his stuck up mother, Agnes. We anxiously wait, our reasons vastly different, by the door for his father. When I hear the engine of Charles's F-150 outside my door, my stomach rumbles with anxiety. I swing the door open and Chuckie runs and jumps in his father's thin but ripped arms.

Charles no longer has a smile for me. He now greets me with a disgusted snarl. I mirror his facial expression. The memory of his affection is distant.

"I'll bring him back tomorrow."

I grunt at Charles. I smile adoringly at Chuckie. I turn my back and go back into my apartment, ready to start my day. I have to earn some money. The rent is due.

*E.R. McNair*

# fourteen

**Nicky**

I need to talk to someone. This shit is a trip. Shootings in Gary are as common as the nickname Pooky is in the hood. But when someone close, close like DayDay was to me, gets shot, it really makes you think.

I'll try to call Bre, but she's been acting fucked up toward me lately.

I dial her number. She answers on the second ring.

"Hello?" Bre asks.

"It's me," I say, not sure how to proceed. I know she doesn't approve of my relationship with DayDay.

"What's up?" Bre asks. I hear water running.

"What are you doing?" I ask.

"Getting ready to jump in the bathtub," Bre answers.

I'm irritated. But I can't figure out why.

"I miss him, Bre. I miss him so much." I blurt it out and wait for her reaction.

"I'm not sure how to respond," Bre answers, turning

off the water.

"I've been visiting him at the hospital." I tell everything.

"What do you want me to say, Nicky?"

"I don't know. I don't know what I want you to say," I say quietly. "Say that it's okay. Say that it's okay for DayDay and I to be together."

"It's not, Nicky. It's not okay. You need to leave him alone and let him have the chance to make it right with CeeCee. They have a family together..."

I cut her off. "Fuck CeeCee, Bre! You act like she's your best friend. I'm your best friend, Bre. Me and you. I met you first. It was me and you. Remember the day we met? We played jump rope together? Why can't you be in my corner? Why CeeCee? I love him, Bre. Me! I love DayDay! CeeCee doesn't. If she did she wouldn't have been fucking Tone." I can't hold it back any longer.

"I understand all that, Nicky. But, all that other stuff is over. Let them start over."

"Fuck you, Bre," I say, coldly.

"You called me, Nicky."

I just sit on the phone hoping Bre will change her mind.

When I see that she's not going to change her mind about me and DayDay, I tell her that I have to go.

"Nicky?" Bre says.

I don't say anything. There's nothing else to say.

"I still care about you, Nicky." Bre says. "I care about you a lot. I just don't want to see you get hurt."

*E.R. McNair*

"You've hurt me," I say, finally finding words.

"You know what I mean," Bre says. "I didn't mean to hurt you. I love you."

My doorbell rings.

"I have to go," I say.

"Who is it?" Bre asks.

"I don't know," I lie.

"Call me back, Nicky," Bre begs.

"Maybe," I say and I hang up.

I pull the door open and Slick slides a balled up plastic bag into my hand.

"Are you coming in?" I ask him, smoothing out my hair.

"I've got a couple other runs to make," he tells me, jumping into his Jeep. "If you need something else, hit me up."

I nod at him and close the door. Who needs someone to talk to? I've got my new best friend right here.

*E.R. McNair*

## fifteen

**Bre**

It's been almost a week since the fight at the Upscale. DayDay's still unconscious, Tone has been set on fire and killed and I'm supposed to go on a date with Mello tomorrow.

I'm sitting in my living room relaxing after a long day of work. The television is on, but instead of watching it I'm thinking about everything that has happened. I take a drink of my soda and the telephone rings.

I answer it and a smile spreads across my lips.

"Hey Bre, what's going down, baby?" Mello asks.

"What's up? Mello, I haven't heard from you in a couple days. It's great to hear that you're still alive," I say with an attitude, unable to mask it. "But I'm busy right now so I'll need to call you back!" I slam the phone down, pissed that this dude has the nerve to speak to me like we've been talking everyday this week.

*E.R. McNair*

The phone rings again and I know exactly who it was.

I let it ring more times than I usually would.

"Hello?" I answer, my eyes roll up into my head. I fold my arms across my chest and listen for an explanation.

"Look Bre, don't hang up on me. I'm sorry I didn't call you but I was out of town. I had an emergency that I really had to deal with. Do you accept my apology?"

"I don't know Mello, I have to think about it. I was worried about you. I know you heard all the shit that's been going on around here?"

"No, I haven't heard shit. What's up?"

I don't know why, but it seems to me as if he knows exactly what I'm talking about. It's something in his tone. I go ahead and explain even though I don't believe him. "That nigga Tone got shot up and set on fire! They found dude in his car burned to a damn crisp. Nicky called me yesterday and told me that Slick is tripping talking about if Tone's boys find out this had anything to do with DayDay, they fucking up everything that nigga love."

Mello is quiet for a few seconds. "Get the fuck outta here. They set dude on fire. That's some gangsta shit right there. Damn, what can I say? I ain't heard nothing about that shit. But, my phone has been off for the couple of days. Hey, karma is a mother fucker for real. That nigga got his just due. All the shit he did to niggas in the hood, ain't no telling who was getting his ass back. Day was just the tip of the iceberg for that nigga."

"I hear you Mello. I just think that's crazy. I talked to CeeCee and she's on edge. She got her number changed because someone keeps calling her house and threatening her and the kids."

"Really?" Mello asks, interested in this new development.

"It's just been real crazy around here and I think that's why I was so mad at you for not calling. I was worried about you." I sigh.

"I know baby and I'm sorry. I won't let that shit happen again. So are we still on for tomorrow?"

"Where are we going?" I ask, excited like it's Christmas day.

"I'm not going to tell you right now. It's for me to know and you to find out."

"Not fair."

"Bre?" Mello asks.

"Yes."

"I can't wait to see you again."

"Me too."

We hang up.

"Well, enough about me." CeeCee tries to lighten her voice. "Have you talked to Mello? Do we have a love connection or what? It'd be nice if one of us fell in love and got married. I can't wait to be in the wedding."

"Whoa, slow your roll," I tell CeeCee. "We haven't even been on our first date yet."

"So?" CeeCee says.

*E.R. McNair*

"So, if the brother has no moves, then I can't be expected to spend the rest of my life with him," I tease.

"Girl, from what I've heard, he doesn't have a problem there."

"Good to know," I say.

I tell CeeCee that my pasta is done and that I'd better eat it while it's hot. I tell her I'll call her tomorrow and if she needs me to call me at any time.

I skipped lunch today because of all the work I had to get done and so my stomach is growling with anger, having been starved all day.

I eat my dinner in quiet. My friendships and now my relationship with Mello is taking a lot of my energy.

After dinner I wash up my dishes and then I decide to call Nesha. I haven't talked to her a few days.

I dial Nesha's cell phone number. It rings a couple of times and then goes to voice mail. I hang up, deciding not to leave a message.

Two seconds after I hang up, my phone rings. I see that it's Nesha.

"Hey, Nesha, what's going down, sweetie?"

"Who's this?" Nesha asks.

"Nesha? It's me, Bre. You don't remember my phone number?"

Nesha laughs. "My bad. What's up? To what do I owe this call? I ain't heard from you in a minute," Nesha says.

"I know. I'm sorry. But I wanted to call and check on you and the kids."

"Thanks, B."

"Don't sound so excited to hear from me," I say, faking disappointment.

"I hear you, Bre. It's okay. I know you only fuck with me because you have to." She laughs. "It's all good, you're still my girl, Bre Bre."

"See there you go, Nesha. I care about you. You know I love you, girl."

"Yeah, I hear you but for real. I'm good. The kids are good. I've just been chilling hanging out. Just trying to lay low. I decided to take a break from the streets."

"I hear you. I've been chilling, going to and from work. And just thinking about where were all gonna be in five years from now."

"Five years, please. I'm just hoping I make it to next summer," Nesha says.

"You heard about Tone getting killed?"

"Yeah, heard it all," Nesha says.

I can tell she's doing something or someone with me on the phone. I decide to hurry up and get off the phone with her.

"I have a great idea. Let's go out this weekend. What about Chicago? A girl's night out!" I'm excited about the possibility.

"Sounds good to me. I haven't been to Chicago in a minute."

I can hear someone else.

"Nesha, what the fuck are you doing?" I ask.

"Handling mine," she says.

I can hear her breathing start to increase and she's

laughing.

"Oh, hell no. You're not fucking some dude while you're talking to me?" I ask.

Again, Nesha laughs.

"I'm getting off of this phone, right now."

"No. Wait. Wait a minute. Wait." Nesha struggles to get the words out.

I'm horrified.

"Okay. Okay. I'm done," Nesha informs me, laughing into the phone.

I can't say anything.

"Bre. Oh, stop being so stuck up. Shit, a girl's got to get hers when she can. The kids will be home soon." Nesha lights up a cigarette and inhales deeply. "Okay, what, this weekend to Chicago?"

I don't know if I can talk to her. I'm imagining her fucking some nigga at her house with me on the phone and I feel like a voyeur.

"Oh, hell!" Nesha shouts. "Bre, call CeeCee on the three way so we can talk about going to Chicago."

I'm still unable to talk. I click over and dial CeeCee's number. I click back over.

"Hey, CeeCee," Nesha says.

"Hey CeeCee." I'm finally able to speak.

"What's poppin', Nesha and Bre?"

Nesha laughs, "CeeCee, Eddie was over and helping me blow off some steam and Bre called in the middle of it. She's upset cause I was handling business with her on the phone."

"Fuck you!" I scream.

"Get over it, Bre," Nesha says.

"Bre, we always do that. We have kids, we have to multi-task," CeeCee explains.

They both bust out laughing. I can feel myself turn red.

Ignoring them both, I start with my plan, "CeeCee, what about a girl's night out this Saturday?"

"Come on, CeeCee," Nesha pushes, "we could use a break from Gary."

"I don't know," Cee hesitates.

"Come on, CeeCee," I urge. "The kids can stay with DayDay's mom."

"They do miss her, but I can't trust that bitch. She would turn an overnight trip against me. You know I can't take that chance," CeeCee says. "I'm really trying to get along with her, you know. I call her. But she continues to be such a bitch. I'm just tired of arguing with her."

"I understand, CeeCee. But you can't stay stuck up in the house forever," I say.

"No you can't," Nesha agrees. "You are still young. You've got a lot of living to do."

"I told Ms. Jackson I want us to get along for the kids' sake. You know what she said? She told me to kiss her ass. Can you two believe that? Now what the hell kind of shit is that to say? Then she tells me she wishes her son would've met someone like Nicky before he went and layed up with my ass. I don't even know where that shit came from. What the hell does Nicky have to do with

*E.R. McNair*

Day and me? Then she says Nicky's a better woman than I am and that at least she respects her son."

"What do you two think?" CeeCee asks us.

I don't say anything. I try to stay quiet. My heart begins to beat fast.

"Oh, hell no!" Nesha hollers out. "That bitch is a trip. So, what's she trying to do, hook up DayDay with Nicky? That bitch is a trip."

CeeCee continues. "I don't know what to think. I'm like, is Nicky fucking with Day behind my back? I mean, what is really going on? Then I start thinking about all that shit she's been talking. But if she was, how would his mom know that shit?"

I stay quiet letting Nesha talk for both of us.

"Fuck that bitch!" Nesha barks.

"Bre, what do you think?" CeeCee asks.

Damn.

"I don't know, CeeCee. You know his mom is very upset. She would say anything to hurt you right now."

"No, fuck that bitch. Both them bitches need a serious beat down," Nesha says. "Stop making excuses, Bre."

"Yeah, that may be the case," CeeCee says, ignoring Nesha, "but I've been calling Nicky to see what's going on and she won't call me back. That right there, that tells me there's something going down, and I'm gonna find out just what it is."

"I got your back!" Nesha screams. "I got your back. You tell me when and where."

"For real, Bre, if Nicky stabbed me in the back like

that while she sat up in my face acting like my friend...
I'm going to seriously fuck her up. And you can put
money on that."

I try to change the subject. "Well what about
Saturday? CeeCee are you in?"

"I'll have to let you know, Bre."

"Nesha?" I ask.

"I'm in. I'm always up for a party."

"Come on, Cee?" I beg.

"Fine. I'll go."

"Can Nicky come?" I ask, not sure how many curse
words I'll hear.

"Fuck no!" Nesha screams.

"Did you hear what I just said to you?" CeeCee asks.
"That bitch has been smiling in my face and fucking my
man behind my back. You want me to sit in a car with
her for an hour and not beat her ass?"

"We are girls!" I remind them both.

"Fuck that shit. Are you living in a fantasy world,
Bre?" Nesha asks. "Grow the fuck up. That bitch Nicky
isn't CeeCee's friend."

"We don't even know if what CeeCee's saying is
true." God, I hate myself. Trying to keep things the way
they are, I'm lying to everyone I care about.

"Whatever," CeeCee says, flatly. "I'll go."

"We're going to have so much fun," I say, hoping that
that's true.

"We'll see," CeeCee says.

"You better hope so," Nesha warns. "I got to go. I

*E.R. McNair*

have to clean up before my kids get home."

"I got to go too. I'll talk to you tomorrow, Bre," CeeCee says.

They both hang up.

I try to call Nicky, but she doesn't answer my call. I leave her a message on her voicemail about the plan to kick it in Chicago this Saturday and I tell her to call me back.

It's getting late. I take a shower and iron my clothes for work the next day. While getting into bed, my phone rings.

"Hey baby!" Mello calls into the phone.

I hear music in the background.

"Where are you?" I ask.

"I'm at the spot. But I wanted to say goodnight."

"I'm glad. It's good to hear from you. I kind of miss you," I say, surprised by my honesty.

"I miss you too. I can't wait to see you tomorrow."

"Me too."

"Dream about me."

"I will."

"Be good."

"I will."

I could tell he was smiling.

"Peace," Mello says.

"Bye." I hang up; a smile on face and one on my heart.

# sixteen

**CeeCee**

I've met so many new people at the hospital. I greet the nurses by name.

"How are you?" I ask Karen, a nurse assigned to take care of DayDay. "How's he doing today?"

"He's great!" Karen responds, her attitude always upbeat, always positive.

I take the children to the cafeteria to get a snack. While we're eating we talk about what happened in school today. DJ tells me that he got an A on his spelling test and Alexis tells me that she fell off the swings because she and her best friend, whose name is also Alexis, was pushing her too hard. She shows me the scrape on her arm and I kiss it trying to make her feel better.

"Ashley, how was school today?" I ask my six-year-old while wiping off an apple for Alexis.

*E.R. McNair*

Ashley shakes her head and turns away from me.

"What's wrong, Ashley?" I ask again, moving closer to her, concerned by her quietness. I put my arm around her and she leans into me and begins to cry. "What's wrong, baby?" I ask her again, becoming more concerned.

Her words are sort of incoherent and muffled, but I strain hard to understand.

"Donald told me today that daddy was going to die. He said that his uncle got shot and he died." Ashley's tears flowed fast and furious.

My heart was breaking. I hold Ashley in my arms and rock her back and forth trying to calm her. I ask DJ to take Alexis to the play area while I talk to Ashley.

"Ashley, Daddy's not going to die," I say, not even knowing that Ashley knew what death is. I hope my prophecy is true.

"Donald said that he was. He said that all people that get shot die." Her soft, meek voice a vast contrast to the subject of our conversation.

I shake my head. "That's not true. Not true at all." Now I know that for a fact. I feel myself getting upset and my voice rising to indicate my dislike for this Donald kid. Who was this child, this child who filled my precious daughter's head with negativity?

Ashley looks up at me and I wipe at the tears in her eyes. "Daddy's not going to die?"

I shake my head no.

"Do you promise?"

I shake my head yes.

"Double pinky promise?" Ashley asks.

I'm sure that's something she learned in on the playground. She shows me how to double pinky promise. And I do.

Ashley smiles at me and I can clearly see the gap her three missing teeth have left behind.

I hope I haven't lied to my daughter. She'll never trust me again.

I walk Ashley over to her brother and sister who are in the hospital's play area.

I sit down and I can feel my anxiety level rise. I'm worried about DayDay, I'm worried about how the kids are affected by this and how they're affected by all my drama. It's my mother all over again. I feel tears begin to well up in my eyes and before I can stop them they flow from my eyes and drip down my face and land on my bare arms.

As I'm searching my purse for a tissue, I see a hand extended before me with a tissue dangling from the end.

I look up and see a friendly face I've never seen before.

"Hi," she says. "I'm Beverly Stephens." She sits down beside me and hands me another tissue.

"Hi," I say back, smiling. But I don't feel like smiling. I force myself.

"I hope you don't mind me sitting?" Beverly asks.

"No," I say back. But I do mind.

"Your children are beautiful."

*E.R. McNair*

"Thank you," I answer, not sure what she wants.

"My father is here," Beverly tells me. "This is his second heart attack."

"I'm sorry to hear that." I wonder if she's waiting for me to tell her why I'm here.

"It's the waiting that's the worst part."

I shake my head. I agree.

"What helps me is to pray."

I look at her. I wonder if she can see the confused look on my face.

"Do you know how to pray?" Beverly asks me. Her words aren't condescending, they're calming, helpful, peaceful.

I shake my head no. I don't think I've ever prayed for anything.

"It's easy," Beverly says. "It's just asking God for what you want. Watch," she says. She bows her head and closes her eyes, "Dear God in Heaven, thank You for working in me to make me a better person. I thank You for this day and for every opportunity You've given me."

I look over at Beverly as she prays. Her eyes stay closed.

"I come to you, Dear God, with a grateful heart. Help me to honor You in everything I say and do. In Jesus's name. Amen." Beverly opens her eyes and looks at me.

I don't know what to say. I feel a little choked up.

"That was beautiful," I say quietly. I could feel tears in my eyes.

"I just spoke from my heart."

"I don't know if I can do that," I say, watching the kids.

"Of course you can."

I shake my head no. I know I can't do that.

"I know you can. If not today, then tomorrow. God knows what's in your heart."

I smile, feeling better by her words. "I hope so."

*E.R. McNair*

## seventeen

**Bre**

After I hang up with Mello, I grab and hold tight the T-shirt he left at my house. It still has his smell in it.

Again, my phone rings. Only bad news comes when the phone rings late at night. I grab the phone fearful of what I'm going to hear next.

It's my mom.

"Hey, mom."

"Hey, Bre. Sorry to call so late. But I wanted to meet you tomorrow morning for breakfast."

I think about it. Other than the fact that it's Friday and I'd be anxious for my date with Mello, I don't have any other plans.

"Sure, mom. What's up?" I ask, wondering why she wants to meet so early.

"Well, Bre," mom is slow to continue, "I received a letter for you from your father today."

"For real? A letter from my dad?" I snap. "I haven't

heard from him in years. And now he sends a letter. What could he possibly have to say now?"

"I know it's been a long time, Bre, but he's still your father. So, let's meet for breakfast and I'll bring the letter so you can read it."

"Okay, mom. I'll see you in the morning. Morning Watch?"

"Absolutely."

"Mom, are you okay with me getting this letter? I know you and dad split on bad terms."

"You know Bre, it doesn't matter one way or another, he's your father regardless of our issues. But we'll talk tomorrow. Get some sleep."

"Okay, mom, see you in the morning."

We hang up. I grab the T-shirt and hold it even tighter. My stomach is in knots. My date, the letter, DayDay, Nicky, it's all too much. I pray that sleep will come fast.

Morning comes before I know it. I'm still holding the T-shirt. I don't even feel like I've been to sleep. I dress quickly. I'm anxious to get to Morning Watch. I want to see what my dad has to say for himself.

When I get to the restaurant my mother is already seated. She has a cup of coffee in her hand and she's talking to the waitress.

"Mom," I say as I place a big kiss on her cheek.

"Hey, baby." She smiles at me.

She smells great.

*E.R. McNair*

"You're looking beautiful this morning," I say to her.

"Thanks, right back at you." She smiles. "I just realized that I don't get to see enough of you. What are you doing for dinner tonight?"

"I have a date," I tell her.

"Really? Anyone I know?" mom asks me.

"No," I say, staring into the menu.

"What?" mom asks, noticing my body language.

"What?" I ask back a little defensive.

"There's something that you're not telling me," mom detects. I can tell she's staring at me even though I'm not looking at her.

"No, mom. There's nothing to tell right now. If it becomes serious, you'll be the first to know." I smile hoping she'll back off.

"I hope so," mom says. "Go ahead and order."

Not only is Morning Watch a great place to eat, but it's also just around the corner from my job. I always get the same thing when I come here. Bacon, scrambled eggs and French toast with a large glass of tomato juice. I'm always stuffed when I get to the bank and it takes me about an hour before I can finally do any work, but it's worth it.

"Mom, have you talked to Aunt Boots?" I ask between bites of food. "We're thinking about going to Chicago on Saturday. I'm thinking about stopping by to see her."

"Well, I talked to her a few days ago. She said your cousin is thinking about coming home this weekend from school. I know that he'd love to see you and so would your aunt. Why don't you give her a call and see what she says? Here's the letter from your father."

I stare at the envelope looking at the handwriting, not sure how to feel.

"I'll read it later," I say, unable to put the letter down. "I'll call Aunt Boots to see if Terry is really coming home." I'm suddenly a little less hungry.

"Mom, did you ever think about my dad after you two broke up?" I'm curious about him. "I mean, you know, he was your first love? I know you've had boyfriends since him, but why didn't you ever remarry? Was it because of him?"

"Bre, I thought about your dad, a lot. I loved him, but there were a lot of issues between us. There were so many things that I don't think we would have ever been able to fix everything. There is so much that you don't know. Your father was a good guy, he just made a lot of bad decisions."

She drinks the last of her coffee. "Bre, promise me that when you really fall in love you won't lose sight of who you are just because of your love for that man. That's what I did. I was so in love with your dad that I put up with everything that he was doing for years. The women calling and coming by the house and the other kids he was having. I lost who I was. It took a long time to build up the nerve to leave. But I did. I wanted to be a good example for you.

"Your grandmother used to say 'if you're crying more

*E.R. McNair*

than you're laughing, then it's time to hit the road.' So I left. He was my first love and it hurt for a long time. And I have had other loves. I guess I never got remarried because I never really found anyone who I thought I could spend the rest of my life with. Besides, I'm not old, Bre. My boat hasn't sailed yet. You could still end up with a step-daddy one day," mom teases.

"Oh God, no mommy, that is the last thing on my mind, an old, gray-haired step-daddy. I don't even want to think about that," I laugh. "Mom, did my dad really have six other kids? Was that the issue with you all?" I ask, getting serious again.

"Bre, I don't know for a fact. That was the word on the street. There were a lot of women and some who said they had his babies. But there was no test." My mom raises her hand to get the waitress' attention. "Can I get the check?" She smiles.

Mom pays the check and we walk outside.

"Mommy, I hope you're not upset. You know that I love you, right?" I ask, shielding my eyes from the sun.

"I'm fine, baby, and I love you too," she says. "Have a good day at work."

"You, too," I say. We hug goodbye and I walk away toward the bank.

I look at the letter in my hand and a part of me wants to rip it up and throw it in the trash. But then there's a part of me that's curious. I want to know what he has to say for himself. I decide to open it up.

I tear it open and see that it's only one page. I expected more from someone who'd been missing for years. I can't understand how a man could just let his family walk away and not even try to get in touch with them.

It makes me think about Mello and what he said about his son. It sounds like he's a good dad. I hope so for his son's sake.

I hold my letter and look at the address and wonder where he lives, who he lives with, and how long he's lived there? I wonder if it was his family that kept him away from me. But why have they changed their minds now? There are so many questions and I know he couldn't have put all the answers in this one page letter. I decide to go ahead and read it to see what he says. I stop on the street in front of the bank.

*Dear LaBrea,*

*I know it's been a long time. And I know I'm probably the last person that you expected to hear from. I have made a lot of mistakes, and allowing your mom to leave was the biggest one I ever made. She was a good woman. I am sure you know that. I know that you have a lot of questions you want answered, and I am really not sure if I can answer them all. I was young when your mom and I were together, and although that is not an excuse, it's the only explanation I have.*

*I know you have heard that you have brothers and sisters. You have two younger brothers and two younger sisters. They all know about you, and I hope*

*one day you will all meet and get to know each other. I love you very much, and I am sorry that I could not have been a better man and do right by you when you needed me most. I missed all of the important things in your life, the things that a father should be there for. But I hope we can begin to mend our relationship and at least become friends.*

*I don't want to miss out on any more of your life. I hope you can find it in your heart to forgive me for not being there for you. If you would like to talk, please call me. My number is 330-555-2642. I am looking forward to talking to you. There is so much I want to say to you. I love you, baby girl.*

*Love, Dad*

After reading the letter, I just stand there. I can't breathe and it seems as if all the air in the world has disappeared. I realize that I'm blocking the door to the bank.

"Excuse me," a customer says with a little more attitude than necessary.

"Oh, I'm sorry."

What am I supposed to think? I haven't heard from him in years and then all of a sudden he shows up out of the blue and wants to start a relationship. Where the hell was he when I needed to talk about boys and other things my mom couldn't explain to me?

I ball the letter up in my hand. I hate him! How am I supposed to feel about the fact that I have brothers and

*E.R. McNair*

sisters? That makes me hate him even more. I mean, was he there for them? Was he in their lives? I need to know, but I'm afraid if I find out the answer will hurt my feelings.

"Bre? LaBrea?" I hear someone calling my name.

I turn to see my boss standing behind me.

"Are you okay?" Ms. Calloway asks.

"Yes. Yes, ma'am, I'm okay," I say embarrassed.

"Then let's get to work," she instructs as she sashays away from my desk.

I put my stuff away, throw the balled up piece of paper into the trashcan and then clock in. Then I rush to the bathroom and pull out my cell phone to call my mother.

"Mommy," I whisper into the phone.

"So, did you get the answers you were looking for?"

"Not really mommy, it was only a page long. Did you know he had other kids?"

"You knew that, Bre," mom says.

"I didn't know for sure. But now I do." I roll my eyes. "He wants to start a relationship with me."

"Well you know, Bre, that's a good thing. Don't punish your dad for his past mistakes. You should give him a call and see what his story is."

"I threw the letter away," I say, still upset.

"Okay."

"Okay!" My mother always has a way of getting me to do what she wants without even mentioning it. "I'll call him."

*E.R. McNair*

"I think you should," she says calmly. "When?"

"I need some time. I have too many other things going on right now to add him to the pile."

"Well, Bre, I know you're worried about your friends. You can't save everyone. Sometimes you have to let people take care of themselves and allow them to tend to their own business. If you weren't around, what would they do then? You handle your business." My mom drops knowledge on me. "And your father is your business."

"I hear you, mom. I hear you." I sigh.

I go back to my desk. I grab the letter out of the trashcan. I try to straighten it out, making sure that I can read the telephone number. I notice that Ms. Calloway staring at me. I smile at her and then pull out my keyboard and start working on the project she gave me earlier in the week.

Break time, I grab my cell phone and go to the cafeteria. I call CeeCee.

"What's up girl?" I ask CeeCee.

"Not much, just sitting here with Nesha and her bad-ass kids."

"My kids ain't bad," Nesha hollers in the background.

We talk about going out this weekend and my big date with Mello tonight. They joke that I might not be up to going out after Mello puts his thing down on me. I tell them I just might need the break after all of the action. I tell them that Nicky has agreed to go with us Saturday and that she left a voicemail at my house. They aren't really happy about it, but they agree that they'll behave.

I also tell them about my dad writing me and Nesha says I should call him. She says she would do anything to know her dad and that at least my dad is trying to contact me. She says she's often wondered if her dad even knows she exists. I tell her to talk to her mom and see if she'll tell her about him since she's older now and she has her own kids. Maybe her mom might just give her the information she needs to find him, or at least she might give her a name. She says she'll try, but she's not holding her breath.

CeeCee says, "I talked to DayDay's mom. She called me yesterday, out of the blue for real. She said that she had just come from visiting Day. She said Mello took her and they talked."

I hear Nesha in the background. "Man, fuck his mom. What else did that bitch have to say?"

I just listen, looking at my watch, making sure I don't go over my fifteen minutes.

"Come on, Nesha, that ain't cool, I'm trying to get along with her for the kids. Anyway, his mother said that she was going to try to be cordial," CeeCee says. "So we came to an agreement that the kids will stay at her house on Saturday. So I can go and kick it with you. Hey!" she continues, "we also came to an understanding about me and the kids visiting Day in the hospital. She'll visit in the morning and afternoon and leave the evenings for me so that I can take the kids when they come home from school."

"I'm happy to hear that everything is working out," I say, still checking out my watch.

"Bre, I know that you helped get us to this point. Thanks a lot, girl. I really just want my kids to be happy. And they really miss their Nana."

Again I tell CeeCee I'm glad to hear that Ms. Jackson is getting better. I tell her to tell Nesha I said bye and that I have to go back to work. "I'll talk to you soon."

I have to make sure there is no reason for me to have to stay after work. I work my ass off until lunch, not even taking time to use the bathroom, even though I thought I was going to bust.

At the stroke of twelve, I grab my purse and dash to the door.

# eighteen

**Nicky**
The noise is unbearable. My head has been hurting for days.

"Here, take this."

Slick hands me a couple of capsules. I look at them and wait for something to drink.

Slick looks at me and sucks his teeth. "Bitches." He leaves the room and returns with a bottle of beer. "Go ahead, take it. It's not going to work sitting in your damn hand."

He watches as I choke down the pills and take a hard drink of the beer. I cough uncontrollably and he continues to watch. I wonder if he's waiting for me to die.

"Get dressed," Slick says. His words are cold. He's a different person. He doesn't seem to care anymore. Not to say that he had the type of feelings for me a man has for a woman he wants to spend the rest of his life with, but there was a time he wanted to get with me. Now it

*E.R. McNair*

just seems like our relationship is one of employer/employee.

I can feel my body disconnect from its inhibitions. While this is a feeling I searched for before, right now I am repulsed by it. I can hear the crowd on the other side of the stage become loud and unruly and I want to run, run far away from this place, but I can't figure out where to go, or how to get there.

My cell phone is in my pocket and it begins to ring. I look at the caller ID and see that it is my mother. I can't deal with her right now. She'll for sure bring my high down and I need it to get through this.

"Now, Club Pinky's patrons, get ready for our newest addition to the Pinky family—the tantalizing, the tasty, the tempting, Naughty Nicky!"

I push back the curtains and step onto the stage. The overhead lights blind me and the music is so loud that the bass makes my insides jump. I can't see anybody and I guess that's a good thing. I can hear the applause and the feeling is good. Now my head and body are totally disconnected from each other. I start to move. The applause grows louder. I love this feeling. I get the sensation that I'm floating out of my body and I can see myself dancing. I'm smiling and the niggas are throwing their money on the stage.

I can't tell if I'm dancing to the beat of the music from the DJ or if I'm dancing to the beat in my head. But, whatever I'm doing, the niggas are loving me. I see Slick in the corner. He's got a toothpick in his mouth and he's smiling, a beer in his hand. He must like what he sees. I'm moving faster now. I dance down to the end of the stage. I hear the cheers and hollers of the niggas as I turn toward them. I shake my ass at them.

I'm on fire. I'm throwing clothes here and there and now I'm totally nude. I dance some more and then I feel myself falling. I'm falling down, down until I'm in the lap of a nigga I've seen before but don't know.

"Fuck! Nicky, fuck! Are you all right?"

I see Slick's face right in front of me, but I can't focus. I feel his breath, hot on my skin. And the smell of alcohol burns my nose. He's pulling me up and he throws me over his shoulder. My head begins to pound harder than it was before I took the stage.

I moan.

"Shut the fuck up!" Slick hollers at me.

I moan again.

"Bitch, you better work this shit out. Do you know what I had to do to get you this job?" He's throwing cold water on me.

I open my eyes and I'm lying, naked, on the pink leather couch in the dressing room.

I see the same guy whose lap I was lying in, he's smiling at me. I see Slick take money from him. I see him walk toward me. I close my eyes again. I shut them tight. I will myself to be someplace else, any place else but here.

*E.R. McNair*

## nineteen

**Bre**

Mello and I made plans to meet at my apartment right after work. I'm so excited about our date. I had planned to hold out and not go there on our first date, but every time I talk to him I want him more.

I know Mello isn't just interested in sex because he didn't try anything when he stopped past my house to visit and talk last Saturday night. I always try to wait until the fourth or fifth date with a nigga before I let him hit, but I would say that this isn't even really our first date, just our first outing together since technically we've been together before. Hell, we even slept in the same bed, so I'm not going to feel guilty about giving him some if I do.

In an effort to make tonight extra special, I schedule a Brazilian wax during my lunchtime. You know, to make it extra sexy for him.

Salon You is around the corner from my job so the

procedure will be a quick stick, pull and go. Jocelyn is ready for me when I get there. Perfect, because there have been times when her ass has almost made me late getting back to work.

"What's up girl?" Jocelyn asks as I prepare for the procedure.

"Hot date tonight!" I say, bracing myself.

"Are you ready?" she asks.

"As ready as I'll ever be," I say, holding my breath.

*Rip. Rip. Rip.*

I check myself out in the dressing room and I'm happy with what I see.

"Thanks, J," I say, dropping a hefty tip on her counter. "See you next time."

I leave Salon You feeling a little sexier than I had when I walked in. I wink at the security guard at the door of the bank and I even lick my lips at Jamie, hoping he doesn't get too hot in the pants.

God, I can't wait until tonight! The wet dreams about Mello are driving me crazy, and I really don't know how much longer I can take it. I just hope that this is going to be all that my mind is telling me it is.

I really like Mello. He's the first guy I've gone out with that I can really see myself being his woman. I have had my share of guys, but I've not really been crazy about a guy since high school. It's times like this I really miss not having a dad to talk to, to get a male opinion. I think about his letter and pull it out of my purse. I tell myself I'll call him, just not right now.

*E.R. McNair*

Right now my mind is on my date with Mello and I don't want to think about anything else.

# twenty

### Nesha

I'm sitting in the lobby of the courthouse and I'm nervous. I can't believe that after all the threats and arguments Charles and I have had over the last couple of years, he's finally going through with this bullshit.

I see him drop his mother off at the front door while he goes to the park his car. She sees me and turns her head away from me. Ms. Young never had too many words for me. She never thought I was good enough for her son. I know I'm not. Never claimed to be. But Chuckie is my son too. I'm a good mother even though she doesn't believe it.

Mrs. Young is dressed in a black suit. I like it. But I would never tell her that. I look down at my clothes. I had to borrow this suit from Bre. I had nothing in my closet that would be presentable. The judge would for sure take Chuckie if he saw me in my regular clothes.

Here comes Charles. He looks at me and rolls his

*E.R. McNair*

eyes. *Bitch.* Niggas don't roll their eyes. He wouldn't last one day on the streets. Not one day.

I get up and walk to the courtroom we've been assigned. CeeCee asked me if I wanted her to come with me. But I told her no. I wanted to do this on my own.

I walk into the courtroom and this is the first time I'm not afraid that I'll be put behind bars. This punishment would be a hundred times worse. I look around the room and it's small. No jury. No bailiff. Just me, Charles, his mother and the judge. Yes, a hundred times more scary.

The judge enters and I swallow hard. I'm on one side of the courtroom and Charles and his uppity mother are sitting on the other side. Me against them. We stand up and I make eye contact with the judge. She acts like she's seen me somewhere before, but I don't think so.

"Ms. Perry, do you know why you're here?" Judge Hill asks me.

I nod my head and then I say, "Yes, ma'am."

"Can you tell me?"

I point over to Charles and his mother. "They think I'm not a good mother and they want to take my son away." I feel myself want to cry, but I inhale deeply and suck the tears and the emotion back up.

"Are you a good mother, Ms. Perry?" Judge Hill asks me.

"Yes," I say. "Yes ma'am." I nod my head.

I hear Charles' mom grunt and she says something under her breath so that only I can hear her, not the judge.

I will myself to not look over there because I know if I do, I'll cuss that bitch out.

"Do you have a job, Ms. Perry?" the judge asks.

I look down. I nod my head no. Here we go.

"Ms. Perry, I asked you a question," the judge says to me. I hear her catch an attitude and I could cuss her out too. I look over at the sheriff placed conveniently to the judge's side.

"No, ma'am," I answer and I know I'm done.

"How do you take care of your child?" The judge looks through her files. "Your children, how do you take care of your children without a job? You have more than one, correct?"

"Yes, ma'am," I answer, worry filling me up from the inside. I feel the same butterflies Bre talked about, but mine are from a whole other reason. "I have three kids."

"How do you take care of your children?"

"I'm on assistance," I say. I feel hot and then a blast of cold air hits me and I get goosebumps.

"Is that all? Do you also get child support?"

"No, ma'am, not from the other kids' daddies."

I hear Charles' mother say something smart and I'm ten seconds off her ass. I look over at the sheriff and he's looking at me, his hand securely on his firearm.

"Well," the judge says. She then starts to ask Charles and his mother questions. I listen but their words flow together and they might as well have been speaking German. I feel my chance to keep my son rush down the toilet. I'm dazed, confused. I can't concentrate. I feel hot,

*E.R. McNair*

even hotter than before and all of a sudden I'm on the ground.

"Ma'am. Ma'am, are you all right ma'am?" I wake up and I'm in the arms of the sheriff who was once threatening me. He hands me a glass of water and I drink it till it's all gone. "Can you get up?" the sheriff asks and he helps me to my feet and escorts me to the bench behind where I was originally sitting.

"Ms. Perry?" the judge begins.

I look up at her and I see two of her sitting there.

"Ms. Perry, you scared us. Are you all right?"

I nod and rub my back where I hit it on the bench before I landed on the floor.

"I need more time to make my determination. Your children haven't been in the system before and to take your parental rights just because Mr. Young and his mother don't approve of your need to be on assistance isn't a plausible reason to take a child from his mother. But," the judge continues and I wonder where she's going, "but, Ms. Perry, you seem to be an able-bodied female, despite your fainting spell, which I attribute to your fear. You need to find gainful employment or enter a training program, but I don't want you to continue on assistance. There's no need."

I'm starting to feel better. I guess I should have eaten something before coming here today. I guess lunch with the Youngs is out of the question. I want to turn to them and revel in my win, but I'm not sure I won.

"Do you have anything to say, Ms. Perry?"

I cleared my throat. "I'll work on it, your Honor."

"I hope so, Ms. Perry. You want to be a positive role model for your children. There's nothing wrong with assistance if you need it, but I'm totally against abuse of the system."

She stares at me. I nod my head.

"I'll continue to monitor this case," the judge says and she dismisses us.

I look at Charles and his mother and all the words I want to say to them bubble up in my throat and I have to fight hard to keep them down.

"Let's go, Charles," Mrs. Young says.

Charles looks at me and for a minute I think I see a hint of past feelings. Then again maybe I don't. I can't wait to get home so I can hug Chuckie. He's my son. My son. My son! And there's nothing they can do about it.

# twenty-one

**Bre**

Finally, it's 5:30 p.m. on Friday! I feel like I've been waiting for Santa Claus on Christmas Eve. I talk to Mello and he says he'll be at my house at six o'clock.

I want everything to be perfect so I rush home, nearly running head-on into an ice cream truck, to take a quick shower. I dress in a black strapless silk dress that stops right above my knee. I find a cute pink furry poncho in my closet to go over it. I pick out a pair of pink Gucci sandals that tie up to my knee and a matching pink leather Gucci clutch. I check myself out in the mirror and am pleased with what I see. I hope Mello is just as pleased.

My phone rings and my stomach starts to turn with anticipation. Mello tells me that he's right around the corner and that he'll be at my door in a few seconds. I decide to wait outside for him and I watch as he pulls up.

He rounds the corner in his cranberry Lexus RX300

and I almost jump out of my skin. He gets out and opens the door for me and I can't help but smile. Most of these sorry-ass niggas in Gary just honk the horn and expect you to come bouncing out to the curb. My baby's a real gentleman.

"Hey, sexy," Mello says. "Damn, you look good tonight." He inhales deeply. "And you smell good, too!"

"So, where are we going?" I ask, excited. The leather seats feel good beneath my silk dress.

"I'm not telling you where we're going, but you're going to like it, for real," Mello says. "Now," he smiles at me, "I need to know if you have a curfew or can I kidnap you for the night?"

"I'm a grown-ass woman. I don't have a bedtime. If you want me for the night you got me, baby," I say.

Now, I knew I should have been playing a little harder to get, but I had waited too long for this night. I mean after all, it had been a couple of years that I had been digging on Mello. I decided to fuck worrying about it, whatever happens, just happens. I sat back, relaxed and enjoyed the ride.

Once we got on I-90 I knew we were heading to Chicago. It took us about an hour to get there due to traffic. He says he has reservations at a nice restaurant called 312 Chicago and he hopes I like Italian.

"I love it!" I say, maybe going a little overboard.

Mello pulls the car up to the valet and hands the guy his keys.

"It's beautiful," I say to Mello, holding onto his arm as

*E.R. McNair*

we walk through the crowd of people at the front door. "I need to use the ladies' room," I say. "I'll be right back."

The maitre'd points to the bathroom and I walk through the room toward the back of the restaurant. I think I may see some famous people, but I'm not sure. I check again on my way back to the front but they are no longer there.

When I get back the waiter takes me to our table where Mello is already seated. He's looking over the menu when I walk up, he stands and smiles at me. The maitre'd pulls out my chair and I sit down.

"What looks good?" I ask, putting my napkin in my lap. "Have you been here before?" I look around the room trying to see if I see anyone else famous.

"A couple of times," Mello answers, taking the first sip of the drink the waiter sets in front of him.

I tell the waiter I'd like an iced tea and he leaves to get my drink order.

"Mello, this place is the shit," I say, trying to keep my voice down.

"Stick with me, baby, and you'll see more places like this."

I smile and look at the menu. I decide on the steak with shrimp pasta. Mello orders steak and lobster with another glass of beer.

I didn't know what to talk to Mello about and I didn't want to talk about the situation with DayDay. So I tell him about the whole situation with my dad and ask him for his opinion.

"Well, Bre, I think that you should give him a chance to explain himself. But that could just be the man in me talking. Like I told you, I only get to see my son every other weekend, and holidays. I'm glad to get that time but I wish it could be more. I couldn't see myself just letting him leave and never looking back."

"It's so funny, I'm still trying to see you as a father. Don't get me wrong," I say, putting my hand on his, making sure I don't offend him, "I'm sure you're a great father. It was just a shock when you said you have a son."

"Yeah, I'm a private kind of guy. I have to be. When too many people know too much about you, it makes you an easy target. When it comes to my son you have to be a pretty special person to even know about him."

"Well, I hope I will get to meet him someday since you think so much of me to tell me about him," I say. "I bet he's a cutie."

"Yeah, he looks like his old man. That would make him a handsome dude, you know?" Mello teases.

"Well, aren't you the modest one?" I tease back.

After we finish dinner, we go to see a movie. It was the new Martin Lawrence movie, but I can't remember what it was about because we did more kissing and touching than we did watching.

Mello says he has another surprise for me after the movie. Once in the car he tells me to close my eyes. I try my hardest to keep them closed but as we pull up to the Swiss Hotel Chicago, one of the top hotels in the city, I

*E.R. McNair*

giggle letting him know I'm cheating.

We pull up to the valet and again Mello hands him his car keys. We check in and then head up to the room. At the nineteenth floor, we exit the elevator and I see Michigan Avenue out the window. The view is spectacular and downtown Chicago is so pretty in the moonlight.

Mello unlocks the room and it's Christmas day all over again. I run in, kick off my shoes and look at each room. It's a suite with a separate living room from the sleeping area. Mello goes through the mini bar, pulling out a beer. He offers me a drink. "Oh yeah, you don't drink."

I think about asking Mello to light the fire in the fire place, but it isn't cold enough outside. Champagne is chilling in a bucket and there are rose petals all through the rooms and on the bed. I feel like a princess.

"Look on the bed," Mello instructs me before he goes into the bathroom.

There's a box on the bed. I open it and inside is a beautiful Victoria's Secret nightgown with the matching robe and panties.

Mello calls from the bathroom. "I hope you don't mind. I just wanted you to be comfortable." He also has a sweat suit for me to wear home the next day and some sneakers. "I got the sizes from CeeCee."

I jump up and down, excited by what's going on around me. I'm going to kill her when we get back, but not really. I'm so excited!

It's after midnight now and I want to take a shower

143

to get more relaxed. Mello also has a bag of all my favorite toiletries, including my honey dust. That CeeCee!

I shower and put on my smell good and dust. When I come out Mello is sitting on the bed watching SportsCenter. When he sees me he puts down the remote. He puts his hands behind his head and looks me over.

"I like what I see."

"Me too," I say. He looks so good lying there I want to jump him. I go over to him and stand between his legs. I put my arms around his neck.

"Damn, girl, you know you smell good as hell," he says.

"Thank you." I smile.

"I'm glad to see that everything fits. Do you like it?" he asks.

"Yes, it's beautiful. CeeCee must have told you that purple is my favorite color."

"Well, she hinted to that fact, so I thought you would like it," he replies.

"I don't know how to thank you for everything. I've really had a good time tonight," I say. "I don't want the night to end."

"You know, Bre, I never thought you were really interested in me," Mello says. "When I would come around you would never say anything, so I figured you just weren't interested until I said something to you that night in the club."

*E.R. McNair*

"Mello, I've been interested for a long time, I just didn't know how to approach you. But I can show you my interest better than I can tell you."

I look into his eyes and he holds my face in his hands and starts kissing me. His tongue tastes so good. I can't get enough. I suck on his bottom lip as he slowly sucks on my top lip. He then slides his tongue into my mouth and I suck on it.

He slowly reaches up and peels the strap of my nightgown down. "You didn't even need to put this shit on because it's gonna be on the floor."

"Is that right?" I ask, wishing that it would happen sooner than later. He starts sucking on my right breast and then moves to the left one. I think I'm about to explode.

I kiss his forehead and then his neck while he plays with each breast. "Oh my God, Mello. You're driving me crazy. I don't know how much more I can take. I've waited so long for tonight."

Mello pulls me down on his lap. I can feel how hard his magic stick is through his clothes. By the time he gets me on his lap my nightgown is around my waist. "Damn Bre, you taste good as hell. Oh girl, why you taste so damn sweet?" Once he says that I know the honey dust has worked. I just hope that the wax was well worth the pain.

He picks me up and lays me on the bed. Then he pulls his clothes off and I take my gown off the rest of the way and then slide off my panties.

"Oh my God, Bre, you have the prettiest pussy I have ever seen! I can't believe that you don't have any hair there!" Mello exclaims. "Damn, you shave that shit off?" He stops everything as he stares in amazement at my stuff.

"No, I get waxed, but you haven't seen anything yet," I whisper.

Mello stands there and stares at me for another minute and then he starts kissing my feet and toes. He works his way all the way up my thighs and when he gets right to my hot spot, he says, "Turn over."

I'm breathing so hard, and I want him so bad. I turn over onto my stomach and he starts again at the back of my neck and works his way down to my ass. Then he licks real slow between my ass cheeks. He works his way down until he gets to the opening of my playground. He slides me open with his tongue and works it out!

I have to cover my face with the pillow to keep from waking the entire hotel with my screams. He works me until I can't take it anymore. I have to pull away. I flip over and he starts from the front. I swear he sucks on me until my legs start to shake. I reach down, grab him and lift him to me. I kiss his chest and lick on his nipples. He moves to his side and I kiss his waist and work my way down. I decide that tonight I'm going to use everything that CeeCee and Nesha taught me.

I kiss him until I get down to his dick, and then I begin to lick the tip. I suck it and I can tell by his reaction he's really enjoying what I'm giving to him. I put my

*E.R. McNair*

hands under his balls and I squeeze them as I suck on them. He starts moving his hips as I move his dick in and out of my mouth.

I guess it's getting good because he grabs my head and holds it while he fucks my face. Right before he comes, I get up and put the condom we have in my mouth on his dick and roll it down his shit. He grabs me by my shoulders and pulls me up to his mouth.

While we kiss I put his dick in and start to ride him. He has his head back and his eyes are closed. I put my hands on his chest and lean back. Then he grabs my hips and while holding me down he thrusts that dick up in me. He's pounding my shit, and I'm loving every moment of it. I lean forward and lick his lips. Then I bring my feet in front of me and put them on his chest while still riding his ass and he's loving it, for real.

"Damn, girl, this is some good-ass pussy," Mello moans. "I wasn't expecting this at all. Turn that ass over so I can hit that shit from the back."

I flip over and get on my knees. He grabs the back of my hair and sticks his dick in. I let out a moan and move with his every move. It's so good. He keeps pulling my hair and talking shit. I put my arms under my head on the bed and keep my ass in the air. He's smacking it and talking shit at the same time.

"Yeah, whose pussy is this now? Is this my pussy?" he asks. "Huh, is it mine?"

I tell him, "It's yours, baby. It's all yours." The way he is making me feel I'm serious! He's hitting all the right spots and I'm about to cum and cum hard. I bury my face in the pillow because I know I'm going to scream, and I didn't want someone from the front desk knocking the door down.

We cum at the same time, and I fall out on the bed exhausted and ready to go to sleep. He's behind me and holds me. This is the first time I really feel wanted by someone and I can tell he really wants me with him. I have never been happier. This is what I've waited for, and was well worth the wait.

He falls asleep holding me and I cuddle up in his arms and go right to sleep. We wake up in the morning horny as hell and we do it all over again. After we have some good morning sex, we are both hungry as hell so we order room service.

I hit the shower while we wait for breakfast. He joins me, and it's on again. We finish in the shower just in time. Room service is at the door and knocking. We eat and then get dressed. Check out is at twelve and it's already eleven thirty. So after a quickie we get ready to go.

On the way home, we talk about the night.

"I really enjoyed myself," I say, smiling at him.

"I'm glad," he says.

"I hope this won't be the last time I see you," I say, trying to feel him out. Is this just a one time thing or is he really interested in starting something with me?

"I plan on seeing you tonight if that's okay with you."

"Well," I pause wanting to kick myself for planning

*E.R. McNair*

this trip with my girls. "My girls and I are having this girls night out thing tonight. We're going to Chicago. But I'll be home Sunday morning. I'll call you first thing."

"You're not planning to go out and cheat on me already, are you?" Mello asks, a smile on his face.

I shake my head no, returning his smile.

We pull up to my apartment at two o'clock. I don't want the date to end. He leans over and kisses me. But I don't move. He kisses me again.

I smile at him.

"I'll call you later," Mello says.

"Don't forget."

"I won't. I promise."

# twenty-two

**CeeCee**

I've been invited to a revival at Ms. Stephens' church. I'm a little nervous about attending. Who goes to church on a Friday night? But Ms. Stephens promises me it will be an awesome experience. Those were her words, 'awesome experience.'

The kids and I visited DayDay early today so we would be able to attend the revival this evening. When we get home I lay out the kids' clothes. I had to go to the mall and buy us all outfits to wear because none of us had anything suitable. It's hard to believe that I'm actually going to church ... and on a Friday night.

I tried to talk to Nesha about church but she's still not trying to hear me. I keep telling her that we can't keep going on like we have been, but she just doesn't see it.

The kids and I walk into the church, First Baptist. The music is loud and we see a woman shouting, her words

*E.R. McNair*

incomprehensible. The kids look sort of scared. And truth be known, I'm sort of scared myself. What have I gotten myself into? I grab Alexis's hand and turn to make a mad dash toward the door when Ms. Stephens pops up out of nowhere.

"I'm glad you came," Ms. Stephens says. She leans in and hugs me whispering, "Grace and peace," in my ear.

Her embrace is hypnotic. The fear I was experiencing earlier is now replaced with an overwhelming sense of serenity.

Ms. Stephens says hi to the kids and she tells me she's going to take them to the children's room. She says they'll be able to color, paint and they'll hear stories. I tell DJ to keep an eye on his sisters and I wander toward the main sanctuary. The room is stacked, people everywhere. It's so similar to being in the club, but the big difference is I don't have to worry about getting shot or having to cuss someone out. The looks from the people are pleasant and everywhere I turn I'm greeted with the words grace and peace. So very different from the club where I get evil glares and vicious words.

I find someplace to sit and I listen intently to the rhythmic drums, the soothing horns and the melodic signing. I close my eyes and then I jump as my cell phone vibrates in my jacket pocket. Nervous, I bend down to answer it, trying to be discreet. "Hello?" I ask.

"Where the fuck have you been?" Nesha asks me, her voice booming so loud I wonder if the worshipers can hear her profanity.

"Nesha, I'm at church right now."

"What the fuck did you say?"

"I said, I'm in church. I'll call you back." I want to hear how her court date went.

I'm not sure if she hung up or if the reception disappeared, but Nesha is no longer on my phone. I push the off button and I try to find the same serene place I was once visiting. It felt good. For the first time in a long time, I feel good.

*E.R. McNair*

# twenty-three

**Bre**

As soon as I walk in the door, I call Nicky. I'm still floating on cloud nine and I have to tell her how my night
went. I call her house, but she doesn't answer so I hit her
on the cell.

"Hello?"

"Nicky, where are you, man?" I ask. "I just tried to call
you at your house."

"Well, damn! If I ain't answer the phone, then I must
not be at home, right?" Nicky says with an attitude.

"Look, bitch, don't be a smart-ass," I say. "I was just
calling so I can tell you about my night with Mello, but
since you have a stick up your ass, I'll call you later." And
I hang up.

I don't know what's gotten into Nicky, but her attitude has been real funky lately. I decide to call CeeCee
and see what's up with her.

"Hey, Bre! What's up, girl! How was the big date?" I

can tell she's smiling.

"What up, C? It was all that, girl!" I exclaim. "I can't even begin to tell you how good it was. Oh, and thanks for giving all my secrets away!"

"Girl, please. That nigga went shopping for your ass. If a nigga asks you some shit about me so he can buy me some shit, your ass better spill the damn beans!"

"I was so shocked when I opened that box with all the right sizes and my favorite color. I could have screamed." My voice rises a couple octaves. "Girl, we went to 312 Chicago to eat," I say. "Then we went to the movies. We saw the new Martin Lawrence movie, but don't ask me what it was about because we were too occupied doing other things to watch." I'm a little hot thinking about last night. "We'll have to check it out together because I really did want to see the movie. Then he had me close my eyes when he took me to the hotel, the Swiss Hotel. Girl, it was so beautiful. He had rose petals on the bed. And, CeeCee, girl, the sex was so damn good."

"Tell me everything," CeeCee begs.

"No. I don't think so. I'll have to fight you bitches off my man!" I laugh. "Anyway, is it on for tonight or what?"

"You are funny! That's so sweet. I'm glad that you two hit it off and had a good time. Sure, tonight is still on. I talked to Nesha and her kids will be with their dads. Ms. Jackson came by and picked up my kids this morning. So the only one who no one has talked to is Nicky. Have you heard from her?"

*E.R. McNair*

"I called her right before you, you know, just to confirm, but her attitude was so stank I had to hang up on her."

"Well, I've been trying to call her to ask her about her and DayDay, but she won't return my calls."

I thought, would you call the woman of the man you've been fucking? But I kept that to myself. "I don't know, CeeCee, maybe she's going through some things, and she just don't want to talk about it," I say. I try to change the subject. "I don't know about Nicky, but let's just have a good time tonight with no drama. You can talk to her about Day another night."

"I feel you on the no drama thing, Bre, but I just can't let this ride, not how I'm feeling right now. I mean, he's not just my man, we have kids together, and to think that my girl, my dog, was sleeping with my man behind my back, that shit is just unforgivable. I mean, I know that she was upset about Tone, but he didn't want her. And she knew that shit. But to call yourself getting back at me by doing my baby's daddy, now that's foul."

"I know, CeeCee, I really do. I'm just saying that with everything that's going on right now you don't need any more stress and bringing that up is just going to be more stress." I hope I'm getting through to her.

"I tell you what, Bre, I'll let it go until after our night out. But I'm warning you, if that bitch steps out of line just one time, BAM! It's on. And I don't give a damn where we are. Okay?"

"Okay, I can live with that. Now how is DayDay and

how did the exchange go with his mom?"

"He's still unconscious. When we go to visit, I read and talk to him. The kids tell him about school, their homework and they sit up on the bed with him. I just don't know how much more I can take, Bre." She takes a deep breath. "I need him to wake up. I miss him so much," CeeCee starts to cry, "and so do the kids. I never thought about everything that I've done to him until now. And you know what, I'd hate me if I was him. But he didn't hate me, Bre. He just wanted to love me and I pushed his ass away. I know I don't deserve him, but I can't lose him."

"I feel you, CeeCee. I'm so sorry." I feel awful.

"Why didn't you say anything to me, Bre? Why didn't you tell me to stop being such a ho?"

"What was I supposed to say, uh, CeeCee, stop spreading your legs to every Tom, Dick and Harry you meet?"

CeeCee didn't say anything. I wonder if I offended her.

"Was I that bad?"

Now it was my turn to be quiet. "Um, I guess I exaggerated it a little bit," I say, but I didn't exaggerate.

"No you didn't," CeeCee says. She sounds deflated.

"Come on CeeCee, what's up with DayDay's mom? How is that going?"

The tone in her voice is a little different. "She came and picked the kids up this morning. I was glad that I had cleaned the house and the front door has been locked

*E.R. McNair*

since that night. She looked around the house and then she told me that she still doesn't like me, but that she would try to make it work for the kids. I told her I was sorry for everything and that I really do love her son.

"We talked about what'll happen when he comes home. She wants DayDay to stay with her so she can take care of him, but it's really up to him where he goes when he leaves the hospital. I'm just hoping for the best, Bre. I hope everything turns out okay. I know once this is over he'll never have to worry about me being with anyone but him, and that's real, Bre. On my kids, he's all I want."

I can tell from her tone that CeeCee is serious. "We just have to keep praying for him. It'll be all right, I know it will," I assure her. "I'm going to get off the phone. If we're going up to Chi town we need to hook up by at least eight o'clock. And I want to take a nap before then. I need to rest up from my date." I smile from ear to ear remembering my date. "So, I'll see you around then. I'm just wearing some cute jeans tonight. I don't feel like getting all dressed up. Oh, and I want to stop by my Aunt's house if it ain't too late."

"Cool. Well then I'm gonna wear jeans, too, so I'll see you later."

"CeeCee, don't worry. Everything will be fine. I'll talk to you later," I say.

We hang up and I start to look for something to wear. I decide to wear my blue jean Capri pants with the matching blue jean jacket and a red tank top. And then

I'll wear a pair of red tie-up stilettos. I lay my outfit on the bed and then I lay down. I grab the remote and flip through the TV channels waiting for sleep to take me over.

Sleep doesn't come as quickly as I'd like. So, I decide to try to call Nicky again to see if she's in a better mood.

"Nicky, what's up? Are you better now?"

"What's up, cow? I was cool then. You didn't have to hang up on me!" she says. "How was your big date?"

"It was all that and then some. He took me to Chicago for dinner and a movie then we went to a hotel, and damn, it was well worth my wait." I wonder if I'm giving up to much information. I still have my doubts about my ability to trust Nicky.

"Damn, Bre! So is there love in the air? Are you two kicking it now or is he just something to do when you get that urge? Tell me more!"

"I don't know." I decide that I'm a little hungry. I go into the kitchen and make a sandwich. "He says he wants to see me again. And we did have a lot of fun. I'm not going to lie, Nicky, I'm digging the shit out of him, for real!"

"Just take it slow, girl, don't rush anything. Just let it happen," Nicky advises. "Mello's a nice guy. I think you two make a cute couple."

"I hope so, girl, I really do. So is it on tonight? Are you still coming out with us?" I ask. "Nesha and CeeCee got sitters and we're meeting at CeeCee's around eight o'clock. I think we're going to go to The House of Blues

*E.R. McNair*

or maybe Spy Bar. I don't know."

"I don't know, Bre. You know with everything the way it is, I don't want the drama," Nicky says. "Besides, there is a lot going on with me right now and I just don't know if I feel like dealing with Cee or Nesha. You know how Nesha is, Bre. Her and that fucking mouth; the way I feel right now, we'll be fighting."

"Damn, Nicky. What's going on? You can talk to me. I don't want it like this, we're all supposed to be friends. Besides, CeeCee promised that we would be like old times tonight. Just four friends kicking it on the weekend."

Nicky just listens. "That's what you say. Bre, there are some things happening that you can't help me with. I love you, girl, but you can't save everybody and quit trying to be Captain Save-a-Ho."

"I could have worse habits." I laugh. "Look, Nicky, I'm just going to go ahead ask you. I've heard some things and honestly I didn't want to believe them. Are you on that shit?"

"Bre, I'll be fine. Ask me no questions. I'll tell you no lies," Nicky says. "Look, Bre, forget about it. Just know that you can't believe everything you hear! You know I smoke here and there. That ain't nothing I can't quit any time. If I want to. I just need to deal with this myself. But I'm glad to know you're here for me. As for tonight, I still don't know. I just can't deal with the drama right now."

"Okay, Nicky." I'm tired of begging her for information. "Whatever you say, I'm not gonna push the issue.

When you're ready, you'll tell me. Tonight... it's a drama free night. I promise. Just keep your cool and your comments to yourself, and I promise, we'll have a good time! Come on, Nicky, it'll be like old times. Please!" I beg.

Nicky pauses for a few minutes. "Okay, I'll go."

"I promise. No drama."

"What are you wearing? I'm not getting dressed up."

"That's cool, We're all just wearing jeans. We're keeping it casual. So I'll come pick you up about seven thirty. We can talk then." I pause. "That's if you want to. I'm getting ready to take a nap. I'm exhausted. Mello wore me out."

Nicky laughs. "All right. I'll be ready at seven-thirty."

"Nicky, seven thirty..." I warn.

"I'll be ready."

"See you then."

"See you, then. Peace!"

I hang up with Nicky and lay down on my couch. Before my head touches the pillow, my phone rings again.

"Hey, Mello, what's up?"

I tell Mello that I miss him. He says he misses me too. I tell him I was about to take a nap because he wore me out. He laughs and says that he looks forward to more dates just like last night's. I tell him that I'll call him before we leave for Chicago. It is odd how he pauses before he says goodbye. For just second, I think he's going to tell me that he loves me. Am I rushing things? I think I may be rushing things. But I want to tell him I love

*E.R. McNair*

him. I know that I need to hang up quick or I might say something I'll regret. This time when my head hits the pillow I'm out like a light.

I sleep until six thirty. After eating a couple slices of pizza I had in the fridge, I start to get ready. I call CeeCee to let her know that we'll be at her house by eight so that we can hit the road.

I shower, dress and am at Nicky's by seven-thirty. She's ready when I get to her house. She swings the door open to show me that she's all dressed. I honk my horn to express my excitement.

We make it to CeeCee's by seven forty-five. She and Nesha are smoking when we get there.

"Hey, hoes, what's up?" I say when I open the door.

"Oh, no you didn't. When I heard you was up all night getting that ass waxed by Mello last night!" Nesha says, throwing up her middle finger.

"Nesha! What would make you think I would do something like that? I'm a good girl!" I laugh.

"Yeah, okay, that's what your mouth says, but your face, it's saying something completely different," CeeCee laughs.

Nesha looks Nicky up and down, "What's up Nick?" she asks, taking a long drag off of her cigarette.

"You," Nicky says, lying back as not to cause any problems.

Nesha passes her cigarette over to Nicky. She grabs it and inhales.

"Bre, did Mello mention anything about Tone to you?" Nesha asks.

"No, girl, he's been quiet about everything since Tone's ass turned up dead. He said he didn't even know anything about it. He says he was out of town on a family matter. I don't know. Why? What have you heard, Nesha?" I ask.

"Girl, I don't know. I keep hearing Chicago niggas and gang shit, that's what the streets is saying anyway." Nesha throws up her hands.

"Yeah well, I know those niggas better quit calling my house about Tone!" CeeCee screams over the music. "Hell, between them niggas and the police I don't know who's getting on my nerves more."

"Still? I thought when you had your number changed the phone calls would have stopped," I say.

"I thought they would have too. But some buster is giving out my number left and right and not many of you heifers have the number." CeeCee tries to give us the evil eye to decide which one of us is the culprit.

"Don't look at me," I say.

Nicky turns her head. We all know CeeCee didn't even give her the number, so it couldn't have been her.

CeeCee looks at Nicky. "What's up, Nick? I've been calling your ass."

"I've been busy. Shit been kind of crazy at home."

CeeCee looks at me but speaks to Nicky. "Looks like life is rough all over. Well, I ain't really want nothing. I'll just holler at you another time."

*E.R. McNair*

"That's cool. How's DayDay?" Nicky asks CeeCee.

The tension is thick. I hope they both keep their cool and their promises.

"The same. We go see him every day," CeeCee says, "me and the kids. His mom and I rotate times. She goes in the morning and I go in the evening so the kids can see him."

"I hope he gets better. I'll keep you all in my prayers," Nicky says.

"Yeah, well, thanks because we need all the prayer we can get." CeeCee takes one last hit on her blunt. "Now, are you trolls ready to blow this joint or what?"

# twenty-four

**Bre**

We're finally on the road. I'm glad everything with Nicky and CeeCee is good, so far. God knows I can't handle a catfight between those two. We hit I-90 and head for the Windy City to get our club on.

About forty-five minutes later we hit the Chicago city limits, so I tell my girls that my cousin Terry is in town and I want to stop by my aunt's to check him out.

"He may know something about a party tonight," I say.

They're cool with that. Besides, I know Nicky has been digging on Terry for as long as I can remember.

It doesn't take us any time to get to my aunt's house. We pull up and we can smell the food from her driveway. My mom is a good cook, but her sister, my Aunt Boots, she can cook her ass off. I told my aunt a long time ago that she needed to open up a soul food restaurant because people would pay good money for her cooking.

*E.R. McNair*

She always just laughed and said she liked to do it for her family but cooking for other people would be too much of a headache.

"What's on the menu?" I ask as soon as we get in the door

"Damn, girl! All you think about is eating. Can't your aunt get a hug before you decide to eat me out of house and home?" Aunt Boots hugs me so tight I can barely breathe.

After I release myself from her bear hug, I say, "Aunt Boots, you remember my friends? This is Nicky, CeeCee and Nesha."

"Hey girls. Make yourselves at home." Aunt Boots goes back into the kitchen and I follow her. My eyes almost pop out my head when I see everything she's cooked— barbecue chicken, greens, macaroni and cheese, corn bread, chocolate cake and sweet potato pie.

"All this is for Terry?" I ask, rubbing my stomach to show that I was in heaven. My girls do the same. It is his favorite meal.

"Bre," Aunt Boots calls to me, "Terry and his friend are down in the basement. Grab yourselves a plate before going down."

We fix our plates and then head down to eat.

Aunt Boots' house is huge and her basement had been turned into a clubhouse for Terry. He has everything down there—a pool table, projection TV, vintage Pac Man and Space Invaders video games and a ridiculous movie collection.

As soon as my cousin sees me, he grabs me and spins me around almost making me drop my plate to the ground. "Cuz! You look great! It's been too long."

I can't believe how big he's gotten. Even though he's eighteen, I still think of him as my little cousin. "You have got to be seven feet tall!" I say to Terry, trying to take all of him in.

"Not quite. But I wish. I'd do damage on the court for sure then." Terry turns to his friend and gives him a hard high five.

Behind me I hear Nicky clearing her throat and then I hear Nesha whisper under her breath, "Hound."

"Terry, you remember my girls, Nicky, CeeCee and Nesha?"

Before Terry can say anything, Nicky is in his face, her hands wrapped around his.

Nesha and CeeCee bust out laughing.

"It's great seeing you all again." Terry pulls his hand away from Nicky. "This is my friend from school, Anthony Johnson."

"What are you guys playing?" I ask as I shovel another fork full of mac and cheese into my mouth.

"Halo," Anthony answers, his eyes never leaving the television screen.

I look at Nesha and CeeCee and I whisper to them, "Damn, these college niggas got it going on! Now why didn't I go to school?"

"Terry, what's going on tonight? We're looking for

*E.R. McNair*

something to get into," I ask.

"A friend is having a big party on the South Side." He stops the game. "You and your girls should come and hang out with us. It's going to be on and popping."

I look at my girls and they nod in agreement.

We clean up after dinner, all four of us vying for mirror time in the small bathroom in the downstairs hallway.

I'm back in the kitchen. "Aunt Boots, everything was delicious," I tell her.

"I'm glad you enjoyed it, baby." Aunt Boots looks at Terry. "You going to show the girls where to go tonight?"

"Yeah, Mom. We'll see you later." Terry kisses his mom and I give her a kiss as well.

"Bre, tell your mom I'll call her this week sometime."

"I will, Aunt Boots. I love you."


We follow Terry and Anthony through the traffic. We're rolling, our heads bobbing to Lil' Wayne and all of a sudden, a siren wails and a light shines behind us.

"Damn!" I shout. "Nesha, please tell me you left that shit at home," I say, scared that this night might end behind bars.

"I don't have anything," Nesha says.

The police officer walks to the car. "Do you know how fast you were going, ma'am?"

Honestly, I had no idea. With the combination of the music and the idea of hitting a party, I got caught up in the moment. "No, Officer," I admit.

"Well, you're in fifty-five mile per hour zone and you were doing sixty. I see that you're from out of town."

He shines the light in the car, looking at my passengers. My stomach's twisting and turning. I see that Terry and his friend have pulled over up ahead.

"I'll need your license and registration."

I hand the police officer everything he's asked for and wait as he goes to his cruiser to run my plates.

"It didn't seem like you were speeding," Nicky says.

"That's bullshit!" Nesha says. "Five fucking miles over the speed limit! That motherfucker must have a quota to fill."

"They don't have quotas," CeeCee corrects.

"What?" Nesha says.

"Jody's brother is a cop. He said they don't have quotas," CeeCee tells Nesha.

"And why should I believe a cop? They're all dirty." Nesha turns up her lip. "This is bullshit!"

The officer knocks on the window when he's done. "Ma'am here's your ticket. Can you sign here?"

I sign for the ticket. I know I have a scowl on my face.

"Slow it down tonight, miss. We want you to make it back to Gary safely."

I grunt at the officer, roll my window up and pull off.

"I can't believe that shit," I say.

"Oh, it's time to party now," CeeCee says. "Ask Mello to pay it for you, Bre. He's got the cash."

"I don't need him to pay it. I have money," I say irritated. "It's just the fact that I don't want to spend it on

*E.R. McNair*

this bull."

"You need a drink," Nesha suggests.

"If I drank, I sure would take a couple," I say.

I continue to follow Terry until we pull up into the driveway of this bad-ass house.

Terry opens my door. "You okay, cuz?"

"I'm cool," I answer, still pissed from getting the ticket.

I hear someone call Terry's name.

He spins around to four fine brothers reaching out to shake his hand.

Again, I wonder why I skipped college.

I look around for my girls and just like old times, they've already found the party. Nicky is off in a corner with some dude but CeeCee and Nesha are missing in action.

Terry introduces me to his friends. "Bre, this is Mark, Tim, Chico and Allen."

I shake hands and I can't help but smile.

All four smile back, and Tim says, "Make yourself at home. Mi casa es su casa."

"Thanks," I say, watching them walk away toward four bikini-clad females.

The house is huge, like a mini-mansion. I walk through the foyer and there it is, the pool. That's where the party is. The music is on point, old school Tupac.

I'm looking around and there are men everywhere. I can't believe what I see, so many fine brothers. I think to myself I could drown in all this fine ass.

"Hey, cutie," I hear a baritone voice coming from behind me.

I spin around to see a cute, chocolate brother in jean shorts and a black T-shirt. "Hey, back at you," I say.

"I'm Scottie." He holds out his hand.

I shake hands with Scottie and a funny feeling overcomes me.

"Are you going to tell me your name?" Scottie asks.

"I'm sorry," I say, "I'm Bre." I laugh. "I have a boyfriend," I say, nervously.

"I was just going to ask you to dance, not to get married," Scottie says and walks away.

I feel my face burn up with embarrassment. I look around to see if anyone saw the awkward exchange.

Terry walks over. "Stop being a wallflower." He pulls me to the dance floor. "Let me see what dances they're doing in Gary."

We kick it for a minute, and then I tell him I have to use the ladies' room. I wander through the house and run into Nesha on my way up the stairs to find the bathroom.

"Hey, girl, what's up? Are you having fun?" I ask. "Oh my God! There are some fine-ass brothers up in here tonight."

"Yeah, girl," Nesha says. "I met this little white dude. He's cool as hell and he's got some fire-ass weed."

"I should've known that if you're hanging with a white dude it has something to do with some weed," I say laughing.

*E.R. McNair*

"Yeah, well, I don't discriminate on the dick either, girl, but I had to find me some fire up in here. Your little encounter with the law put me in a mood," Nesha says, throwing up her hand. "Besides, white boys always have the killer drugs."

"Whatever, girl, have you seen Nicky and CeeCee?"

"Yeah, Nicky was outside with some dude," she says pointing behind her. "They looked like they were having a pretty deep conversation, and the last time I saw CeeCee she was on the dance floor, kicking it."

"Okay cool, well I'm going to the bathroom. I'll see you back out there."

"I have to get back to dude before he smokes all the good shit without me. I'm trying to get some of his stash to take home with me. We got some good shit back home, but nothing like this shit, for real. Your square ass should come and try some, Bre. You might like it!"

"Nesha, come on. Don't bring that shit in the car. I'm paranoid as it is. Please," I beg. "You and CeeCee have enough of that shit at home. You don't need to bring it from here."

Nesha dances away, smiling in my face. I hope she understands the consequences if we get caught with that shit in the car.

After using the bathroom, I wander into the den. I see CeeCee still kicking it. She looks like she's having a good time. She has changed so much in the past week. Before, she was wild as hell. But there is something different about her. She is still smoking her weed but she seems to be reflecting on her life and wondering whether or not she should make some changes. I'm glad she's having a good time. She needs to get her mind off of everything that's going on in her life back home.

I see Nicky. She's standing by herself staring into space.

I walk over to her. "Hey, Nicky. What are you doing?" I ask, taking a bite of the fruit salad I picked up in the den. "I thought you were out here getting your mind blown by some dude, at least that's how Nesha made it seem."

"Yeah, well, she had part of it right." Nicky sighs. "You know how they say it's a small world and six degrees of separation and all that shit?"

"Yeah, I've heard that shit before, but what does that have to do with you?"

"Girl, why is my life always full of drama? All the damn time. It's like I can't catch a damn break, you know? I mean, this thing with me and Day, then I got other shit that's going on," she says a little weepy. "I thought coming up here would be cool. I thought I would meet me some drama-free dude, kick it for the night and forget about my problems, but dude," she points across the patio, "he just added to the shit I already got fucking up my life."

"Nicky, what in the hell are you talking about?" I put my hand on her arm. "It's like you just met your long-lost brother or something. What's up, for real?"

"Girl, I wish it was that simple. Dude's name is Kenny.

*E.R. McNair*

He's from Arkansas. He goes to school with your cousin, and they play ball together. I told him that I used to date a guy from Arkansas who was in Gary for the summer, but that he got killed a week after he went back to Little Rock. He asked what my ex's name was and I told him."

She gives me a look that makes me wish I hadn't asked. "Girl, it turns out that him and Ty's dad are cousins. Can you believe that shit?" She shows me a piece of paper. "He gave me his number and told me to call him, but he would understand if I'm uncomfortable being around him. Bre, this is some fucked up shit. I mean, when I first saw him I was attracted to him because he did remind me of Tay, but I never thought this nigga was related to him!"

"Who would have fucking known?" I say, shaking my head. "Nicky, shit, girl, drama has you in its sights, because it follows you everywhere."

Nicky cracks a half smile. "What the fuck, man! I feel like God is getting back at me for not telling Tay's family about Ty. He told me that Tay's mom is still real messed up over what happened to him because he didn't want to come back home, but she needed him there to help her out. She begged him to come back home and then he gets killed. I can only imagine how she feels inside.

"Bre, I feel so fucked up. Like I owe it to her to tell her about Ty, but how do I do that now? He's six years old. I hate myself for this whole thing, but he's all I have, Bre. Ty is the best thing in my life. He's all I have to live for."

*E.R. McNair*

"Damn, Nicky, that is some crazy-ass shit, for real. I don't even know what to say to you. I mean, I can't even pretend that I know how you feel, but you knew that one day this was going to happen." I touch her hand. "I mean, even if you never told his family, Ty would ask you about his father and his father's family and why they never wanted to see him. I think this is a sign that you need to do this while he is still young and can have a relationship with his other family. You never know how this will turn out, and I can't see them trying to take Ty from you. You're a good mom."

While I don't know how Nicky feels, I do know how Ty would feel when he gets older. Not having your father around can have some deep ramifications, especially for a boy.

"Bre, I just don't know. I didn't come all this way to deal with this shit tonight. I really need to think about all of this. And I need to do it by myself. You know sometimes life just makes you want to get so high, you know, so you can leave all the bullshit behind you? For real." Nicky sighs and puts her head down in her hands.

"The problems are still there, Nicky. When you come back you still have to deal with the problems. I keep telling you, I'm here for you when you want to talk. You're my sister, girl, so if you need me just let me know."

Four o'clock rolls around and we're ready to get on the road to go home. I tell Terry that I'll see him soon and that he can come and visit me in Gary anytime he wants.

*E.R. McNair*

I'm tired as hell and even though I'm anxious to get home, I drive slow as not to get another ticket. Tonight ends up being a perfect night, everything except the speeding ticket. I look over at Nicky.

"I'm not asleep," she says. "I'm just thinking."

I nod at her. Then I look in the backseat. CeeCee and Nesha are huddled up, a small snore coming from CeeCee, or is it Nesha? I'm glad she had a good time. At least she was able to take her mind off of everything that was going on in her life.

The sun is rising by the time we get back and I drop everyone off. Once at home, I take a quick shower, wash my hair and jump into bed. They always tease me about taking showers when I come in from the club. But I hate smelling like smoke when I go to bed. I look at the ticket on my bedside table and decide that if the price for a good time out with my girls is a speeding ticket, then it was worth it. I smile and close my eyes.

# twenty-five

**Bre**

My phone rings and wakes me out of a good sleep.

"Hello?"

"Hey, sleepy head, you must have had a real good time last night," Mello says. "You're still asleep? It's two o'clock in the afternoon. Man, I feel bad. I thought I was giving you enough time to rest. I'm sorry."

"Oh, no, baby, you're fine." I lift myself up on one elbow.

"I hope you weren't out there cheating on me," Mello teases.

I smile. "Never. But we did have a good time. I got a speeding ticket, though." I look at it feeling like ripping it to shreds.

"No. How fast we're you going?" he asks, sounding genuinely interested.

"Just five miles over the limit." I pout, hoping that I wouldn't have to ask him to pay it like CeeCee suggested, but that he would offer.

"I got you," Mello says.

Bingo. I smile. "You don't have to," I respond slowly, hoping I don't make him change his mind. "We went to a party with my cousin. It was at his friend from school's house."

"And how many niggas tried to holler?"

"None, I swear," I say trying to remember if anyone tried to talk to me and then I remember Scottie. I blush all over again.

"I didn't get a call from you this morning," Mello chastises.

"My fault, baby. I guess it's my turn to apologize. I was so tired."

"I forgive you."

"How about dinner tonight to make up for my mistake? Can you be here at four thirty?"

"A home cooked meal. I'll be there. Do I need to bring anything?"

I think about it for a minute. "Pepsi."

"Okay, Pepsi it is. See you later, baby,"

We hang up and I'm finding it hard to move. I lay there for a few more minutes and then I pull my legs over the side of the bed. "What am I going to cook?" I ask myself realizing that I may need to run to the store to get the ingredients to prepare the type of meal that will make him fall in love with me. I think the only thing in my fridge now is an onion, a quart of half and half and a bottle of ketchup.

I get out of bed and decide to call my mom and see what she thinks.

"Chicken," she says. "You can't go wrong with chicken."

Mom is right and chicken is easy to cook. Plus, all black men love them some fried chicken. Now isn't that some stereotypical shit? But she was right.

I'm glad that my mom had taught me how to cook. She would always say, "When you get a husband you'll know how to keep him happy, if you can cook." She said men want a woman who is good in the kitchen and the bedroom. I never expected to hear that from my mom, but she is real open like that. We have a close relationship, and I always tell her everything. I even told her about the first time I had sex. She just wanted to know that I used protection. When I said I did, she was cool.

I run to the store and grab some wings, potatoes, corn bread mix and stuff for a salad.

While I'm cooking Nicky calls me.

"Hey, Nicky. How are you feeling today, girl?" I ask, concerned about her.

"Hey, Bre. I'm cool, man, I've just been chilling. I called dude and we talked."

"Did you tell him about Ty?" I ask Nicky, trying to avoid being popped by the chicken grease.

"No. I didn't tell him." Nicky was quiet. "But he said he would be coming to Gary in about a month. He's coming for a big party for his aunt's 60th birthday."

"Are you thinking you might tell him then?"

*E.R. McNair*

"Maybe. What if I just let him figure it out? If he sees Ty he could probably figure it out. Ty looks just like Tay."

"You really want to let it go down like that, Nicky?" I ask, chopping up the lettuce.

"Yes." She answers hesitantly.

"Stop lying," I tell her. I burn myself on the stove. "Shit."

"What are you doing?" Nicky asks.

"I'm cooking..."

"For Mello?" Nicky cuts me off.

"Yes and I just burnt myself." I run the cold water over my arm.

"Look at you trying to be all domesticated and what-not," Nicky teases.

I hear something in her voice I don't like.

"I'm supposed to go to the hospital with Ms. Jackson today. To see Day."

I don't say anything.

"I know you think it's fucked up, but she called me and asked me to go. So I'm going. I think she's taking the kids since she has them for today."

I still don't say anything.

"I really miss him. I just want to see him and talk to him. He really became my shoulder to lean on."

"Look, Nicky, I need to finish cooking before Mello gets here. But you know what? You're making this bed, and you're the one who is going to have to lie in it."

"Bre, I've laid in a lot of beds, and this one is just as lumpy as the rest of them. I don't expect you or anyone else to understand what me and DayDay have. But it's real."

"Nicky, all that shit is in your mind. He has children with CeeCee." I'm becoming tired of having this conversation with her.

"He is not her man. She gave up the right to call him that a long time ago. He loves me, too. I know it because he told me."

"He told you while you were fucking him?"

Nicky was quiet.

I had my answer.

"I'm going let you go so you can do your thing," Nicky says with an attitude. "And I'm going to get ready to meet Ms. Jackson."

We hang up and an eerie feeling overcomes me. For some reason I know that today is going to be the day that the shit hits the fan. I just hope Nicky is ready to deal with all of it.

I finish with dinner about four o'clock and Mello will be here soon. I'm not even dressed yet. I jump in the shower and then put on some lounging pajamas and some perfume. The bell rings and I open the door and there stands Mello, with a liter of Pepsi in his hand. Damn, I love a punctual nigga!

"You remembered my Pepsi, huh?" I say, leaning forward to plant a big kiss on his lips.

He kisses me back, slipping his tongue into my mouth.

I back away. "Wait a minute." I smile. "Let's eat first

before we get to dessert."

Mello chuckles. "My fault, you just have that effect on me." He hands me the liter. "I wasn't going to come in here empty-handed." He walks in and I close the door behind him. "Damn, Bre, it smells good as hell in here. Don't tell me I got me a domesticated woman."

I think about Nicky.

"I won't say that, but I know my way around the kitchen. My mom taught me well, you know."

"Yeah, well, I'm gonna have to meet mom and thank her for my good woman." He taps me on the behind.

We sit down on the couch.

"Oh, really? Well, I have to make sure you're meet-mom-material, I don't want just anyone meeting her. I have the same policy you do about meeting your son. Besides, she don't play, so you have to be up to par."

"So you doubt my 'meet mom' skills, huh? Well, I'm just going to have to prove to you that a thug can be a gentleman, too."

"Oh, so you're a thug now, are you? Well, what have I gotten myself into, Mr. Mello?"

"I think you have gotten yourself into a whole lot more than you can handle, Ms. Bre, a whole lot more for sure." Mello leans in to kiss me and he runs his hand up my leg.

"Are you ready to eat?" I ask, grabbing his hand and kissing it.

"I'm ready for anything you offer," Mello says.

We eat making small talk in between bites.

*E.R. McNair*

"This is good as hell."

"Thanks. I'm glad you enjoy it." I smile.

"Now it's my turn." Mello grabs my hand and leads me toward my bedroom.

"What?" I play shy.

"I want to give you dessert."

We lay on the bed kissing and touching. I'm so excited by him I start to remove my clothes. My shirt is off and my bra is halfway removed when the phone rings.

I could scream.

"Hello?" I answer, annoyed by the disruption.

"Bre? I'm gonna kill this fucking bitch." CeeCee is screaming in my ear. The mood is definitely gone.

I sit up and push my bra strap back up and search the floor for my shirt.

"She's been fucking my man and now she's laying up in his hospital bed, like she's his woman!"

I can tell that CeeCee is on her cell phone because the reception fades in and out.

"What the fuck, Bre, for real? You better go get your girl. Because when I get through with her she's going to be in a hospital bed right beside him."

This time CeeCee's threats are real. There is no way I can beg them to squash this.

"CeeCee, calm down. Where are you?"

"I'm on my way to that bitch's house. I just picked the kids up from Ms. Jackson's house."

I can hear the kids in the background.

"I told you to sit down and shut the fuck up!" CeeCee

*E.R. McNair*

shouts at her kids. Then she gets back to me. "They told me Nicky was at the hospital and she was laying in the bed with DayDay. I mean, what kind of foul shit is that? Then she does the shit in front of my kids?"

I look at Mello and shake my head.

"As far as Ms. Jackson is concerned, she won't ever see my kids again. And I mean that shit! I'm on my way over Nicky's house right now!"

"CeeCee, not with the kids in the car." I look for my sneakers.

"That bitch better not have her ass at home! I'm going to tear some shit up when I get there. I don't give a shit about her son. She sure as hell don't give a damn about my kids! I'll talk to you later, Bre!" CeeCee hangs up the phone.

"Let's go, Mello," I say.

"What's going on?" he asks, pulling himself together.

"The shit has hit the fan," I say, brushing my hair back into a ponytail. "I knew it. I just knew it."

## twenty-six

**Bre**

Once we're in Mello's car, I dial Nicky's number.

Nicky answers the phone as if she doesn't have a care in the world.

"Nicky?" I say.

"Bre, what's up?"

"I just got call from an irate CeeCee."

Nicky is quiet.

"She told me that the kids told her you were at the hospital." I try to stay calm.

"So, I can go to the hospital if I want to. It's a public place, or doesn't CeeCee know that?"

"Were you laying in the bed with DayDay?" I ask.

"So the fuck what? I was talking to him. What do you want Bre? I'm busy. Maybe I'm cooking dinner for some nigga." Her tone is obstinate.

"Look," I say, tired of her mess, "CeeCee is on her way over there to kick your ass."

*E.R. McNair*

"Whatever, Bre. I don't have time for these childish games. If CeeCee wants to come over here and start some bullshit, than she can come on. I ain't scared of her." And she hangs up the phone.

"I'm so sick of this shit." I look out the window. "I'm tired of trying to fix everything for everyone."

"Nicky's ass is tripping," Mello says. "Yeah, your girl got a lot shit going on you don't even know about, Bre. I told you she was on that shit."

"I asked her about that. She said she was fine."

"Fine? Right. Well, then why is her ass stripping at Pinky's outside of Gary?" Mello asks matter-of-factly.

I'm shocked. I look at Mello. "Stripping?" I ask, "Have you seen her stripping?"

"I didn't have to. Slick told me he gave her some E pills and she's been doing heroin. She's turning tricks and shit for him. His boy Dog owns Pinky's, so hell, put two and two together. Stop being so damned naïve, Bre."

I hit Mello on the arm.

Mello shakes his head and sucks his teeth. "Look, babe, I know that's your girl, but she's a ho. And she has issues. They all have issues. I mean, CeeCee has been getting it together, but shit, that's gonna take some time. Then Nesha, her ass is flipping more birds than I am. Shit, I'm ready to holler at her. I know you love them. But Bre, you're on something different. You don't need to be hanging around them."

I sigh and turn back toward the window.

*E.R. McNair*

*E.R. McNair*

## twenty-seven

**Nicky**

I look out my window and I see CeeCee and Nesha in front of my house. I can see their mouths moving, but their words are muffled by the closed windows. These bitches are truly a trip. I call my mother and tell her to get over here so she can take care of Ty. He's taking a nap right now and I'm glad. He doesn't need to see this mess.

Why can't CeeCee just get it through her thick head that DayDay and I are going to be together? How can she be over here talking all this shit? I thought her ass was supposed to be in the church now.

I take another hit off my blunt. I swing open my front door. "Why are you bitches in my front yard?" I ask.

"Look bitch," CeeCee starts, "I should have known you wanted my man." She points her finger in my face. "But I'm here to tell your skank ass that ain't happening."

"DayDay wants me," I say. "So why don't you leave us

the fuck alone!" I see my neighbors look out their windows and doors and I wonder how long until one of them calls the police.

"Bitch, please. He don't want you."

"That's not what he said while we were fucking ... in your bed!" I scream back at CeeCee.

CeeCee reaches out and grabs me by the top of my head. I can feel the strands rip from my skull.

I swing and I feel my fist connect with her jaw and she lets go of my hair, but she's still holding a handful of it. I scream and run toward her.

"You bitch!" I holler at CeeCee.

We jump on each other and are punching, some blows are connecting, others are missing big time.

"You fucked my man in my bed?" CeeCee screams.

It feels as if her grip is tightening and then I feel her teeth in my arm. I knew this bitch fought dirty. Again she grabs a handful of my hair and she bangs my head into the concrete. It feels as if my head is cracking open.

I get one more hit in, knocking CeeCee to the ground.

I hear Nesha's voice telling her to get up and it's like she has a burst of energy. I can't move. CeeCee jumps on me. I'm lying on my back and she wraps her meaty fingers around my neck and squeezes. Her eyes are dead.

Before I pass out, I hear Bre's voice scream, "Mello, go get CeeCee off of her!"

The last thing I think about is I hope my mother has Ty and then I pass out.

*E.R. McNair*

I wake up and Bre is sitting in the chair next to my bed.

"What the fuck do you want?" I ask, wincing in pain.

"I came to see if you're all right. I told your mother I would check on you and give her an update."

"Whatever." I look around the room. There's nothing here. It looks nothing like the hospital rooms I've seen on television. No flowers, no cards. It's like no one cares. "I have a fucking concussion, and twenty-two stitches in my head. I have to stay in this place over night. That bitch tried to kill me. Go tell my mother that."

"Do you blame her? You know you got what you deserved."

"I don't need this shit right now. Don't make me call security," I say to Bre. She gets on my fucking nerves. I just look at her.

"Ty's with your mother."

I nod.

"I hear he's been staying with her a lot."

"So?" I say with much attitude. "That's his grand-mother. He can stay over there. It's not a law against that."

"For days at a time?"

"What's your point?"

"I hear you're stripping now."

"Bre, my head hurts like a mother fucker. You are not my mother. I don't have to answer to you or her or explain anything to you or her. I'm a grown-ass woman."

"You're acting like some kid without responsibilities."

I look for the button to call the nurse.

"I'm leaving. I'll tell your mother that you'll be home in a couple of days."

"I don't care what you tell her," I say and turn my head and close my eyes.

"CeeCee and Nesha are in jail."

"They need to be." I can't remember what Nesha's part in the fight was. But if CeeCee was fighting, the odds are that Nesha was involved in some way.

"Are you going to press charges?" Bre asks.

I don't say anything. "I don't know," I say, barely over a whisper. Why does she care? Does she want to go and prepare them for what might happen?

Bre doesn't say anything. I can feel her eyes on me.

"Where's Mello?" I ask. I can taste the bitterness of my own words.

"He's in the waiting room," Bre answers. "Why?"

"I figured he was close. I'm sure he misses you. Why don't you go be with him? I'm tired."

Bre is quiet for a minute. She stands up. "I'll see you later."

I'm sure she can feel my anger. "Not if I see you first," I say.

Bre leaves the room and I'm glad to see her go. I close my eyes and pray for death to take me away. Why does living have to be so fucking hard?

*E.R. McNair*

# twenty-eight

**Nesha**

I can't believe this shit. I look over at CeeCee and the bruises on her face are becoming noticeable. We're in the cell alone. I'm worried about the kids, especially about Chuckie. I'm sure if Charles hears about this shit, he'll be at the judge's office quick to get her to give him custody. I can only hope he doesn't find out.

CeeCee is pacing the floor.

"Calm down, damn," I tell her.

"Calm down? Calm down? How can you ask me to calm down?" CeeCee asks. Her voice is louder than it should be.

"It's a matter of time. We'll be out in a few hours."

"A few hours? Nesha, this shit ain't cool. We don't belong in jail. We have kids."

"What? CeeCee, you handled your business. That bitch Nicky will think twice before she fucks with DayDay again."

CeeCee looks at me as if I said something in another language. "Nesha, you just don't get it. DayDay was just as much to blame as Nicky. He fucked her. He allowed her in my house. Nicky didn't have the key, he did." Again, she paces. "We are always going after the girl and letting the nigga slide for his indiscretion."

I stare at her. "So, you want to fuck DayDay up too? I get it."

"Yes. No. He's just as much to blame. Nesha, where are your kids? Where are mine? Who the hell knows? We are mothers. We shouldn't be sitting in a jail cell." CeeCee turns from me and stands in the corner of the cell as if she's picking the farthest spot away from me. I feel sick.

I think about what CeeCee said. I have no idea where my kids are, but most likely they're with one of my brothers.

"Nesha Perry, you have a visitor," I hear a voice say. And then I see Charles. I feel everything I've eaten today rise to the top of my throat. I steady myself against the bars. CeeCee moves closer sensing that I will need her support.

"All I can say is thank you." Charles looks at me and smiles. "I knew it was only a matter of time before you fucked up and I'd have all the proof I'd need to get Chuckie. Your stupid ass never learns. When will you grow up?"

I spit at him. "Fuck you!" It lands on his jacket.

"Bitch," Charles says to me. His one word is a testa-

*E.R. McNair*

ment to his true feelings for me. I can almost hear his mother cackle with delight that they now have my son. "I hope you fucking rot in here."

For the life of me, I can't figure out how Charles found out that I was here.

"I'm sorry," I hear CeeCee say. She wraps her arms around me and I turn to her and cry.

"He's gone," I moan. "He's gone, CeeCee. My Chuckie is gone." I can't stop crying. All I can think about is the fact that it's my fault that my son is gone.

## twenty-nine

**Bre**

I fall down on my couch exhausted by everything that has gone on. I can't believe my life. I see the letter from my dad sitting on the coffee table and I grab it and reread it. "As good a time as any," I say to myself and I dial his number.

I'm not sure what I'm going to say. I have so many things I want to get off my chest and questions that only he can answer. I think about DayDay lying in that bed not being able to talk to or see his kids. And then I think about my father, I mean, how can a man just walk away from his kid and never look back? No calls, not even a letter or a visit for years.

I dial the number three times, but I hang up before it begins to ring. I read his letter again. "Forget this," I say and I pick up the phone once more. I dial the number. This time I allow it to ring until someone answers it.

"Hello?"

*E.R. McNair*

I pause for a second, my stomach is doing jumping jacks. "Um yes, may I speak with Matthew Watkins?"

"This is Matt. Who's calling?" he asks.

"Hi, it's LaBrea, LaBrea Watkins." My voice gets lower, "your daughter."

"LaBrea, I'm so glad you decided to call. So you got my letter!" Matt asks. "I'm glad your mother gave it to you. I wasn't sure if she would or not."

"She's not like that. She gave it to me the day she got it in the mail," I say, defensive and probably with a little more attitude than necessary.

"I wasn't sure if I wanted to call you. I mean, it's been a long time. Why after all these years did you decide to get in touch with me?" I can feel myself becoming upset. I feel like I want to cry but I hold it in.

"I know that it's been a long time. I'm sorry for that," he says. "I wanted to talk to you and see you, I've wanted to for years. But, I guess I wasn't sure how to do it. I was a little scared of being rejected. I caused your mom a lot of pain. I couldn't blame her if she decided not to give you the letter. I couldn't blame either of you. I stayed away because I thought it was best if I just left you all alone, less trouble that way."

"Less trouble for who? You? Do you know what it's like growing up thinking that your dad doesn't want you?" I ask. "I didn't have a father to talk to about boys. You missed my first date, my prom, my graduation. You missed everything!" I scream at him. I can't believe I'm talking to him like this, but my emotions won't be contained any longer. "Were you there for your other kids? Did you teach them to ride a bicycle or see them off on their first dates?"

"LaBrea, I'm sorry." He's quiet. Then he coughs like something is caught in his throat. "I really am sorry. I wanted to be there," he says. "I love you and your mom so much, but how do you tell someone that you have hurt so bad and so many times that you're sorry again? Your mom was a good woman and she always did right by me. She stood with me through thick and thin, but I did her wrong so many times. She just couldn't deal with my deceit any longer. I don't blame her. I would have left, too. So you see, I thought I was doing what was best by going away. I was selfish, I know. I just couldn't hurt her or you anymore. Do you understand?" he asks.

"Hell no I don't understand!" I scream again. "The stuff between you and my mother, that was between you and my mother, not you and me. What gave you the right to make the decision that it was better for me if you weren't around? All I wanted was to be loved by my dad. I used to sit and hope that one day you would knock on our door and say you've been looking for me and you're so glad you finally found me. You would hug and kiss me and tell me how much you love me and what I meant to you." I start to cry. My other line clicks telling me some- one is calling but I ignore it. "I mean don't get it twisted, I knew mom loved me. I never had any doubts about that. But all I knew was that you were gone and never did you look my way." I grab a tissue from the bathroom

*E.R. McNair*

and dab at my eyes. I can't believe I broke down.

I continue. "That's why all of my relationships with men are shit. I give them everything they want because I want them to love me no matter what it does to me in turn. I give more of myself then I need to trying to please them and forgetting about me and my happiness. Do you know I was raped when I was younger? I never told any-one because I felt it was my fault!" I'm crying like a baby now. "I used to wonder what I did that was so wrong that you didn't want me."

"It wasn't you, Bre."

"Try to make an eight-year-old understand that," I say. "It used to hurt so bad. But it doesn't hurt anymore."

"Please don't cry, LaBrea. I'm sorry. All I can say over and over again is that I'm so very sorry. I guess I never realized that me not being there would have this effect on you. I need you to know you were always on my mind."

"That doesn't help," I say coldly.

Matt says nothing.

Matt's words are quiet. "After so much time passed, I didn't even know how to approach your mother about seeing you."

"I don't know what to say."

"You don't have to say anything," Matt says. "Please, just listen. To answer your question, yes. I was with my other kids, your brothers and sisters. I lived with them after you and your mom left."

A knife to the gut couldn't hurt more. I close my eyes

wondering if this was a mistake.

"They know all about you and they really want to meet you, and I really need to see you, too," Matt says, trying to sound positive.

I say quietly, "After all this time, so many years, why do you need to see me now?" I ask. "I'm an adult on my own. You missed everything, and you ruined my ability to have healthy relationships with men so why now? Is there more shit you'd like to add to my life?"

"Look, LaBre, I'm not perfect. I know that I can't make up for all of the time that I've missed but I really want to try and start from now. I have to make this right with you for myself and for you, well, before it's too late." Matt gets quiet. "I've watched my daughters grow and I thought about you growing up and me missing it." He laughs. "I wondered what your first boyfriend was like. Did you play sports? How did you look at the prom? What were your grades like? Were you a cheerleader like your mom? I thought about all of those things. Please, LaBrea..."

"Bre," I correct him.

"Bre, please, I really need to see you. I don't have a lot of time left to make this right." Matt pauses. "You see, I have colon cancer and my doctors don't know how much longer I have."

My head aches and a sharp pain strikes me behind my left eye.

Matt continues. "I just want to make things right with you and with your mom if you'll let me."

*E.R. McNair*

I hold my head. "I can't believe this! I don't hear from you for years and now you call me to say you're dying and you want to make amends for all the wrong you've done! How could you leave this on me?" The room is spinning. "I don't know," I say. I don't want to deal with this right now. "You're dying?" I ask, just to make sure I heard him right.

"Yes."

"Why couldn't you have written sooner?"

"I don't have an answer to that. Things just happen in their own time."

"Of course," I say, rolling my eyes. Now I'm pissed. "I don't know, Matt."

"I understand."

I'm hating that he's so accepting.

"I hope you change your mind."

"I want to hate you," I say.

"I understand that also."

"But I can't. I want to tell you to go to hell, but I can't." I start to cry again. "How can you do this to me? Why?"

"I'm so sorry to lay this all on you, baby girl." I can hear tears in his voice. "I really am. If I could turn back time, I would do a whole lot of things differently, but I can't."

I sniffle and sneeze.

"Right now is all that we have. So please, I'm asking if I can come and see you. You don't have to answer now. Take a couple of days to think about it. But I want to spend as much time with you as I can. I want to know my baby girl. I want to be a part of your life while I can."

"Wow, this is really some shit," I say, clearing my throat. "I'll call you tomorrow. I have to go because there's someone on my other line," I lie.

"Okay, baby girl. Well, I hope to hear from you soon. And, LaBrea, Bre? I love you."

"Yeah, okay. Well, I gotta go. Bye."

I hang up and I scream. I'm so confused. I pace my floor talking to myself. "My father, who I haven't seen since I was six years old is dying and he wants to see me." I wave my hands in the air. "This is some bullshit!" I laugh. If someone saw me they might have me committed. "Who the hell does this kind of shit to their kid? I mean it wasn't like this bastard didn't know where I was. Like I need this shit. To find out he's dying. Well fuck him. He can burn in hell for all I care! I don't want to see him. Maybe I do so I can spit in his face. Hell, I don't know what I want." I start to cry again, "I just want this pain that I feel right now to go away, I know that much." I sit on my couch and rock back and forth holding my stomach. "I have to call mom. She's not going to believe this shit."

I dial my mom's number.

"Hello?"

"Hey, mommy, are you busy?" I sniffle and sneeze again.

"Bre? What's wrong, baby?"

"Mommy, you're not going to believe this. I just got

*E.R. McNair*

off the phone with my dad." I feel myself calming down.

"Oh, really? Well what did Matt have to say for himself?"

"He's dying!"

"He's what?" my mom screams. "Dying of what? Are you sure he said dying? I can't believe it!"

"Dying. And he wants to see you and me and make right what he did wrong!" I pace some more. "After all this time he calls to say he's dying!"

"I can't believe that," my mom says to herself.

"Believe it," I say. "He says he has colon cancer and his doctors don't know how long he has to live. He wants to know if he can come here to see us. He told me to call him with an answer. I don't know what to say, mommy," I whine.

"Baby, you can say whatever you want to, whatever you feel. If you want to say no, then say it," my mother says. "You're not obligated to see him, but he is your father and he has always loved you. You don't have to do this by yourself. If you want me to be with you when you see him, I will. You know I am always here for you."

"Oh, he wants to see you too," I say, moving my head from side to side. "How can you say that he has always loved me, mom? He never tried to contact me in all of the years we've been here."

My mother is quiet and then she continues slowly. "Well, Bre, that is not exactly true. When I first left your father he did try many times to see you. But I told him to leave us alone, that we didn't need him. He finally respected my wishes and never came back around or called."

I think I'm dreaming. The room begins to close in on me. I think I might hyperventilate. Everything I knew to be true was now all a lie. It isn't my father I should hate, it's my mother.

She goes on. "He would send you Christmas and birthday cards for a while and I would throw them away. But then after a while those stopped, too. I thought it was the best for you and me to make a complete and final break. I knew what he was capable of and it wasn't good." She gets quiet and then takes a deep breath. "I see now that it was probably the worst thing that I ever could have done." I think about Nicky and Ty. "I hope you don't hate me for this. But I thought I was doing what was right. I'm so very very sorry, Bre." My mom breaks down, crying.

"Oh my God! I can't believe I'm hearing this shit from you. What the hell, mom!" I scream.

"I'm sorry, Bre."

"I'm sorry, too. I don't mean to disrespect you. I can't believe you kept him from me. I thought he hated me. I thought he loved his other kids more than me and he wanted them and never wanted me."

"I know baby, and I am truly sorry but you have to understand when I left your father I was young and hurt. My life was in shambles. Your grandparents practically disowned me. They felt I let him ruin my life, our lives. You were the only good thing in my life." Her words were

*E.R. McNair*

coming fast and furious. "They kept you while I finished school. And they thought that I was over your dad. That he was out of my system. Then I married him when I finished college. They were livid. They didn't speak to me for years. Not until I left him. Then I only had a few years with them before they died. Please forgive me, Bre," mom begs me. "I can't lose you too. You know how much I love you. Please understand and know how much I regret doing this to you. Do you forgive me?" I hear her sniffles.

"My head is pounding. I don't know what to think. I feel like my whole life has been a big fat fucking lie." I can't take any more. "I have to go, mommy. I'm sorry for cursing. I'll call you later. I need to think. I just can't deal with this right now."

"Ok, baby." I hear sadness in her voice. "I'll let you go to think but I need you to know I love you. Please call me if you need me. I am still your mother."

"Whatever, mommy," I say flatly and then I hang up.

I feel so alone. I don't want to call any of my friends. They're all going through enough. I understand now Nicky's need to smoke weed. I want to be lifted away from here, but I never want to come back.

I call into work and tell them that I'm sick. "I think I have the flu," I say.

# thirty

**Nesha**

I walk into the back room of the pawnshop and I see Mello.

"Thanks," I say to him. He didn't have to bail me out when he bailed out CeeCee.

"No problem," he answers. "I'm sorry to hear about Chuckie."

I nod and push back the tears. This is no place for emotions. Charles and the sheriff came to pick Chuckie up yesterday. Me, Marsean and Angel slept in his room last night. Our way of paying our respect to our missing soldier.

The pawnshop room is cluttered with drug paraphernalia—scales on the counters, bags of white powder and piles of the best weed from Cuba. A couple of guns lay on the table and six bulletproof vests are piled on the beat-up couch on the opposite wall. The room smells of stale cigarettes and body odor. You can't get these nig-

*E.R. McNair*

gas to bathe for nothing.

I empty my pockets and backpack of all the money I have and pile it on the table in front of me. When I counted it last night before I went to bed, it was $25,000. I search the room for the alternate exit and make sure that I would have a clear path should I need it. I am the smallest one in the room so I would be able to squeeze through the opening no problem.

"How much?" Paul asks.

"Twenty-five," I answer just as coolly as he asks.

He nods his head. I can see that he's pleased.

I'm tired of working for someone else. I'm smarter than all these niggas put together. I could run this business and make ten times as much as they can. They have no vision. No planning. No ingenuity. I'm just biding my time.

I see Mello leave with another nigga he was talking to. I wonder where they're going.

"What do you need?" Paul asks me.

We begin our transaction and before we can finish there's a loud knock at the door. We're alone in the room and we both jump. I grab one of the guns from off the table and dive under the table. Another set of knocks and I fire. *Bang. Bang. Bang.* I shoot, not at anyone or anything. I stash the gun in my backpack and dash for the exit.

Once in the back alley, I see four or five police cars surround the building. Then the siren of an ambulance fills the air. I listen closely trying to hear who or what I hit when I was shooting but I can't tell. I move slowly, making sure not to draw attention to myself.

I feel in my bag once I'm sure I'm far enough away from the commotion. I feel the gun and I also feel the $25,000. I smile to myself.

I put the key in my front door and turn the lock. Tito and Michael are sitting in the front room, their feet propped up on the coffee table. I smell chicken and I know they've fed Marsean and Angel. No one says anything.

"What the fuck is wrong with you two?" I ask them. My heart has finally stopped beating wildly and I'm breathing at a steady pace.

They both shake their heads. I can sense that something's wrong.

I grab a beer from the fridge and join them in the living room.

"Where's the kids?" I ask.

"Marsean is over at Terry's playing video games and Angel is at the library."

This time I nod.

"What are you watching?' I ask, finishing my first beer. My nerves are on edge and one beer would do nothing.

"The news."

"Why?" I ask.

"Paul's dead," Tito says.

"What?" I jump up.

*E.R. McNair*

"The police shot him."

"Fuck," I say. No other words would come out. "Fuck."

"What happened?" Michael asks.

"How the hell am I supposed to know," I say, looking at him, daring him to ask me more questions. This nigga is living, rent free, in my crib. He'd better stop questioning me.

The room is silent.

"I need to fucking think," I say. I'm nervous. I wonder if he talked before they killed him. What do the cops know? I know I'll have to lay low for a couple of days. "Fuck," I say again.

Fuck.

# thirty-one

**Bre**

I took my phone off the hook and on Day three Mello is at my door banging as if he's the police.

I see his car when I look out the peep hole, he's around the corner, trying to get a look into the apartment. I guess to see if I'm lying on the floor passed out from carbon monoxide poisoning or something like that. I debate on whether or not to let him in. I look horrible. I haven't combed my hair in days and just this morning I took my first shower.

I swing the door open and the look on his face is one of relief.

"Where the fuck have you been?" he asks, a liter of Pepsi under his arm.

I smile at him and wrap my arms around his waist and lay my head on his chest. I hear his heart beat and the rhythm is soothing.

I usher him in and tell him everything that happened

*E.R. McNair*

with my dad. And I tell him it was my mom who kept me from my father.

"Damn Bre, that's some crazy shit, for real. I can understand why you're so mad. But don't be too hard on your mom or your dad. At least you have both of your parents. Some people only wish they still had parents to argue with, you know," Mello says. "And never do that shit again, taking your phone off the hook. I was tripping when I couldn't get in touch with you."

"I'm sorry." I flash my sincerest apologetic look. "I know that," I say, propping my feet up on his lap, "and I'm trying but it's hard as hell. She lied. He didn't. But what I can't figure out is why he didn't fight for me."

Mello shrugs his shoulders. "The only person that can answer that is your dad."

"I think I'm going to see him." I sigh.

"Good. I'm sure you'll be happy once everything is cleared up." Mello smiles.

I kiss him. He tastes good.

"Mello?" I say his name.

"Yeah?" He answers with his eyes closed and his head resting on the back of the couch.

I look at him. "I need you to define our relationship."

He lifts his head and looks at me. He takes my right hand and kisses it.

"Is that your answer?" I ask.

"It's part of my answer."

"What's the rest?" I ask, anxiously.

"I like you a lot, Bre. You're special. You give me a

funny feeling in my stomach."

I smile. "How many cool points do you loose for that one?" I ask.

"Who are you going to tell?"

"Are you ashamed of us?" I'm curious.

"Hell no," he says, a serious look on his face. "But all they need to know is that you're my girl."

I smile and lay my head on his shoulder.

"Are you hungry?" he asks me.

"I'll just live on our love." I say worried by what I've said.

"Well, while your love is good, I can't live on that shit. I need some food." He stands up. "Pizza?"

"Cool." I watch him go into the kitchen and get the phone book. He orders a supreme extra large pizza, tells them to deliver it and comes back and sits next to me.

"Mello, you just being here with me is making it better. I'm glad you're here."

Mello smiles, turns on the television and flips through the channels. "I went to the hospital to see Day today. Ms. Jackson was there. I told her it was messed up what she did. She said CeeCee was going to find out eventually, and it was better that she found out now." He shrugs. "I don't know."

"Mello?"

"Yeah," he says. I can tell he's dozing off to sleep.

"I don't want to talk about that. It all makes me sad." I look away.

"I know what you mean," Mello says. His eyes close

*E.R. McNair*

again.

"Mello?"

"Yeah, babe?"

I wonder if I'm bothering him.

"I'm hungry." I look at him and he opens his eyes.

"I thought you said you weren't hungry." He looks at his watch. "We got about a half an hour before the pizza gets here. Can you wait until then?"

"I'm not hungry for food," I say with a smile on my face.

"I feel you." He grabs me by my hand and leads me into the bedroom.

In my room Mello begins to rub my back and shoulders. I moan, it feels so good.

He kisses my back and neck and I feel myself getting hot all over.

Mello whispers in my ear. "I'm gonna make you feel like you never felt before for real, Bre." Mello pulls my clothes off and then he starts at my neck and kisses all the way down my back until he gets to the crack of my ass.

"Oh, my God!" I scream out.

He's playing with my love button and I'm going crazy. We kiss and kiss and kiss some more. Then he enters me from behind. I think I cum about three or four times.

Afterwards, I lay next to him and play with his ear.

"I'm going to take a quick shower," Mello says.

The doorbell rings.

"Grab some money out of my pants," he calls from

the bathroom.

I dress and head to the door, pay for the pizza and take a slice realizing that I'm hungrier than I thought. We both eat and then we go to bed. We sleep wrapped in each other's arms. I'm happier than I've been in a while. I think that I should have called him three days ago. I would have saved three days of vacation. Or, I might have taken them anyway.

I wake up Thursday morning and I feel like a new woman. Mello leaves when I leave to go to work. We kiss in the parking lot like a husband and wife. I smile at him, he winks at me.

When I get to my desk I call my mother first thing, "Hey, mommy?"

"Hi, baby. I'm so glad you called. I was starting to worry."

"I know. I needed to think. I'm still a little upset and hurt about everything. But I forgive you. I don't understand it but I know that you only did it because you love me." I say, looking over my shoulder for Ms. Calloway.

"I knew you needed time, that's why I didn't call you. Maybe one day when you have kids of your own you'll understand my reasoning. Have you made your decision? Maybe then we can get everything out into the open."

"I'm going to call him. He can come here, if that's okay with you?" I say.

"That's fine with me, Bre, I want to do this. I have

*E.R. McNair*

some things I need to say to your father as well. He needs to know that I have forgiven him. And I want his forgiveness also so that he can die in peace and I can be at peace as well. Call me with the details."

"Thank you, mommy, I know this will be hard for both of us," I say, "but we can do it."

"Talk to you later," my mom says.

I work nonstop until lunch. When the clock strikes noon, I rush out to the plaza behind the bank and dial my dad's phone number.

The phone rings six times and then a woman answers. "Hello, Watkins residence."

My stomach aches and I can barely get the words out. "Umm, yes, may I speak with Matthew please?"

"May I tell him who's calling?" she asks. It must be his wife. She sounds older than a teenager.

"This is, um, his daugh— I mean, this is LaBrea Watkins," I say, stumbling over my words.

"Oh my, hi, LaBrea. I'm Matt's wife, Diana. He's been anxiously awaiting your call. Please hold on one minute while I get him?" Diana leaves the phone.

She seems nice enough. I shoo away a few pigeons that try to get my food and I decide I'm not hungry enough to eat. I'm no longer angry at Diana. I realize she was a passenger on this bus to hell that is my life. None of this is her fault.

"Hello, Bre," Matt says into the phone. He coughs, that same scary cough. "I'm so glad you called. For a minute, I didn't think I would hear from you."

*E.R. McNair*

"For a minute, I didn't think you were going to hear from me, too," I say. "This has been a lot to take in. I talked to my mother and I found out that you are not totally to blame for this." I feel a little more courageous during this conversation.

"I understand. There is so much that we need to talk about and there is so little time. I don't mean to put pressure on you but have you thought about seeing me, Bre?" Matt asks.

"I have. I am going to see you and my mother would also like to see you. We can all sit down and get everything out into the open."

"Look, Bre, don't blame your mother. She did what she thought was best for you at the time. All I could do was to respect her wishes."

"Ok Matt. I am sorry to cut the conversation short, but I'm at work. I look forward to seeing you. How about Saturday at six o'clock at my mom's house. She lives at 44 East Main Street?"

"Okay Bre," he says after another coughing fit. "I need you to know that I love you very much."

I nod. I'm not ready to say it back to him.

Matt pauses before speaking. "I will see you on Saturday at six o'clock."

*E.R. McNair*

## thirty-two

**Bre**

My phone rings. It's CeeCee.

"Look, Bre. Mello bailed us out. That bitch wouldn't press charges. But we need to talk, for real. Open your door. I'm out front."

CeeCee looks a mess. Her hair is all over her head and her clothes are ripped up. She walks in.

"Look CeeCee, I know you're mad."

"I'm more than mad. I can't think of what I am." She paces my living room floor and then she stops. "I'm hurt." She stares pointedly at me. "I really want to kick your ass right now. But I'm trying to be calm and rational about this shit for real, Bre." CeeCee gets a glimpse of herself in a mirror and she tries to pat down the hair standing up on her head. "You're my girl, Bre, but I would never keep something like this away from you. I'm trying to be understanding but it's hard to be cool."

"Look, CeeCee, I know that you're upset and I can

understand why. I'm sorry I wasn't honest with you. I wrestled with this shit for a long time. I didn't know what to do. I really didn't want to be in the middle of the fight." I laugh. "And look where I end up. Right smack dab in the fucking middle."

CeeCee sits down and looks at her feet. "How do you think I felt when my kids tell me that Nicky was laying in the bed with Daddy and she kissed him? She has absolutely no respect for them or me and his mom. That bitch is canceled in my book!" She stands and continues to pace the floor. "It all makes sense now. The little comments Nicky would make. The way they would stare at each other. Hell, even the shit his mom said. It all fits now."

"Honestly, CeeCee, I just found out the night that DayDay got shot."

CeeCee stares at me as if she's trying to determine whether or not my words are the truth. "Yeah, well, it's going to take me a while to get over this." She walks over the door and swings it open. "I guess I still love you like a sister." CeeCee turns around and hugs me.

I worry she might sneak me.

"But, I'll need some time to get over this, Bre." She looks out into the street. Carl from down the block honks his horn and we both wave. "If the shoe were on the other foot, how would you have handled the situation?"

I shrug my shoulders not sure what I would have done if I found out Nicky was fucking Mello too.

"Do you know how long they been kicking it?"

*E.R. McNair*

CeeCee asks.

"Nope. Nicky wouldn't give me too many details."

"Well, she can't have DayDay, Bre. I won't let that shit happen. I know that I have done some foul shit, and maybe I don't deserve Day, but he's mine right now and I love him," CeeCee says.

"I did tell her that what she was doing was wrong. If that makes you feel any better?"

CeeCee put up two fingers to show me just how much better it makes her feel. Not much.

"I've been praying a lot," CeeCee says, looking at me to get my reaction.

I smile.

She continues, "I met this woman at the hospital. She's been praying with me and talking to me. She told me that I should get God in my life and that he could turn every situation from bad to good." CeeCee nods her head.

I nod too.

"I figure, what do I have to lose? So this lady, she asked me to go to church with her. I'm going to go and see what her God can do to make my life better. I mean, I don't know if this is going to work but I'm going to give it a try. Anything is better than this shit." CeeCee sits down on the porch. "I'm tired. I have three kids and no education. I quit school in the tenth grade. How can I teach my kids anything when I don't know shit my damn self? I can't say that this is going to make me any different but anything is better then the life I'm living right now."

I sit down next to her and wrap my arms around her. "CeeCee, I'm proud of you." I can feel tears forming in my eyes. "I think that this is a good thing. Church can't hurt, and it may help the kids, too. I hope you really find what it is that you are looking for."

"I do, too. I'm scared though, Bre. I don't know if I can change or even if I want to. I know that sounds crazy. I mean, what if it's too hard? I don't know how to be a good mom or a good woman. Look at who my mother is. I mean, she's clean now but who knows what she'll be next week. This ain't the first time that she has gotten clean."

CeeCee stands up and brushes the dirt from her behind. "I can't worry about my mom. I have enough to deal with. The lady said she's going to come and get me on Wednesday. I'm going to go to bible study with her after I go visit Day. She said they have classes that the kids can go to, and she thinks they would really enjoy it. I don't want you to make a big deal about it just yet, but I took my GED test. Who knows, if I pass, maybe that'll open up some doors for me."

"That's cool, CeeCee! I hope everything works out for you and I am going to keep you in my prayers. Keep your head up. I hope that this works out for everyone."

I walk CeeCee to her car. "Where's Nesha?"

"Nesha's at home, still pissed. She still wants to fuck Nicky up. But I told her it's over, let the shit go. I told her this is my fight not hers, but you know Nesha. She can't

*E.R. McNair*

ever let anything go. I just hope that she lets me deal with this how I want to deal with it."

"I stopped by to see DayDay when I was at the hospital."

CeeCee smiles.

"He looks good."

"I miss him, Bre. We were like best friends." CeeCee allows a few tears to drop from her eyes.

"He'll be back to you soon."

"I hope so," CeeCee says as she starts her car. "I hope so." She backs out and leaves.

# thirty-three

**Nicky**

I've had a headache for the past three days and nothing will make it go away; at least nothing that they can give me at the hospital. That's fucked up! I have to take a cab home. Where are my girls when I need them? Bitches.

I called my mother, but she didn't answer. I wonder where she is. I look around my apartment and everything looks the same. And that's not good. I check my messages and there's only one. It's Kenny. He says he's going to be in town for his aunt's birthday party. He wants to hook up. I roll my eyes.

The phone rings and scares me away from my thoughts.

"Hello?"

"You're home?"

It's Slick. I'm pissed I answered the phone.

"Yeah," I say. My head begins to pound harder. I'm scared about what he's about to say.

*E.R. McNair*

"We need you at work."

I can hear loud music in the background.

"Slick, I don't feel like working." I can only imagine what he's about to say.

"Bitch, you don't have sick leave. I don't give a fuck how you feel. Your ass better be here tonight." He hangs up before I can respond.

I drop the phone to the floor. There's no one else I want to talk to.

I go to the bathroom and run the water in the tub. Hopefully the hot water will relax me. I search through the drawers in my bedroom and I find a small bag full of weed. I roll a small joint and take it into the bathroom with me. I inhale deeply and cough. It's been a couple of days since I've smoked and I guess I'm not used to it. Again, I inhale deeply and this time the smoke enters my body and it's welcomed like a long lost friend. I smile, ease down into water. The sensation is familiar. Like what birth might be like. Warm water surrounding me. Peaceful. Quiet.

About a half an hour later I finish up in the bathroom and I head downstairs. With Ty not being around, my time is my own. I don't have to answer any questions. I don't have to fix any broken toys. I can sit and stare at the wall if that's what makes me happy. As if anything now makes me happy.

Again, I'm scared away from my thoughts, this time by a knock at the door.

I swing open the door and it's Ms. Jackson. "Hey,

baby."

I can see by the look on her face that she's not pre-pared to see the bruises on my face. She extends her hand to touch them and I wince before she can even make contact.

"I'm sorry," Ms. Jackson apologizes. "That bitch is going to get what's coming to her."

I nod. I sit. She sits.

"Are you okay?"

"I'm fine," I say. I'm really not in the mood for talking. I glance at the clock near the television and realize that the time is moving fast. Almost time to go to the club. A sharp pain stabs me behind the eyes.

"You don't look fine. I'm on my way to the hospital. Do you want to come with me? I'm sure DayDay would like to see you." She smiles and exposes her crooked teeth. I pray that I don't look like her when I get older. She's lived such a hard life. I guess I'm on the same path.

I shake my head no. I don't want to see the hospital anymore, ever. I just left there. Going back would be a big mistake, for so many reasons.

"Are you sure, baby? Don't let that bitch keep you away from my son. You are destined to be with him. I know it. I just know it."

I try to smile, but her prophecy doesn't seem to be my destiny. At least right now it doesn't. "Maybe another day," I say. "I'm just a little tired right now."

Ms. Jackson nods, as if she understands my reason. "Of course you are, sweety." She grabs her purse and

*E.R. McNair*

heads to the door. She looks down at the phone. "It's off the hook." She bends down to put the phone back in its cradle. "Where's Ty?"

"At my mother's house," I explain. I really don't know where he is. I haven't talked to either of them in a couple of days.

Again, Ms. Jackson nods. "I'll call to see if you're up to it tomorrow." She leans in and kisses me on the cheek. I smell her breakfast, the cigarette she smoked in the car over and her strong perfume. I feel sick to my stomach.

I force another smile. But the action causes my head to pound and the stitches under the bandages to itch.

"Take care of yourself," she says and walks out the door.

Before I can close the door, Ms. Jackson turns around. "Have you eaten?"

"No, ma'am," I answer. The thought of food makes my stomach turn and so now my head is pounding and my stomach is churning.

"I can fix you something," she says, walking back toward my door.

"No," I say a little louder than I probably should. The look on Ms. Jackson's face is one of alarm. "I mean," I say, trying to clean up my mess, "if I eat, it might just make it worse. I'll be fine. I promise."

"Okay." Ms. Jackson gets into her car and drives away.

I close the door and rush to the bathroom to splash

some cold water on my face. I finish up in the bathroom and try to find a comfortable spot on the couch. Sleep attacks me before I know it and I'm on my back with small, soft snores drifting from my lips. I hear a pounding and can't tell if it's the pulsating beat inside my head or if it's someone actually at my front door. I try to drift back to sleep, but the beating continues constantly.

Slowly I leave the comfort of my leather couch and I swing open the door.

"I knew your ass wouldn't be ready!" Slick barks at me. Spittal from his full, rose-colored lips hits me in the forehead.

"Come on, Slick," I say. I sit down on the chair by the door and hold my head in my hands. "I just got out of the hospital. I haven't seen my son in days. I just need a couple days."

"Look at my face!" Slick screams. "Look at my face."

I look up at him and he doesn't look like the same man. His once chubby, hairless, boyish face has been transformed into an evil, money hungry devil. He burns me with his glare.

"Do I fucking look like I care about your head, your son or for that matter, you? You've been gone for three days and like I told you before, you don't have sick leave. When you don't work, you don't eat. Get your shit and let's go!"

Slick grabs me by my arm, pulls me from my house and throws me into his car. A pair of panties and a T-shirt are the only things that cover my body. I sit in the

*E.R. McNair*

backseat of his car, tears streaming down my cheeks, he tells me to shut up or he'll kill me. Where did I go wrong?

# thirty-four

**Bre**

My work day ends and I'm exhausted. On my way home from work, I try to call Nicky. I need to let everyone know I'm okay. I keep getting her voicemail. She was supposed to be released from the hospital yesterday. I hope she's okay. I'm not ready to deal with Nesha, and she probably didn't call me anyway.

When I get home from work, Mello is sitting in his car in front of my house. I smile at him, glad to see him.

"How'd you know I wouldn't have anyone else with me?" I ask him as I'm unlocking my door.

"Because I know that I lay that pipe so good you wouldn't need to go to anyone else." He kisses me on the back of my neck.

I laugh. "Busted. Is that dinner in those bags?" I ask, looking at the grocery bags in his hand.

"It's my turn," Mello says, taking the bags into the kitchen.

*E.R. McNair*

I think he's going to cook, but the bags are filled with pre-prepared food. At least he took the initiative to bring me something to eat.

"I'm impressed," I say, going through the bags.

We eat and I'm stuffed when we're done. We clean up the kitchen and retire to the couch.

Mello and I have a great night. We make love for half the night. When we finish I can't fall asleep. I'm feeling so many emotions I feel like I need to do something. I get up and go into the kitchen and rummage through the fridge, eating everything left over from dinner.

I'm stuffed and now I'm so tired I can't keep my eyes open. I go back to bed and lay next to Mello. Small snores are escaping from his full lips. I smile at him and kiss him on his forehead. I lay next to him and next thing I know it's morning.

I smell bacon. I sit up in my bed. I look around the room and Mello's not there, but I smell bacon.

I go into the kitchen. Mello's standing at the stove, in his boxers only, frying bacon.

"Now that's a sight," I say. I grab a slice that's already finished, kissing him on his bare shoulder.

"You don't have your cell phone taking pictures do you?" Mello's asks, flipping pancakes.

"No. But your boys don't know you cook?" I ask, leaning against the sink.

"They know I cook, but not that I cook for girls."

"So, you have a lot of firsts with me, huh?"

"I guess I do," Mello says, placing my plate on the

table. "Breakfast is served," he says, kissing me on the cheek.

Mello leaves the room.

I put a fork full in mouth and I'm happy with what I taste. "You're not eating with me?" I call after him.

"I've got some business to take care of," Mello says, coming back into the kitchen, now fully dressed. He leans down and opens his mouth waiting for me to fill the space with pancakes.

"I'm a bad nigga," he says with a mouth full of food.

I smile. "Will I see you later?" I ask, finishing up.

"I'll call you." Mello walks to the front door.

I follow him, stopping at the front door. He turns and glides toward me.

"Thanks," he says, planting a kiss on my lips. "You taste like syrup."

"Thanks for what?" I ask, sad that he's leaving.

"For being you." He jumps off the front porch. "Peace."

Damn. I'm falling for this nigga.

*E.R. McNair*

# thirty-five

**Bre**

At work I'm feeling a little anxious. My father will be here tomorrow.

I'm nervous.

I get through the eight hours of work, barely. I leave the bank and head to CeeCee's house.

CeeCee answers the door.

"Hey, Bre." She moves out the way. "Come in, please."

We sit in her living room. The kids are in front of the television, glued to the show they're watching.

"I feel so bad," CeeCee says.

I look at her but don't say anything.

"Nicky."

I nod. I understand. I feel just as bad.

"Something just came over me." CeeCee shakes her head. "I didn't know what it was, but I do now."

I raise my brows asking the question without words.

"The devil. No other explanation."

"The devil made you do it." I smile, making light of what she's said, but I can tell she doesn't find it funny.

"Absolutely."

I nod again.

"I wish I could talk to her. I want to apologize."

"Have you called her?"

"I've tried. She doesn't call me back."

I shrug my shoulders. "She's not real responsive late-ly."

This time CeeCee just looks at me.

"I've heard..." Before I can continue, CeeCee cuts me off.

"I've heard too." She looks down. "So sad. Are you thirsty?"

I nod, yes.

CeeCee tells me to follow her into the kitchen.

I tell her about meeting my dad. She says that I have to forgive my dad. She says if God can forgive us for all that we've done wrong, who are we not to forgive those who hurt us? All I can do is agree with her. I realize this is a completely new CeeCee that I'm talking to, one I never imagined I'd see. I thought she would be a hood rat forever. I like this new CeeCee. She's growing up. We go back into the living room.

"I enjoy talking to the new CeeCee," I say.

"I'm enjoying being the new CeeCee," she says, fold-ing up a basket of clothes beside her. She holds up a pile of clothes. "DJ, take this up to your room, please."

*E.R. McNair*

The boy grabs the pile, trips over his sister's shoes and stumbles to the floor. CeeCee rolls her eyes and helps him collect the clothes.

"What a clumsy kid." She smiles at me. "What brings you over my way?"

"I'm so nervous about meeting my dad."

"When is it?" CeeCee asks, sitting back in her chair.

"Tomorrow." I close my eyes. "I'm confused. I used to hate him. But I don't know how I feel."

"You know, Bre, I hated Day and Nicky. But, I realized that it only made me miserable. When I forgave them, I knew that I was a better person. And I feel better." She looks at me. "You should forgive your dad and your mom," CeeCee says. "Hate can eat away at you."

I nod my head and stare at the television. There's a commercial on and it makes me giggle. "You know with my mom it's harder because I feel so deceived," I say.

"I always did like your mom even though she never liked me. I used to wish that my mom was like your mom. Your mom did what she did because she loves you and wanted to protect you."

CeeCee continues. "Now I'm working on forgiving my mom. I realize a lot of who I am is because of all the anger and hate I feel for her. I'm tired of living like that. I want to change. I want to be a new person, Bre." She shrugs. "I just hope I can. I have a lot of issues I still have to work through."

"Don't we all?" I say. CeeCee's four year old daughter, Alexis, climbs on my lap. She likes me because I gave her a doll one time, but she's always looking for a toy when I come around.

"It's because of my mother that I haven't seen my sister and brother. I still feel guilty." CeeCee puts her head down in her hands. "Bre, I'm glad that I have you to talk to. I love Nesha and she's my girl but she thinks this is just my emotions and that I'll be back to my old self soon. But I don't want to be that person again."

"Well, from what I can see you're already a new person." I reach for CeeCee's hand. "I'm here if you need me. It's not going to be easy, but I know you can do it. Just be patient with yourself. Change takes time."

CeeCee nods her head and she starts to cry. Alexis leaves my lap and goes to sit on her mother, patting her back like I'm sure CeeCee does when she cries.

"You might slip with some things and other habits will take a while to break but like you said, 'God is forgiving.' You help me, too. Talking with you about my dad is making me feel better about the meeting." I whisper, "Thank you."

Tears are falling down both of our cheeks.

"Okay, you guys, let's start cleaning up," CeeCee says to her kids. She pushes the remaining clothes out of the way. "We need to get to the hospital. Pastor Redman is going to meet me there. We're going to pray for Day." CeeCee grabs my hand. "I think today is the day we're going to get him back. If it isn't I'll thank God anyway for him just being alive."

"Amen," I say.

CeeCee and Alexis walk me to the front door. I hug them both and then Ashley comes over to join the group hug. CeeCee laughs.

"I've got some pretty good kids, don't I?" CeeCee asks, smiling down at the girls. "I guess I didn't screw you up as much as I thought I did."

I drive home a little lighter and clearer about how I feel. Maybe I should take CeeCee's lead and pray about it. It couldn't hurt the situation, and it seems to be helping her.

*E.R. McNair*

# thirty-six

**CeeCee**

Since the fight at the Upscale, so much has changed. DayDay is still in the hospital. One of the bullets is still lodged near his spine and he'll still have to have more surgeries. The doctors are confident that he'll eventually be back to running the streets like he did before. Those weren't the words they used, but that's what they meant.

I open the envelope I received from the GED test I took. I'm scared to look at the results.

"Alexis, baby, come here." I call her to come and stand next to me. "Here," I extend my hand, "hold mommy's hand."

Alexis holds my hand and I read. I scream louder than I've ever screamed before.

"I passed! I passed!" Alexis and I dance around the kitchen. "Mommy passed! Mommy passed!" I pick her up and swing her around.

*E.R. McNair*

I call Bre.

"I passed! I passed!" I scream into the phone.

"CeeCee?" Bre asks.

How can she not know it's me?

"Bre," I begin out of breath, "I passed the GED! I'm officially a high school graduate." My cheeks are tired from smiling so much.

"CeeCee, I'm so happy for you."

"The director of the program told me he can get me a job at his sister's real estate office in Charlotte once I pass my test!" I scream into the phone.

"What? Huh? What a minute. North Carolina? What are you talking about CeeCee?" Bre asks.

"I'm moving, Bre. I'm moving to Charlotte. I can't stay here. I've got to go. Everything is falling into place." I can't stop smiling. "I'm moving in three weeks."

"I'm happy for you!" Bre says.

I can hear her real feeling though.

"No you're not," I say.

"I guess it's bitter sweet. I'm glad you're getting everything you want. But I'm going to miss you."

"I'll miss you too. You best believe that. You're my girl. I love you, Bre." I can feel tears begin to form in my eyes. And I swear I can hear her sniffle on the other end of the line. "But Bre, I'll have a house for the kids. Can you believe that? A house, with a back yard?"

"That sounds great, CeeCee. Let's get together before you go."

"Of course. I wouldn't leave without us getting

together."

"I mean all of us."

"I'm not sure, Bre. Maybe we should just remember things as they used to be."

Bre doesn't say anything.

"I don't know if I have the energy to argue, fuss and fight with them. I'm tired of trying to defend the new me with Nesha and Nicky, she just can't understand that I forgive her. I'm sure she just wants to fight and I don't want to."

"You won't have to," Bre says.

"Still trying to referee us, huh?" I laugh. "Bre, some people don't deal well with change. And when you run into people like that, it's up to the person trying to change to cut those people out of their lives. I'm there, Bre. I'm cutting. Snip, snip, snip."

"One more time. If they say no, I won't try again."

"You're begging," I say.

"I know. Please? Friday?"

"Let me know who's coming," I concede.

"I'll call you back."

I can tell she's smiling. I am too.

*E.R. McNair*

## tḫirty-seven

**Bre**

It's Saturday. I kind of hope that my dad will stand us up. I'm very nervous and concerned about what we will talk about, how he'll look, if he'll be disappointed in how I look. I'm not sure I'm ready for this.

Should I hug him or shake his hand? Do I continue to call him Matt or will he rather me call him dad? I'm a nervous wreck.

My mom is calm. She cooked his favorite meal—pork chops, fried cabbage with cornbread and mashed potatoes.

"Why cook his favorite meal?" I ask her, irritated that she's catering to him.

"Don't you think he's going to be nervous enough? I'm just trying to make him feel relaxed, as much as I can."

I don't get it.

It is 5:35 p.m. when he rings the doorbell.

My mom answers the door and I just stand there, looking stupid. She hugs him and while they're hugging he closes his eyes. I just stare. I can't move. My stomach is churning and my heart is beating fast. I think I might pass out.

"Hello, Matthew, it's been a long time," mom says.

"Hey, Shelia, how are you?" he says back. He looks around her and speaks to me. "Hello, LaBrea, you're just as beautiful as I thought you would be." He stands in front of me and holds out his hands to hug me. "You look just like your mother when she was your age." He smiles at me and then looks at my mom.

"Hi, Matt, dad... I'm sorry. I don't know what to call you or if I should hug you or what." I'm nervous and I feel myself start to sweat.

"It's okay. It's awkward for all of us," Matt says.

I'm glad we're getting this out of the way now. But what will we talk about later I wonder.

"Forgive my rudeness," mom says. "Please, Matthew, come in and have a seat." Mom closes the door and then shows Matt into the living room. "Can I get you something to drink?" she asks.

"Water would be nice," Matt says, taking a seat.

I see that he's walking with a cane. His gait is slow. He looks so frail and he's balding. His clothes hang off his body. I wonder how he looked when he was younger.

"How was your drive?" mom asks, handing Matt a glass of water. I see she's giving him one of her good glasses. The ones she fussed at me for using.

*E.R. McNair*

"It wasn't bad," Matt says, drinking almost all of the glass.

"Did you drive by yourself?" my mom asks, looking concerned.

"No. My wife is at the hotel. She drove me."

My mom looks surprised. "Why didn't you bring her? She is more than welcome to come to dinner."

"We thought it best to just be us this time. Maybe next time."

Mom nods.

We're all quiet for a minute, unsure where to go from here.

Mom says, "I made your favorites." She smiles.

Now Matt nods and smiles. "Let me start by telling you both how sorry I am for all of the pain that I caused."

"Look, Matt, that was a long time ago, and I forgave you a long time ago. We were young and things moved way too fast for both of us," mom says. "Right now I just want Bre to be happy, that's all."

We sit still. The quiet is uneasy and awkward.

"Matthew," I say. "I accept your apology and I'm trying hard to forgive you, mom. I'm glad to see you, even if it has taken all these years for it to happen."

"I'm glad I finally got up the nerve to do it, too. I guess it has taken this tragedy to make me realize that I needed to get my stuff together. I decided that I needed to make amends for some of the crazy stuff I did when I was younger. There are many people I was unable to contact because they are no longer around. But, I'm

*E.R. McNair*

lucky that you're still here." He smiles at me.

I can't believe that he admitted that he was scared. I always pictured him living phat and fabulous without me. Not that he was thinking about me at all.

Mom says, "Well, why don't we eat?" She helps Matt up from the couch seeing that he's having trouble. I wish I could be like her, she's pushed the past away, forgiven my dad for all he's done and is even willing to allow his new wife to eat at her table. She continues, "Matt, you can tell us what has been going on in your life."

My mom's the bomb! She could always could break tension in a room.

Matt sits at the table. "Can we pray?" he asks.

My mother smiles and nods in agreement. They look at me and I shrug, not sure what's going on. I guess the years have healed and changed them both.

"Can we hold hands?" Matthew holds out his hands.

I grab his hand and I feel the many years of abuse in his grip.

He begins, "Dear Lord, thank you for your many blessings." He coughs, not the fits I've heard in the past, but his movement jerks me in my seat. "I'm here today because you are a merciful God." Matt pauses and he squeezes my hand. "Thank you for allowing me the opportunity to ask for forgiveness from Bre and Sheila. If it is your will, Lord, I pray that they forgive me for my wayward days. I'm a changed man thanks to you, Lord." He sniffles and he looks up and sees that I've been look-ing at him. He clears his throat, bows his head and con-

*E.R. McNair*

tinues, "Lord, bless this food and bless the hands that prepared it. Amen."

My mother and I say, "Amen." And we begin to scoop out the food.

As if on cue, Matthew continues, "Well after you and Bre left, I was a mess. I was hurt that you took my baby away. But deep down I knew you had good reason to. I moved in with Diana and the kids. We had the two boys, Eric who was three and then Anthony was practically a newborn."

I can tell he's embarrassed by his past indiscretions.

Again he clears his throat and he drinks the water my mother pours for him. "Once our divorce was final, I married Diana." He searches his wallet for pictures of his wife and their children.

I look at my mother wondering how she feels. She keeps a smile plastered on her face, but is it a mask for other emotions that she's trying to keep inside? Mom accepts the pictures he hands her and she looks at them nodding her head, her smile still in place.

They give the pictures to me and then stare at me as I get a look at the family that made my family nonexistent. I want to rip the pictures to shreds, but I suppress the urge. I see, looking back at me, faces that look similar to mine. I see my nose, my eyes and my curly hair. I want to scream. I want to cry. I want to stomp away from the table and go to my old room and slam the door.

"What are the girls' names?" I ask, not taking my eyes off of the pictures.

*E.R. McNair*

"Nicole is sixteen and Natasha is fifteen," Matthew says. "Bre, Sheila, I guess I

wanted to do right by her since I had already screwed us up. I really am sorry for how I treated you both." Matt puts his head down in shame.

"It's okay Matt, I've forgiven you a long time ago. It took me a while, though. But I'm a better person for it," mom says.

"Mom, after you forgave him and got over it why didn't you try to bring him back into my life?" I ask, pushing my food around the plate. Normally I would have torn this food up.

"I didn't know how to approach your dad about you. I did call back home and I talked to a few friends to see what Matt was doing. When they told me he had remarried I just felt it was best that I leave well enough alone. It was probably the worst decision I could have made."

"Sheila, don't beat yourself up. I'm the reason that you took Bre away. You were a good woman and I walked all over you. You deserved better. I have no one to blame but myself for you leaving. But I realized later that you leaving was the best thing that could have happened to me. I love Diana. She's been a wonderful wife and mother to our children." He's quiet and then looks at my mother. "You will always be my first love, though, Sheila."

My eyes well up with tears.

My mom clears her throat. She pushes herself up in her chair. "Matt, so how long have you known about the

*E.R. McNair*

cancer?"

"Well, I just found out a few months ago. But my oncologist said that I've been sick for a while. It looks like I have an aggressive form of cancer. I've been through chemo and radiation treatments. But the doctors aren't sure just how effective the treatments have been." Matthew looks away and wipes at his mouth with his napkin. "That's why I needed to see you two. Bre, I need you to know that I love you no matter what you think. I want you to meet your brothers and sisters so that you can keep in touch when I'm gone."

I nodded yes unable to speak. The words are stuck in my throat. I don't

understand how he can be so calm about the fact that he is dying.

We continue to talk through dinner. We cry some more and we laugh. The night isn't as bad as I thought it would be. I learn that he did see me graduate from high school. He was sitting in the balcony of the arena. He describes everything mom and I were wearing.

When Matthew leaves, I hug him. I squeeze him a little tighter than I normally do for fear that this may be the last time I see him.

"Will I see you again?" Matthew asks.

I nod yes.

He gives me a look that says he doubts me.

"I promise," I say.

"Shelia, it was good seeing you again. You still know how to rattle those pots and pans."

Mom smiles. She blushes a little bit. He was her first love, too.

Matthew hugs mom and then me one more time. We stand on the porch watching the cab drive away.

I'm glad I got to meet him before it's too late. I hold my mom's hand and I cry a little, missing him already.

*E.R. McNair*

# thirty-eight

**Nesha**

I jump when I hear the phone ring. Too much shit going on. My nerves can't take it all.

"Hello?" I ask. I pretend to be asleep giving me a good excuse to get off the phone if it's someone I don't want to talk to.

"Hey!" CeeCee hollers into the phone.

"What's up bitch?" I say.

"Nesha!"

"What?"

"Please don't call me that."

"Oh my fucking God," I say. I can't believe this shit. "CeeCee, come on now."

"Nesha. Please, for me."

"Whatever. What's up?" I sit on my bed and I look at the money and the gun lying next to it. I'm working on a plan but this will help me to lay low for a couple so I can perfect it. I can pay the bills without having to be on the block.

"What are you doing next Friday?" CeeCee asks me, bringing me back from my thoughts.

"I don't know, why, what's up?"

"I'm moving."

"Back with your mother?" I light a cigarette and take a long drag. "That's some shit. I never thought you'd forgive her."

"No, North Carolina," she says.

I can't think of any words to say. "CeeCee, stop being a sucker."

"I'm tired of all of this, Nesha."

"There's bullshit everywhere," I say. "If it ain't one kind of bullshit, it's another. You can't run from it." I'm quiet for a minute and I consider what she's said. Maybe if I changed, I would still have Chuckie. I look at his picture beside my bed and I can feel tears. I push them away and continue, "But if that's what you want CeeCee I gotta respect that. If it were me, I would still be beating Nicky's ass, but that's me."

"We can't stay in the same place, Nesha. It gets us nothing but the same result."

I nod my head. "I'm happy for you."

"Thank you." CeeCee's quiet for a minute. "Will you come and visit me?"

"CeeCee?"

"Come on. You can come and visit. You might like it and come to live down there with me."

"What about DayDay?" I ask. I take another drag off

*E.R. McNair*

the cigarette.

"What about him?"

"Don't play."

"I can't live for him anymore," CeeCee says. I can tell she's thinking about him though.

"What about Nicky?"

"What about her?"

"Them two together? That don't bother you?" I ask, wondering if I can get her to stay.

"No. If they're meant to be together, they'll be together whether I'm here or there. I wish them the best of luck."

"Get the fuck out of here. You're shitting me."

"Nesha. I still love DayDay, but we had an unhealthy relationship. I guess we all have to grow up sometime," CeeCee tells me. "Maybe one day we'll be together again. But right now, I have to do me."

We're both quiet.

"I'm leaving in three weeks, so Bre wants us to all get together next Friday at her house. You know, just to chill, eat, talk and laugh. Reminisce on old times. Are you down with that?"

"I'm cool, what about Nicky's crab ass?" I ask. "That bitch can't say shit to me, and I don't care how far back we go. You may have gotten over that shit, but I'm still pissed."

"Nesha, let it go. Holding on to anger just hurts us. Nicky probably doesn't care if you're mad at her. Bre plans to ask her and I'm fine with it."

"I don't know. Her ass is on that shit, haven't you heard?"

"Yeah, I heard something. But don't you think this is when she needs us the most?"

"So, you've gotten all this talk from church? I'm supposed to believe that?"

"Why wouldn't you believe it? I've heard a lot of good things from church. I'm enjoying it. You've got to come with me?"

"I'm straight."

"Nesha? What about Chuckie?"

Suddenly I'm sad. "What about him?"

"Have you heard from him?" CeeCee asks.

"I talk to him almost every day." I miss him so badly it hurts.

"Is there the possibility of you getting him back?"

"Not right now. We're working on visitation."

CeeCee doesn't say anything.

"I gotta go," I say. I can feel my eyes burning.

"I'll pray for you, Nesha. You're a good person. You make bad decisions sometimes, but you're a good person. Chuckie needs his mom."

The words won't come.

"I love you, Nesha. I'll see you Friday."

I still can't say anything.

We hang up. I leave my room and go into the kitchen. Marsean and Angel are sitting at the table eating whatever it is that Marlon's cooked for dinner.

I grab them both and hug them tight.

*E.R. McNair*

"Mom!" they both scream at me, squirming to release themselves from my grip.

"Shut up and hug me," I tell them, my arms still wrapped tightly around them.

I see Marlon in the kitchen, standing by the sink. He's wiping out the frying pan he used to cook in. Tears are dripping from his eyes.

"You're a sensitive-ass bitch," I say to him before I leave and return to my room.

# thirty-nine

**Bre**

When I get home, I have five messages on my phone. I wonder if I feel like hearing them. From now on, I'm going to think that the message is bad news about Matt.

The first message is from Mello. He sounds like something is wrong. I call him before I listen to the rest of the messages.

"Mello, what's up? I got your message, what's wrong?"

His voice sounds excited. "Hey, baby, you're not going to believe this shit, I'm at the hospital and DayDay is awake! CeeCee is here with some preacher dude, and they were praying and shit and he woke up! The shit is crazy, man. My nigga just woke up!"

"Oh, my God!" I shout. "Is he talking? Is he okay? Does he know who everyone is?" I throw questions at him so fast he doesn't have time to answer them all. "Where are you now? Oh my God!" I say again. "I have

*E.R. McNair*

to call CeeCee. Is she still at the hospital?"

"Damn, calm down, girl. You're asking so many questions. I can't keep up. Yeah, CeeCee should still be at the hospital. They called his mom as soon as he opened his eyes. He still had that tube down his throat, so I don't know if he can talk or not."

"Well, where are you?" I ask, so excited about the news. Today is turning out to be a great day.

"I'm at the crib."

I can hear him opening and closing drawers. I still haven't been to his place. I wonder why? Nope, keep those bad thoughts out your head, Bre.

"Baby," Mello says, bringing me back from an ugly place. "How was your meeting with your dad?"

"It was great! I'll tell you about that later. I want to hear about DayDay. Are you going to the hospital?"

"Yeah, I'm about to go. I came home to change my clothes. You want me to come scoop you up on the way?"

"Yeah, baby, would you please? I'll be ready when you get here. Hell, I'll be outside."

Waiting for Mello I call my mother to tell her the good news. She's excited but I can tell that she's exhausted, too. Today's events were way too much for her. I tell her I'll see her later and we hang up.

Mello honks the horn and I run out

He plants two kisses on me. "What's up, baby girl?"

"I'm good now that I see you. You're the icing on the cake," I say, smiling at him.

*E.R. McNair*

Mello pauses before speaking. "I talked to Ms. Jackson. She was on her way back over to the hospital. I think I should tell you now she went to pick up Nicky. I hope all hell hasn't broken loose by the time we get there."

I roll my eyes. "I can't believe her. Is she trying to cause him to relapse? She can't let well enough alone. Why bring Day the stress? He just woke up."

"I hear you, baby. But you know she's got an agenda. We all know how she feels about CeeCee." He shakes his head and readjusts the radio station.

"But you know what, since CeeCee has been going to church, I really see a change in her. We might be surprised by her reaction to seeing Nicky."

"I hope she has changed because my boy really don't need that shit right now. And just because he's awake, that don't mean he's okay."

"We'll see how it's going when we get there," I say.

We pull into the parking garage and we see Ms. Jackson's car. I take a deep breath and prepare for the worst. Ms. Jackson, Nicky, CeeCee, the kids and Nesha are all in the waiting room.

"The police are in there with him now," CeeCee says, brushing Ashley's hair. "They want a statement about what happened that night."

You could cut the tension with a knife. But the tension was coming from Nicky and Nesha.

CeeCee waves her hand and asks me to come over to where she's sitting. She smiles and introduces me to

*E.R. McNair*

Pastor Redman and Ms. Stephens. "It's nice meeting you," I say.

The police leave DayDay's room and there's a mad rush to the door. Nicky and Ms. Jackson jump up.

"Where the fuck are you going, bitch!" Nesha shouts to Nicky.

"Nesha, take that ghetto shit someplace else. I don't have time to deal with your ass today," Nicky says. Her wounds are still covered with bandages and she doesn't look her absolute best. She looks a little tired and I think she's missed a couple hair appointments.

"I got your ghetto right here!" Nesha hollers back, walking up on Nicky.

Mello stands between them.

The nurse leaves the nurse's station ready to confront the two women. "Look," she says. "I will not have this mess in here."

Nicky and Nesha look away.

"There are sick people in this hospital," she continues, "and if I have to put you all out, including you mom," she looks at Ms. Jackson, "I will. Now. DayDay is doing better, but he's not out of the woods. If you want to continue to see progress, then keep this mess outside of the hospital." She gives us all the evil eye. "Am I clear?"

We all shake our heads. CeeCee smiles.

"Now, two of you in the room at a time," the nurse warns as she walks away.

Nicky and Ms. Jackson rush into the room ignoring

the need for DayDay's children to see him first.

I sit down next to CeeCee. "You look good, CeeCee," I say. She does. The smile on her face does millions for her appearance and her clothes are respectable. No more hoochie, she looks more like a suburban mother— jean skirt, twin set, boots. I'm so proud of her. "I'm so happy for you. Is he talking yet?" I ask. "Tell me everything."

CeeCee explains how when she and her pastor were praying over DayDay, he moved his hand. She says then his arms twitched and then his eyes opened. It was like someone coming back from the dead. CeeCee says all she could do was scream. The nurse rushed in and CeeCee hugged her.

"Pastor had to pull me off of her. I think she thought I was going to try to beat her up." CeeCee laughs.

Ms. Jackson and Nicky finally come out of the room. They're snickering to themselves and I know they're up to no good. CeeCee goes into the room next taking the kids with her.

I hear Ms. Jackson say to Nicky, "Little does CeeCee know that when Dayonte gets out of here, he ain't going to be with her ass. I'm working on that as we speak. Nicky, let her and Nesha try and fuck with you today, I been dying to beat an ass."

Then of course as if on cue, Nesha says, "Come on with that shit, you old-ass bitch. I don't have no problem whopping an old bitch's ass!" Nesha says, pointing her finger at both of them. "Nicky, I dare you to say anything.

*E.R. McNair*

I can fuck you up again."

The nurse leaves the chart she's working on and makes her way over to us.

"I'm leaving," Nesha says, grabbing her backpack. Tell CeeCee I'll talk to her later."

"I'll see your ass later, bitch!" Nicky shouts at Nesha, who is now on the elevator.

CeeCee comes out the room. Her smile is wide.

Her pastor makes his way over to her. "I'm going to leave now that I see you're in good company, Cecelia. But you give me a call if you need me for anything." Pastor Redman wraps his large arms around CeeCee.

"I will, Pastor, and thank you so much for sitting with me and the kids. I really appreciate it."

"You're in our family now. Remember what I told you, God will never leave you nor forsake you. All you have to do is call on Him when you need Him," Pastor Redman preaches.

He seems like he could be someone's grandfather.

"Yes, sir. I'll remember that. Bye and be safe," she says.

"He seems really nice, CeeCee. I'm glad he was here with you. I see the vultures are circling," I say.

"I can't get Nesha to shut up. I keep trying to tell her it's over. I wish Nesha would respect that I've changed. But she just won't get it in her thick head. She wants me to fight and cuss and be the old me, but I can't be that person anymore. I have to be an example for my kids."

"I hear you, CeeCee, and I think that this new you is

great. I'm proud of you."

"You know, girl, I really feel good about who I am. And guess what? I stopped smoking! The last time I had anything was when me and Nicky had our fight," she says.

Mello comes out of DayDay's room. He has a smile on his face, too.

"I need to go see DayDay. Everyone that comes out has a smile on their face." I stand up and go in.

DayDay is drinking water when I come in.

"Welcome back," I say.

He clears his throat. "Thanks."

"I'm not going to stay long. I just wanted to let you know that I've been thinking about you and praying for you."

"Thanks," DayDay says again.

I can tell it's hard for him to speak.

"Everyone is happy that you're doing better. And so," I pause, "I'm looking forward to us all hanging out again."

"Me, too," he says, his voice low.

I smile at DayDay and touch his hand. I tell him I'll see him soon and I leave the room.

"We're going to walk CeeCee to her car," Mello says. He helps her grab up the kids and all their stuff.

We leave Nicky and Ms. Jackson in the waiting room.

In the parking garage, CeeCee says, "My mind feels so clear, and I see the difference in my attitude toward my kids. When I was smoking I had no patience at all. I

*E.R. McNair*

was a really angry person. But you know what? I don't have the time or the energy for that anymore, Bre."

I nod. "You have to do what's best for you and the kids, Cee. You can't worry about anyone else, not even DayDay."

CeeCee lowers her voice. "I've been thinking about our relationship a lot." She looks to see where Mello is. He's having a foot race with DJ. "You guys be careful!" she shouts to them. "We've been together since I was fifteen years old, and you know, I think it's time that I give it a break." She looks down at the ground. "I fought so hard to keep him, and don't get me wrong, I love him with all of my heart, but so much has happened.

I just don't want to go back to what we were, where we were." We stop at her car. "I didn't want to tell any of you this, it sounds sort of selfish. I don't want Nicky to have him. At first I thought I could handle it. I told Nesha that they could be together. But now, I don't think I would be comfortable with that." She looks at me waiting to get my response.

I look at her.

"I know, I know..." CeeCee says.

"I don't know what you thought I was going to say. But I don't think it's selfish." I laugh. "No, I feel you."

We both laugh.

"Thanks for being here for me," she says and then CeeCee looks over at Mello. "You too, Mello, I know we've had our difficulties, but I know that you only had DayDay's best interests at heart." CeeCee hugs him.

*E.R. McNair*

I'm not sure but I think that there might be tears in his eyes.

CeeCee gets in her car and she drives away.

I look at Mello. "More of those cool points subtracted."

We both laugh.

*E.R. McNair*

# forty

**CeeCee**

Again, I can't sleep. I look over at the clock and it's eleven thirty. The kids are at DayDay's mom's house. I have to talk to him. I get dressed and head to the hospital.

Once at the hospital I sneak into DayDay's room past the security guard and around the nurse's station. I push open the door and he's sitting there, wide awake. He's watching a re-run of some show I'm sure he's seen a million times before. He's got a smile on face, but he's startled when he sees me.

"What's up, baby?" he asks. His throat is still raw because of the breathing tube he had for so long.

I smile at him and then I break down. I can't stop the tears no matter how hard I try.

"CeeCee..." he tries to sit up, but he's unable. He no longer has the strength he once had. "CeeCee, please stop crying. What's wrong?"

"I'm sorry. I'm sorry," I apologize. I wipe at the tears with a tissue from his bedside table. "Nothing. Nothing is wrong. I've just got a lot on my mind and I want to talk to you."

"Go ahead." He pushes the off button to the television and he listens attentively.

"You don't know how hard I have been praying for this." I put my hand on DayDay's arm.

"Yeah, I do. I could hear you, CeeCee. I wanted to answer you, but everyone was so far away. It was like I was floating, you know?" DayDay smiles.

I look at him to see if his words are sincere.

Then he cracks a smile and I can tell he's playing with me. I smile back at him.

I hug and kiss him and then stroke his hand. "I'm so sorry, Day. I never meant for any of this to happen. I know that I haven't been a good woman to you or a good mother to our kids, but I am working so hard on that now." Again, tears begin to flood my eyes.

"CeeCee, I'm sorry, too. I know I've done some messed up stuff, especially being with Nicky," DayDay says. He reaches up and wipes the tears from my eyes. "It's just that I felt like you didn't want me. Nicky was there. She made me feel wanted and I needed that." Now DayDay begins to cry.

"You know what, DayDay, I am over that, and I forgive you and her for what happened. I just hope that you can forgive me for the hand that I played in all of this."

"I forgive you, girl, I love you, and I always will.

*E.R. McNair*

You've always been my everything. No matter how much wrong you did, you always had my heart. I just don't know where we go from here." Day closes his eyes and puts his hands on his face. "I mean, what's going to happen with us? So much has gone down. So many things have been said, things that we can't take back no matter how much we regret it. What are we going to do?" DayDay asks.

I'm quiet. I look away, not sure how to continue. I inhale deeply and pray for the words to say. I look at DayDay and speak to him from my heart. "I just feel like right now, I can't be the person you need. I can't give you what you're looking for. I have to get my head on straight for myself and the kids, and I can't do it if my mind is occupied on being a good woman for you. Do you understand that?"

DayDay looks down and doesn't speak for a couple of seconds. "Honestly, I do, baby, and I love you more and respect you for saying it. I've always wanted you to be the best woman you could be. I knew you had it in you. I've always felt that you were selling yourself short. We started so young and neither of us really had a chance to grow up. So I love you enough to let you go. If that's what you need to become a better you, I can live with that."

I put my head down on the bed. "How did we end up here, Day? I love you so much. Maybe one day we can start over. I want you to know I'll never keep your kids from you. Anytime you want to see them you can, just call first."

DayDay laughs. "Oh, you got jokes, huh? I know you would never keep my kids from me, CeeCee, that's the last thing on my mind." He grabs my head and pulls it up so that we are eye to eye. "I love you, CeeCee. Never forget how much I have always loved you. Go out and make something great of yourself."

"You were my first love and maybe you'll be my last. You'll always have a piece of my heart." I'm quiet before I continue. "DayDay, I want to tell you something."

I can tell he's nervous. He sits still.

"I'm moving to North Carolina. I passed my GED and I'll start training. I need to get away from here and make a fresh start."

DayDay is still. I can't read him.

"Are you okay with that, Day?" I ask.

DayDay takes a deep breath. He grabs my hand and brings it up to his heart. "CeeCee, you do what you need to do to make you a better person. I'll be fine. I'll miss my kids, but we can figure out a way to make it work. They can spend summers and holidays with me." DayDay smiles. "We'll have to figure out a way to tell my mother. That's going to be a mess."

We both laugh on that one

"I love you, Day," I say. I climb in the bed with him and rest my head on his chest. The beat of his heart is soothing, so much better than the hiss and beep of the machines that were helping to keep him alive. I listen and I fall asleep to the rhythm of his beating heart.

*E.R. McNair*

# forty-one

**Nicky**

I'm so tired. I stare in the mirror and see that the bruises on my face are starting to heal. Those bitches! They're going to get what's coming to them, eventually. It's not the visible bruises that hurt the worst, though. It's my emotional wounds that are causing me the most harm. I'm hurt that DayDay hasn't realized that I'm what he needs. But I can't cry anymore. Not because I don't want to, it's because there are no more tears to cry. I'm dry and it's the Gary streets that made me like this.

I try to run a comb through my hair and patches of it come out. My stomach begins to ache. The face I see in the mirror isn't the one I remember. It's someone else and I'm scared.

I hear Ty downstairs talking to someone. I scream down the steps, "Ty, who are you talking to?"

He doesn't answer me. I still have the same headache I've had for week now.

*E.R. McNair*

"Ty!" I holler again and I can feel the throbbing intensify.

"It's me," Bre calls upstairs. I hear her footsteps across my hardwood floors and I know she's coming up.

"What the fuck do you want?" I ask, turning my back on her as she's ascending the steps. "I ain't heard from you since the hospital. What happened to I'll call you?"

"I'm sorry. I've been busy."

I look up at her as I light a cigarette. "Mello?" I ask.

She nods her head. "And other things. I saw my father again. I haven't seen him since I was a kid."

I grunt at her. I haven't thought about my dad in years. Who needs that mother fucker now?

"Well," I begin, "I'm busy too. I'm getting ready to go."

"Where?" Bre asks.

"So you care now about what's going on in my life? You didn't care when I had to take a taxi from the hospital." I look at her and put my hand on my hip.

"Nicky, the last time I saw you, you didn't look like you cared to be bothered with me. I tried to show you how much I care about you, but you keep pushing me away."

I grunt at her again. I look in the mirror and the dark circles under my eyes are becoming more pronounced. It's the late nights among other things.

"Today's Kenny's aunt's party. He's in town and invited me, us, so we're going."

"Is Tay's mom is going to be there?" Bre asks.

I smile. "Yes, so I thought this was as good a time as

*E.R. McNair*

any to let her know she has a grandson."

"Damn, Nicky, that's foul. You're just asking for trouble. Why would you fuck that woman's birthday up like that?" Bre asks.

"My life's fucked up, why shouldn't hers be, too?"

"Nicky, you fucked up your life."

"Whatever, Bre. There you go again, Ms. Oprah fucking Winfrey. I don't see it as fucking it up. I see it as a celebration." I smile. "They're getting a new family member."

"Don't be mad at me because I can see what's wrong with your life and you can't," Bre says.

"The question is, can you see what's wrong with your life?" I ask Bre. "You're always trying to fix our lives, but you're life isn't perfect."

Bre doesn't say anything.

I try to apply make-up to hide some of the blemishes on my face along with everything else. I'm getting frustrated because instead of making it all better, I'm looking like some little girl that's gotten into her mother's shit.

"CeeCee's going to North Carolina in a couple of weeks," Bre tells me.

I grunt. "Good riddance."

"I want us all to get together, like old times," Bre says. She smiles and her happiness makes me sick.

"There are no more old times."

"There can be."

"No, there can't. We can't go back, Bre. Stop forcing

it." I've given up. Fuck it. They get what they get.

"Nicky, come on. It doesn't have to be like this."

Bre moves closer but I shoot her a look that warns against her moving any more. She stops dead in her tracks.

"CeeCee thinks she's got everyone fooled. Whatever! She's the same bitch from Gary, Indiana she always has been. I see she's got you fooled, too."

"If that's what you want to call it, Nicky, but I think it's you that got us fooled. I'm still hearing stories about you on that shit."

"Can't believe everything you hear," I say and pull on a pair of jeans from the bottom of my bed. The jeans are too big but I fold them over to make them fit better. I pull a sweatshirt over my head and I'm drowning in it also. "Is that why you came over, Bre? You need to see for yourself what your fucked up friend is into? Well, I'm fine. If I get high on occasion that's my fucking business, not yours or anyone else's."

"I'm just concerned about you, Nicky. I know you're hurt behind Day, but that nigga wasn't yours to begin with. You need to get over that shit and get yourself together."

"I told you stop worrying about me. I'm fine."

"Before CeeCee moves, we are going to get together." She says it again. I roll my eyes. "I want you to come by my house. Next Friday."

I look at Bre. I can feel tears but I inhale deeply to make them disappear. "I'm busy and you can tell CeeCee

*E.R. McNair*

I hope she falls flat on her fucking face!"

"That's fucked up, Nicky. CeeCee says she forgives you and that she still wants to be your friend. But I guess that shows us who the better woman really is."

"Yeah, well, tell her to keep her forgiveness to herself because I don't want the shit, and lock the door on your way out."

Bre shakes her head. I can tell she wants to try again, but then she decides against it. She begins downstairs, her steps are slow and deliberate. I've known her long enough to know that she's going over what's just happened and she analyzing it trying to figure out a way to get me to do what she wants. Not this time. Hell no. I can hear her talk to Ty and then I hear another voice, Kenny's. She talks to him and then I hear her car drive away.

I can tell by Kenny's expression that I'm not what he expected. I've lost weight, I've lost hair and I've lost so much more it hurts to talk about it. I try to smile to smooth out the uneasiness in the room, but I can tell my effort is useless.

"Are you ready?" I ask Kenny and Ty who's been playing with his trucks in front of the television all day.

Ty nods at Kenny, his action is unreadable. Ty runs out the door toward the parking area and Kenny follows. I lock up my house and hope for the best.

# forty-two

**Bre**

I look at the clock. It's late, after midnight. I've decided I'm going to Toledo to see my father and meet my brothers and sisters. I also decide I'm going to ask Mello to go with me. For moral support.

I'll call everyone in the morning to set everything up.

I roll over and look at the clock again. It's not seven thirty. I wonder if it's too early to call Mello. I think for a minute and decide that if he's asleep, I can just call later. I'm really excited to ask him to go. I dial Mello's number and my stomach does flips and flops.

"Hey, baby, what's going on?" I ask when he answers the phone. He doesn't sound too groggy.

"Hey, sexy, what's going down with you?"

"Nothing," I say, trying to figure out how to ask the question. "I want to ask you a favor."

"Shoot," Mello says. I can tell he's preoccupied with

*E.R. McNair*

something else. Getting it out quick would be best.

"I've decided to visit my dad next weekend. I was wondering if you'd come with me."

"You want me to come with you?" Mello sounds surprised. "Wow, I'm honored, Bre. You want me to meet your dad and your brothers and sisters?" He pauses for a minute. "Of course I'll come with you if you want."

"We'll get a hotel room and stay for a couple of days."

"Just let me know the day and time."

"I want to leave Saturday morning around nine. How's that for you?"

"Yeah, that's cool. I'll pick you up bright and early."

"Thanks, Mello. I really appreciate this. I'll feel less awkward."

"It's cool. Anything for my baby. I need to meet my future father-in-law anyway."

"Is that right, father-in-law? Huh, well aren't we moving fast? I'll have to see about that." I laugh. Can I imagine myself married to Mello? "I'm going to call my dad. I'll talk to you later."

"Okay, babe, I'll holla at you later."

I hang up with my Mello and call my dad. "Hi, may I speak to Matthew?" I say, still unsure of what to call him. I'm not comfortable with calling him dad, but Matthew sounds so formal.

"Hello, this is Matt speaking." He coughs into the phone. "Excuse me."

I cringe, fearful of how the illness is destroying his body. "Um. Hi, Matt, this is Bre. How are you?"

"Hi, Bre, it's good to hear your voice. I was just thinking about you. I'm doing as well as can be expected. How about you? How are you doing, Bre?"

"I'm good." I pause, wondering if I'm doing the right thing. "I was just calling because I want to come and see you and meet everyone this weekend, if that's okay with you and your wife?"

"That would be great, Bre." Matt coughs again. "Everyone has been wanting to meet you. I'm sure they'll be excited."

"Okay. I've asked my boyfriend to come with me. Is that okay with you? I'll need to get the name of a hotel that close to you."

"No problem. There are a couple not too far from us. But you and he are welcome stay here, in separate rooms of course. But we'd love to have you," Matt says.

"Thank you for the offer but I think we would be more comfortable if we were to get a room, this being the first time meeting everyone," I say, thinking that that would be a nightmare.

"Okay Bre, whatever makes you comfortable is fine with me," Matt says. "Everyone is going to be excited. I can't wait."

I can tell that he really is excited. "Okay, well I'm going to get off of here. I'll call you back to let you know my plans."

"Okay, Bre, I look forward to hearing from you. I love you."

"Okay, Matt , I'll talk to you soon." I hang up. I'm still

*E.R. McNair*

not comfortable telling him that I love him. I'm not even sure that I do.

# forty-three

**CeeCee**

I'm standing outside of Bre's house and I'm a little nervous. I see Nesha's car, so I know she's here, but I wonder if Nicky's in there. I wonder if I'll be able to maintain
my newfound religion once I see her.

I raise my hand to knock on the door but before my
hand connects it swings open.

"Get your ass in here!" Nesha bellows into the dark,
chilly air.

I can't help but smile. She's never going to change.

The house is festively decorated. Three mylar bal-
loons are in the corner that say "We'll Miss You," "Good
Luck" and "Bon Voyage." Soft music is playing on the CD
player and Bre has food on the kitchen counter that
smells so good my stomach starts to growl.

My smile brightens but them I'm saddened. I'll miss
my friends. I search the room and I only see Nesha.

"Where's Bre?" I ask, dropping my jacket and purse

*E.R. McNair*

on the ottoman.

"Nicky ain't here," Nesha bellows. "I see you looking for her. Do you honestly believe she'd show her face here tonight? That bitch may be dumb, but she ain't crazy." Nesha pauses. "Well, yeah, she's crazy, too. But, she didn't come." Nesha chokes out a laugh and then she starts to cough.

"It's not because I didn't try," Bre says, coming into the room with a big brightly colored box in her hands. "Don't say anything," she says. "We had to get you something. It's a house warming gift, you know, for your new house." Bre smiles, puts the gift down in front of me and kisses me on the cheek.

I'm choked up. I'm not sure what to say.

"Say something, heifer," Nesha says.

I hate that she can read my mind. But I guess spending almost twenty years with someone, you eventually get to that point.

"I'm not sure what to say." I start to cry, not even trying to hold back the tears. "I'm going to miss you two so much."

Then as if tears are contagious like yawns, Nesha and Bre begin to cry.

I look at Nesha. "What?"

"Shut up," Nesha fusses.

Bre sniffles, "Let's eat." She goes into the kitchen and brings out the food and puts it on the coffee table.

We eat, talk and laugh until after midnight.

*E.R. McNair*

# forty-four

**Bre**

I'm tired as hell. I throw everything from the party into the dishwasher and go to bed. I'll take care of all of it when Mello and I get back Sunday.

Mello honks his horn at exactly nine in the morning. He rings my doorbell and grabs my bags, but not before he places a big kiss on my forehead.

"Good morning, Sunshine."

I smile at him and follow him to the car.

We have a great time on the drive to Toledo. We talk about everything. He tells me he used be scared of the dark and that he can't swim. I tell him that I used to love playing with worms and that I can't sing to save my life. I feel so much closer to Mello and now I'm thinking I may be able to make him a part of our small family.

We get to Toledo at about one o'clock in the afternoon. We find our hotel and we check in. I take a quick

*E.R. McNair*

shower and freshen up. I'm so nervous I've sweat through my shirt.

I sit on the bed, a towel wrapped around me.

"What's wrong?" Mello asks as he unpacks his suitcase.

"I'm so nervous." I hold up my hands and they're shaking.

He sits down next to me and kisses me on the neck. "You'll be fine. I bet they're nervous, too."

"You think?" I ask. The knots in my stomach have knots.

"I'm sure they are. They're probably thinking, 'what if she doesn't like us.' I wouldn't doubt it. Bre, just be yourself. Everything will be fine."

I look at him and hesitantly I rise from the bed. I go into the bathroom.

"I want to see you in that towel later tonight," Mello hollers to me from the room.

I throw the towel out the door and it hits him in the head.

We get in the car and try to follow the directions Matt gave us to his house. Toledo isn't a very big city. Mostly industry. We drive past a few closed plants, warehouses and car dealerships until we abruptly hit a suburb. Welcome to Mayfield Heights.

"That's it," I tell Mello and then my stomach jumps, flips and somersaults.

We pull up to the house. It's a big brick house and I wonder how it would have been to grow up here with a

*E.R. McNair*

flower-lined driveway instead of drive-by shootings and flowers at my friends' funerals.

I ring the doorbell and then straighten out the pleated skirt I decided to wear. I look at Mello and he smiles at me. I feel a little more relaxed, but not much.

Matt answers the door. It has only been one week since I've seen him last but he looks as if he's lost some weight since then. He looks a little sad to me even though I know he really isn't.

"Hey, Matt! This is my boyfriend Mello, Mello, this is my dad, Matthew Watkins."

"Hello, young man, it's nice to meet you." They shake hands.

"Hi, Mr. Watkins, it's a pleasure to meet you."

"Please, come on in. You have a lot of people here to meet you." He escorts us to the family room. He's still walking with a cane. "Bre, this is your Aunt Jessica. She's my baby sister. She hasn't seen you since you were a baby."

I smile and extend my hand, but instead Jessica grabs me and pulls me to her. She smells like garlic. "It's been too long." Jessica rocks me back and forth, and I almost get sea sick. She pushes me back to get a look at me and then pulls me into her large breasts again.

Everyone is laughing, but she's winded me and I don't think it's funny.

I didn't expect to meet a bunch of people. But then again I didn't know what to expect.

Aunt Jessica looks at Mello. "He's a handsome one,"

*E.R. McNair*

she says. "You have the Watkins taste, we love us some good looking men." She elbows me in the ribs and walks out the room, her loud bellow echoing off the ceiling, walls and hardwood floors.

"Diana," Matt hollers, "Bre is here." He sits in a chair that looks as if it's kept him comfortable for a long time. He seems as if he's out of breath.

I'm not sure how I feel about meeting her. The history is too deep and painful. It's not her fault, totally, but I can't help what my heart feels. Diana enters the room. There couldn't be two women that were such complete opposites, Diana and my mother.

My mom is tall and thin, Diana is short and squat. My mom is honey colored and Diana is dark chocolate.

Diana smiles and exposes a large gap between her two front teeth. She extends her hand after wiping it on her apron. "It's so nice to finally meet you, Bre," she says, her accent from deep down south.

I smile back at her and shake her hand. She smells of sweet pea and the only reason I know that is because it's the flower associated with my birth month. While I want to hate her, Diana doesn't allow me to. She seems friendly, a little shy, but the feeling I get when our hands connect isn't one of hate but one of welcoming and love.

"Are you two hungry?" Diana asks me and then she looks at Mello.

Mello stands up, extends his hand and introduces himself. "I'm starving. It smells great in here."

"Follow me, baby," Diana says and she directs Mello

*E.R. McNair*

into the kitchen.

"If I'm not back in an hour, come in after me." Mello laughs, leaving me alone with Matt.

It's the first time we've been alone. I planned that we would never be alone when he came to Gary. But I don't have any control over this situation here and my nerves are back.

The large screen television is on, but the sound is turned down. I look over at Matt and his eyes are closed. I can tell this is a lot for him.

Diana calls from the kitchen, "Matt, do you need anything?"

"No," Matt calls back, the one word depleting his already low energy level.

"Dad?"

I'm startled by the tall man that walks into the room.

"My fault," he says, seeing me jump.

"Bre," finally Matt moves and he introduces us, "this is your brother Eric."

Eric stands in front of me and his height and mass are intimidating. I stand and he wraps his thick, hulking arms around me. "It's great meeting you, Bre," he says.

"I think I'm in love," Mello says, re-entering the room. He's shoveling a slice of cake into his mouth. He sees Eric and me in an embrace and he's caught off guard.

"Mello, this is my brother," I say, loosening myself from the bear hug.

Mello brushes his hands off on his jeans and shakes Eric's hand. They exchange small talk and both sit down.

*E.R. McNair*

We all stare at Matt whose eyes are still closed.

It's obvious that none of us are handling his illness well. Eric, having known for some months, me for mere days.

Eric tells me and Mello that he is twenty-three and that he is in the Navy but he's on leave so that he can spend some time with our dad.

"Anthony should be home any minute," Eric says and just as he makes the announcement, the door flies open and Anthony walks in. "Speak of the devil," Eric says.

"What's up?" Anthony asks. He's the opposite of Eric. He's thin and the same color as his mother and he has the brightest smile I've ever seen.

"Anthony, this is Bre," Eric introduces us.

Again, I'm swept up by, this time, thin but still very strong arms. He hugs me and I know that I have at least two broken ribs. I don't think I've ever been hugged this much.

"It's nice meeting you," I say, barely getting enough air to breathe let alone speak.

Anthony tells us he's twenty-one and tells us to call him Ant for short. For some reason he looks so familiar and I know that I've seen him somewhere. I just can't place where. Nicky would have been all over him.

"Nicole and Natasha aren't home from school," Anthony says. "They haven't been able to talk about anything else since dad told us you were coming. They're so excited about having an older sister."

We all look over at Matt who's asleep in his chair.

*E.R. McNair*

"He does that a lot," Eric explains. "Since his illness, he's always tired." He gets quiet. "I'm sorry you didn't get to see him in his prime. He was great."

I feel nauseous. That wasn't my experience at all. He wasn't great, he wasn't there. I can tell Eric feels bad about his remark.

I can feel their eyes on me. I ask where the bathroom is and I rush out of the room as if it's on fire. I sit on the closed toilet seat. I want to cry. I want to scream. But I can't.

Finally, there's a knock on the door. "Bre, it's me, Mello. Are you okay?" I can tell he's concerned.

"I'm fine I say." I stand and splash cold water on my face. I open the door.

"Eric feels bad."

I nod.

"He didn't mean it."

"I know."

"Do you want to go back to the hotel?" Mello asks me.

"No," I say. "I'll be fine."

We go back into the room and Eric tries to apologize to me and I tell him, "It's okay, don't worry about it, not your fault."

My sisters finally come home from school and then we eat dinner. The conversation during dinner is so far from my past that I end up really enjoying myself. Mello and my brothers decide to go out to a club, but I tell them that I want to stay at the house and hang out with Nicole,

*E.R. McNair*

Natasha and Matt.

We look at pictures, talk about boys and dating. Our dad won't allow them to date yet. I hear about school, cheerleading and drama club. Natasha wants to be an actress. I tell her I'll come to her next play.

It's late and everyone goes to bed. It's just me and Matt.

"I had a really good time today," I tell him.

"I'm glad," he says, "I apologize for sleeping so much. It's the medication."

"I understand," I say. "Everyone is great."

"They say the same thing about you." He smiles but I can tell it takes a lot out of him. "I have something I want you to have." He gives me pictures of me when I was a baby, pictures of him and my mother in high school, and he gives me a wedding picture.

I stare at the pictures in amazement.

"I used to look at your baby picture all the time." Matt coughs and I'm scared. "I thought about you often. I just want to let you know again, I'm sorry."

"I know," I say.

"I won't mention it again." He laughs. "I don't want to beat a dead horse."

I nod.

"I like Mello. Can you see yourself with him forever?"

I shrug my shoulders.

"Make sure you know."

"I will."

*E.R. McNair*

I'm glad we had this time together. I want to hug him, he looks so frail in his chair. I wonder how much time he has left.

"Matt," I call to him.

He opens his eyes.

"I love you," I say.

"I know," he whispers and falls back to sleep.

Mello and I leave the next day. I tell everyone that I'll be back soon whispering the words into Matt's ear to make sure he hears me.

I'm happy to be home even though Mello and I had a good time.

"Thanks for coming with me," I say to Mello as he's dropping me off.

"I had a great time, too. Thanks for asking me." He kisses me on my lips and slips his tongue into my mouth.

I smile at him and watch him leave. He said he had things to do but he might see me later.

I call my mother and tell her about my experience. She can't remember the pictures I describe to her but she can't wait to see them. I tell her that I'll stop by after work tomorrow to show them to her and we hang up.

I think about Matt and imagine him in his chair. I'm sad. I don't want him to die. I am just getting to know him and now he's going to leave me. It's so unfair. Life is so unfair.

A couple weeks later I go back to Ohio to see my dad

*E.R. McNair*

again, by myself this time. It is nice to see him again and to get to spend more time with him. He had just been released from the hospital for the second time in two weeks. The chemo treatments aren't working and his cancer was spreading.

A week after my last visit, Matt died.

I took his death harder than I thought I would. My mom and I went to the funeral. I'm glad that we did. I think she needed closure, too. I know deep down she loved my dad. I think a part of her always will. I know I will.

# forty-five

**Bre**

It's been a few months since CeeCee left Gary. When I talk to her on the phone she sounds happy. She says the kids love it in North Carolina and that they're doing well in school. She asks how everyone is doing here at home, and I tell her.

"Nesha's still Nesha and I haven't talked to Nicky in a minute." I roll my eyes wondering what has to happen for some people to realize that if you do what you always did, you'll get what you always got.

CeeCee says that DayDay is still in physical therapy and that he'll be running soon. I tell her I'll keep my fingers crossed and she says that she'll continue to pray long and hard for his recovery.

I tell her Mello and I are still kicking it, but that I'm not sure how much longer that's going to last.

"Why?" CeeCee asks.

"I don't know... he's running in the streets more and

more. He's making more money and he seems to be more interested in that than me. He tells me that he loves me but he needs to handle his business and he doesn't want to bring me down. What kind of shit is that?" I ask CeeCee.

"Men will be men," CeeCee responds.

"I'm tired of Gary," I say.

She says, "Maybe it's time to make that change."

I say, "I might come down south. The bank has been bought out by Bank of America and their offices are in Atlanta. I've put in for a transfer, and I think I got it. So, once I find out for sure, I think I'm leaving."

"That's good, Bre. Change is good. Someone once told me that," CeeCee says.

I think back to our conversation when I told her that.

"Look at me!" CeeCee sounds introspective. "Yeah, change is really good."

"Yeah, you're right about that. Nothing here is the same. You're gone, Nicky, well, she's gone, too, when you think about it, and Nesha, she ain't doing nothing but hustling," I say sadly. "Nesha has always been about getting paid by any means necessary. I heard she had something to do with Paul getting shot up."

"I always thought about that. And what about Chuckie?" CeeCee asks.

"He's still with Charles, from what I hear. The way Nesha's going, she'll never get him back."

I can tell CeeCee is shaking her head. "Doesn't sound like it. And the other kids? If it weren't for the fact that one dad is in jail and the other is gone and her brothers, they'd be gone too."

"Nicky's mom isn't too good. She's in and out of the hospital. But she said that Ty is with his dad's family. He's been gone for a while now. I don't think he's coming back."

CeeCee says, "That was messed up but, at least it worked out and Tay's mom got a piece of her son back."

"I'm just tired, Cee. I don't want to be here anymore. I want something more. I guess it's time to grow up and move on."

"How does your mother feel about you leaving?" CeeCee asks.

"She says whatever I choose is fine with her. But the good thing is that she'll retire in about a year and she might come to Atlanta to live with me."

"I hope she does. I think the South would do both of you some good," CeeCee says. "I hope it all works out for you, Bre. You're a good person and you deserve good to happen to you. I'm going to pray on it for you. I know you can do it. You have an even better start than I did. You have a high school diploma and job experience and no kids. So I know if I did it you definitely can make it happen."

"I was thinking about asking Mello to come with me. But if he says no, then I'm just going to have to let him go," I say.

"Bre, I learned that you have to live for yourself. Let go and let God. That's what a wise person told me once.

*E.R. McNair*

I'm telling you the same thing, be about you." She stops and then starts again, "Bre, don't worry about Mello. He's a grown-ass man. Let him make his own way. You take care of you."

I nod my head. I know she can't see me, but I'm feeling what she's saying.

"Bre, I have to go. I have bible study in an hour and I have to get the kids ready. Call me and let me know how the transfer goes. Tell your mom I say hello. If you see Nicky give her my number and tell her to call me. I would love to try and talk to her. If I can change, anyone can."

"I will," I say. "I hope you can get through to her. Someone needs to."

"Before I go," CeeCee says excitedly, "my mom found my brother and sister. I was able to talk to them on the phone! They're both doing good. I'll tell you more when we can talk longer. Take care, Bre and remember, I love you," CeeCee says and she hangs up.

She's right. I need to worry about me and what I'm going to do with the rest of my life.

I dial Mello's number. I need to tell him my plans and see if he fits into them or if it's time to move on without him.

"Hey, what's up?" Mello says.

I can tell he's in a car. I just blurt it out. "I'm moving to Atlanta."

He doesn't say anything for a minute and then he speaks to someone in the car with him. I can't make out exactly what he said.

*E.R. McNair*

"Did you hear me?" I ask him.

"Yeah. I heard you." He seems unfazed by my revelation.

"Well?" I ask, a little hurt that he hasn't jumped on the opportunity to come with me. It seems to me that these past few months, I've just been something to occupy his time.

"Well, what?" Mello asks me. "I can't stop you from going. What do you want me to say?" I hear irritation in his voice.

I want him to beg me not to go. But it's obvious our relationship has run its course.

I clear my throat. "I don't think a long distance relationship will work," I say flatly.

"I understand," he says and then he tells me he has something to do and he'll call me later.

I want to tell him to forget my number but the words are stuck in my throat. I wonder if this will be the last time we speak. Unfortunately, that's the life of a hustler and I can't be mad because I knew what it was when we started. It was fun while it lasted.

When I find out my transfer is approved I start looking for apartments on the internet. I'm told the office is in midtown. That helps a lot. I'm leaving in a month and I can't wait.

*E.R. McNair*

# forty-six

**Nicky**

I'm looking out the window and I see a moving truck pull into a spot in front of my house. I strain my eyes to see who's driving, but the glare from the sun doesn't allow me to make out the driver's face.

The door swings open and I see Bre jump out. I'm not in the mood for her today.

"Nicky," Bre calls up the steps after she enters my apartment.

I walk down and look at her. I sit on the couch and tuck my legs underneath my shrinking body.

"I just couldn't leave Gary without seeing you," Bre says. She sits down and makes herself comfortable.

I'm hoping she's not staying long.

"You're leaving?" I ask, lighting a cigarette. I have an attitude.

"Look, Nicky, I didn't come here to argue with you. I just wanted to see my friend before I leave."

*E.R. McNair*

289

I look at her and then return my stare to the television screen.

"We missed you at CeeCee's little party," Bre says.

"I told you I had plans," I say coldly.

"You did. We had fun. We reminisced about old times." Bre stares at me.

I still don't say anything.

"I'm on my way to Atlanta. I'm moving there. I got a transfer from my job. I don't know when I'll see you again. But I didn't want to leave without trying to resolve our issues."

I move to find another comfortable position. "Well, Bre, that's fucking great. I hope you have a happy life. As for resolving issues, there's nothing left to resolve. As they say, all good things must come to an end. We were friends, now we're not. It was nice seeing you, take care of yourself." I salute her.

"I hate that you see it like that, Nicky. But just so you know, I'll always be there for you and Ty. You're my girl, my sister, whether you want to be or not."

Bre scribbles on a piece of paper from her jacket pocket. She sits it down on the coffee table. "My new phone number and CeeCee's number."

"That's nice to know. But I choose not to be your anything. I'm cool, not that you were really concerned."

I stand up hoping that Bre will take the hint.

"I hope you're happy," I say, almost screaming at Bre. "Ty is leaving me. His grandmother wants him to spend some time with her. She said that if I didn't agree she would take me to court."

I can tell Bre's a little hurt. "But it's not permanent?" she says, hopefully.

"It might as well be. I have nothing else but Ty and now they're taking him from me!" I scream at her, close enough to show how pissed I am.

Bre stares at me. I can tell she wants to say something else, but nothing she can say will fix what's been done. Words are useless now.

"Leave, Bre. Just leave. Your conscience is clear now so be on your way. Don't worry about me. I'm like Tony the fucking Tiger. I'm grrrreat," I growl at her and I can tell she's scared.

"Okay. Okay, Nicky, it's cool. I hate to leave it this way, but I guess it is what it is. If you ever need me, don't hesitate to call."

I watch Bre walk to her truck and get in. She starts it up and drives away.

## forty-seven

**Nesha**

I walk into the courtroom and I can tell this is not going to be as easy as the rest of the times I've been here. My heart is beating a million miles a minute. I look down at the shackles on my hands and feet and I know for sure, this time is different.

The judge enters the room and everyone, including me, rises. My hair is all over my head and I smell. I haven't had a bath in a couple of days. I look to my right and Charles is sitting there, his mother beside him. The smirk on his face is proof that I'll never see my son again.

My attorney speaks on my behalf. I have no clue what to do.

"Counselor, what does your client plead?" the judge asks. Her tone is angry.

"My client pleads not guilty, your Honor." My attorney is a public defender bogged down with a million cases

*E.R. McNair*

and I'm sure mine isn't the one he'll spend nights awake, trying to get me home to see my kids. I'm a repeat offender with an eleventh grade education. I know he probably thinks I'll be better off, the world will be better off with me behind bars.

"Counselor, does your client realize the seriousness of what she's accused of doing?"

"Yes, your Honor, she does," my attorney answers as he haphazardly rustles through mounds of paperwork before him.

"Well, counselor, due to the fact that your client has been here, not just in court, but in my courtroom in the past and the fact that she was in possession of a firearm which is against her probation and the fact that she used said firearm to shoot a police officer, I must remand her to the women's correctional facility without bail." She pounds her gavel on the bench and dismisses court.

"All rise."

The courtroom rises, including me. The judge leaves and I'm escorted from the room with one armed sheriff on either side. I can't cry. The tears won't flow. I don't see a future. I don't see anything.

**One Year Later**

*Bre*

I made it to Atlanta and I live in Buckhead. I was in awe of the city when I first got here. It's such a beautiful place, green trees and flowers all over. I love it.

Atlanta is everything I heard it to be. The traffic is crazy, but I live close to where I work so I don't need to drive. Everything is right here—shopping, restaurants and movie theaters. The people are friendly and the atmosphere is right for upward mobility. Everyone here wants to be successful.

My mom retired and now she's here with me. We're building a house in Alpharetta.

I met a great guy, Al-Kharir Mohammed. He's a Muslim. He introduced me to Islam. I'm still learning about the religion but so far I feel like a new, happier person when I worship at the mosque.

My mom is hoping for grandkids soon, but I keep

*E.R. McNair*

telling her that that will have to wait until after Al and I decide if we're getting married.

My brother, Ant, lives here in Atlanta. He joined the Army shortly after dad died and he's stationed here. So, we hook up on a regular. He and my mom hit it off right away. Now they're so close he calls her his second mom.

I know my dad is smiling down on all of us. I'm sure he's happy that after all the years of us being separated that we're all together and getting along. Both of my sisters are planning to go to college here in Atlanta when they graduate from high school. They come down often to visit and I'm sure they'll spend weekends at my house when they're here permanently. Mom has become a surrogate mother to all of my siblings. I laugh about that. It makes me wonder if she is showering on them the love she had for my dad.

Finally, my mom has a special friend. His name is Mr. Joe Johnson. They met at Wal-Mart. It took my mother coming all the way to Atlanta to meet a boyfriend at the Wal-Mart. He's a good guy, a typical southern black gentleman, and he drives a Cadillac. He was born and raised in Georgia which is rare to find here, but he treats my mom like a queen and that's all that matters. I like him and who knows, a wedding might happen for my mom before it happens for me. But only time will tell.

Mello and I kept in touch for a while after I moved away and he even brought his son to visit me. I knew then that it would definitely be the last time we spoke.

*E.R. McNair*

He had changed so much.

About a month later I received a call late one night from CeeCee. She told me that Mello got busted for drug trafficking. She said that that was his third strike and he would be gone for life. I couldn't breathe while she told me the details of what happened. If he would have accepted my invitation to leave Gary he may not be in the predicament he's in now. I was sad. I wrote him to a few times, and he was talking a good game at first. He would say things like he wanted more out of life and he blamed his trouble on his father. But when it's all said and done, a brother looking at life behind bars will say anything. I could tell that Mello wasn't sincere and eventually I gave up on him. I couldn't waste any more time on something that I knew would never be. I loved him, though, and sometimes I miss the good times we had together. I heard he was appealing his case, but I haven't heard the outcome.

CeeCee is back in school and she says she wants to be a Social Worker. Right now she's working for Charlotte's child welfare system. She says she's using her life experiences to help others.

She and DayDay kept in touch after she left. CeeCee says that she kept talking to him, telling him that there wasn't anything good for him in the streets. She says she prayed for him, on her knees, crying out to God asking Him to guide DayDay to the right path.

After DayDay got out of the hospital, he saw one of

*E.R. McNair*

his partners gunned down one night at the club and he decided it wasn't worth his life. He said he wanted to see his children grow up. The next week he began studying for the GED exam and he passed. He showed up at CeeCee's front door, his GED in one hand and a ring box in the other.

CeeCee says that when she opened the front door, DayDay was on one knee and he asked her to marry him right then and there. When CeeCee told me, I cried. I knew they were meant to be. I flew to Charlotte and was CeeCee's maid of honor.

Ms. Jackson is still a little bitter. But she's adjusting to CeeCee being her daughter-in-law. She's even been down to visit, CeeCee says.

DayDay got a job as a counselor at a detention center for boys, and he coaches DJ's pee wee basketball team. He's an inspiration to the boys in the Center. He has plenty of life experience to help guide them away from the same mistakes he made.

CeeCee's mom has been clean for over a year now. CeeCee says she knows it was all the praying she did. Now that her brother and sister are adults and they both have families of their own, they finally can come together and talk. When they spoke over the phone they both told CeeCee that it wasn't her fault for what happened and they never wanted her to take on the burden. She was just a little girl herself. CeeCee says that made her feel so much better. CeeCee's sister lives in Virginia with her husband and two kids and her brother is a fire fighter in Philadelphia.

And Nicky ... my heart continues to hurt when I think about her. I hate the way our friendship ended. I still love her with all my heart. It just wasn't supposed to end that way. I know drugs can cause a user to behave strangely and it was the drugs that made Nicky flip the script. I also know that until she admits that she is using, she's not going to admit there's a problem and she will never change.

Atlanta was just the change I needed. I'm glad I made the move. I talk to CeeCee once a week. I found in her the friendship I once had with Nicky.

My dream, when I was in Gary, was that we would all find what we were looking for. Unfortunately for Nesha and Nicky, they went looking in the wrong places and fortunately for CeeCee and I, we found our positive through negative, but we found it. I learned that change is good.

The hood made me who I am today. But I used the hood, I didn't allow it to use me. I took from the hood what I needed and I left the rest behind. In the hood, drama is around every corner. Some of us are able to get out of the hood, and some of us will stay there until we die. I'm glad I chose the first path.

But no matter where we are today, I'll always love my sisters, the Hood Rats.

*E.R. McNair*

## ORDER FORM
*Triple Crown Publications*
PO Box 6888
Columbus, OH 43205

| | |
|---|---|
| NAME | |
| ADDRESS | |
| CITY | |
| STATE | |
| ZIP | |

| | TITLES | PRICE |
|---|---|---|
| | Dime Piece | $15.00 |
| | Gangsta | $15.00 |
| | Let That Be The Reason | $15.00 |
| | A Hustler's Wife | $15.00 |
| | The Game | $15.00 |
| | Black | $15.00 |
| | Dollar Bill | $15.00 |
| | A Project Chick | $15.00 |
| | Road Dawgz | $15.00 |
| | Blinded | $15.00 |
| | Diva | $15.00 |
| | Sheisty | $15.00 |
| | Grimey | $15.00 |
| | Me & My Boyfriend | $15.00 |
| | Larceny | $15.00 |
| | Rage Times Fury | $15.00 |
| | A Hood Legend | $15.00 |
| | Flipside of the Game | $15.00 |
| | Menage'A Way | $15.00 |

**SHIPPING/HANDLING**
**1-3 books $5.00**
**4-9 books $9.00**
**$1.95 for each add'l book**

TOTAL      $_____

**FORMS OF ACCEPTED PAYMENTS:**
Postage Stamps, Institutional Checks & Money
Orders. All mail-in orders take 5-7 Business days
to be delivered

# ORDER FORM

*Triple Crown Publications*
PO Box 6888
Columbus, OH 43205

| NAME | |
| --- | --- |
| ADDRESS | |
| CITY | |
| STATE | |
| ZIP | |

| | TITLES | PRICE |
| --- | --- | --- |
| | Still Sheisty | $15.00 |
| | Chyna Black | $15.00 |
| | Game Over | $15.00 |
| | Cash Money | $15.00 |
| | Crackhead | $15.00 |
| | For the Strength of You | $15.00 |
| | Down Chick | $15.00 |
| | Dirty South | $15.00 |
| | Cream | $15.00 |
| | Hoodwinked | $15.00 |
| | Bitch | $15.00 |
| | Stacy | $15.00 |
| | Life | $15.00 |
| | Keisha | $15.00 |
| | Mina's Joint | $15.00 |
| | How to Succeed in the Publishing Game | $20.00 |
| | Love & Loyalty | $15.00 |
| | Whore | $15.00 |
| | A Hustler's Son | $15.00 |

**SHIPPING/HANDLING**
**1-3 books $5.00**
**4-9 books $9.00**
**$1.95 for each add'l book**

**TOTAL     $_____**

**FORMS OF ACCEPTED PAYMENTS:**
**Postage Stamps, Institutional Checks & Money**
**Orders,  All mail in orders take 5-7 Business**
**days to be delivered**

# ORDER FORM
*Triple Crown Publications*
PO Box 6888
Columbus, OH 43205

| NAME | |
| --- | --- |
| ADDRESS | |
| CITY | |
| STATE | |
| ZIP | |

| TITLES | PRICE |
| --- | --- |
| Chances | $15.00 |
| Contagious | $15.00 |
| Hold U Down | $15.00 |
| Black and Ugly | $15.00 |
| In Cahootz | $15.00 |
| Dirty Red *Hardcover | $20.00 |
| Dangerous | $15.00 |
| Street Love | $15.00 |
| Sunshine & Rain | $15.00 |
| Bitch Reloaded | $15.00 |
| Dirty Red *Paperback | $15.00 |
| Mistress of the Game | $15.00 |
| Queen | $15.00 |
| The Set Up | $15.00 |
| Torn | $15.00 |
| Stained Cotton | $15.00 |
| Grindin' *Hardcover ONLY | $10.00 |
| Amongst Thieves | $15.00 |
| Cut Throat | $15.00 |

**SHIPPING/HANDLING**
**1-3 books $5.00**
**4-9 books $9.00**
**$1.95 for each add'l book**

TOTAL     $_____

**FORMS OF ACCEPTED PAYMENTS:**
**Postage Stamps, Institutional Checks & Money**
**Orders,  All mail in orders take 5-7 Business**
**days to be delivered**

# ORDER FORM

*Triple Crown Publications*
PO Box 6888
Columbus, OH 43205

| | |
|---|---|
| NAME | |
| ADDRESS | |
| CITY | |
| STATE | |
| ZIP | |

| TITLES | PRICE |
|---|---|
| The Hood Rats | $15.00 |
| Betrayed | $15.00 |
| The Pink Palace | $15.00 |
| The Bitch is Back | $15.00 |
| Escape from the Madness | $15.00 |
| Still Dirty *Hardcover | $20.00 |
| As Cold As Ice | $15.00 |
| | |
| | |
| | |
| | |
| | |
| | |
| | |
| | |
| | |
| | |
| | |

**SHIPPING/HANDLING**
**1-3 books $5.00**
**4-9 books $9.00**
**$1.95 for each add'l book**

**TOTAL    $_____**

**FORMS OF ACCEPTED PAYMENTS:**
**Postage Stamps, Institutional Checks & Money**
**Orders,  All mail in orders take 5-7 Business**
**days to be delivered**